WHAT PEOPLE ARE SAYING
ABOUT **TROJAN HORSE**...

"Lots of action and an exciting story. My wife actually ordered this book for me by mistake, and I'm glad she did...very enjoyable read. I ended up ordering his other book 'The Sentinel' too—another excellent book."

—Jim Simons

"This was the first of this authors books I have read and while it's not in a genre I usually read, I enjoyed it very much."

—Eric Smith

"Very intriguing and up to date with current world situation. Shows much research of facts."

—Janet Lipscomb

"Bourdon's protagonist Devon McKenzie character is a Jason Bourne sans the super powers — outstanding storytelling!"

—Mike Navarro

"I enjoyed this book and look forward to more of Paul Bourdon's books, having read this and the previous one. I really want to see more romance between the characters in his book's though, I think it would add an extra something to already good characters and stories."

—Barbara Krueger

TROJAN HORSE

TROJAN HORSE

First Edition

Copyright ©2014 Paul Bourdon

ISBN: 978-0-9960789-1-7

Paul Bourdon

TROJAN HORSE

CHAPTER 1

THE DACHA WAS BUFFETED BY NORTHERN WINDS FROM THE Finnish tundra. The roof strained by the weight of three feet of snow. Icicles glistened in the sporadic sun that penetrated low, puffy clouds. As the temperature plummeted, two men were set to meet in secrecy. Waiting inside was Igor Dravenskey, the largest shareholder of Gazprom, Russia's dominant natural gas distribution company. In route was Rear Admiral Popov of the Russian Navy.

Dravenskey was a modern-day mogul. A cautious man, his success lay in the fact that he could find an advantage over both adversary and friend, and that advantage was born of information. Prior to any relationship, he made sure that he knew everything about the other person, including their dirt. He had a network of informants, and their reports showed that the admiral was on the take.

Five months prior, Popov had moved eighteen million dollars' worth of decommissioned and recycled ammunition onto the foreign black market. These successes had made him brazen, and greed began consuming the lifelong navy man. The report said that Popov was working a deal to move thirty anti-submarine missiles and two hundred airplane bombs. The mogul knew that any man who would go that far could be enticed to wade deeper into the muck. Dravenskey ascertained that Popov would be this man.

Igor Dravenskey knew the right buttons to push. He hadn't eliminated ninety percent of his competition playing by the rules. Besides, in post-communist Russia, there were no rules. Money talked, and Dravenskey had dangled enough of it in front of Popov to flush the old fox out of his lair. His terms for their initial meeting were simple:

You and I to start … no one else … my dacha.

When Dravenskey's people first contacted Popov, the admiral was reluctant to meet. Dravenskey knew that Popov was a puppet master who preferred working behind the scenes instead of attending meetings. But the gas mogul knew the rewards on the deal he was proposing were astronomical, and all Popov's previous dirty dealings were petty by comparison.

Dravenskey sat with legs crossed in an overstuffed sofa, waiting for his guest to show his face. He saw Popov get out of his car, walk up to the door, and stand without knocking. He bet that the old fox assumed this act of boldness would somehow give him a leg up. The mogul snickered at the attempt. As Popov entered, Dravenskey put on his game face, looked up, and nodded to the couch. Handshakes were neither offered nor made.

The men sat in silence, each staring at the other, each making their own judgments. Dravenskey saw Popov growing agitated. Popov licked his lips and scanned the room. Dravenskey knew that a good Russian would have a bottle of vodka waiting for his guests. Making the admiral wait was his second move.

Dravenskey was satisfied that round one had gone to him. A master at the game of chess, he decided to make his opening gambit. A cagey smile broke on his face as he rose from the couch, feigned an aristocratic manner, and said, "I am so sorry, Admiral. It was rude of me not to offer you a drink."

Dravenskey saw Popov nod and lick his lips, while his eyes followed him to the liquor cabinet. The mogul felt confident when Popov beamed as he returned with a bottle of Belvedere in his hand.

Dravenskey set the bottle and two shot glasses on the coffee table between them. He smiled and tilted his head toward the bottle, indicating that the admiral could dig in.

Dravenskey continued his stare. Popov turned the bottle in his hands and said, "I see you are a man of exquisite taste. We Russians may consume the most vodka, but sad to say, the Poles are better at making it. We should never have given those filthy dogs their freedom." He filled both glasses and handed one to the businessman. "And may I toast to the beginning of a beautiful friendship?"

"Friendship is of no consequence," replied Dravenskey. "I will drink to money!" Round two was also his. "Now, Admiral, may we get down to our business?"

"Certainly," Popov said, again pouring himself a shot.

"The Norwegians are building another deep sea platform to exploit their most recent discovery, the Gimli gas field. Like the previous Troll platform, it will be towed into the North Sea, and will supply Europe with sixty percent of its natural gas needs for the next fifty years. It will be finished in four years.

"As you know, we have been arguing for seventeen years with Ukraine over the main pipelines that run through their country to supply Europe. We built the pipelines, and now they demand that we sell them their gas at far below market value. It's unfortunate, but we have not been able to reach an agreement with their national gas company, Naftohaz Ukrainy. In response, we cut off our gas supply to Ukraine. But now, they are siphoning off a large portion of the gas that passes through to Europe and keeping it for themselves. You may dislike the Polish dogs, but I can tell you, these Ukrainians are worse. They are nothing but a cutthroat band of extortionists and thieves. Because of the 'uncertainty of supply' that these pig gypsies have caused, Eastern Europe is looking to cut back on its orders from Gazprom and increase their purchases from Norway. This is unacceptable to our profit margins. It is vital to increase our share of the European market."

Dravenskey saw Popov's eyelids begin to droop. He cleared his throat, and said, "Are you paying attention to me, Admiral?"

He startled Popov, who in one motion, refilled his glass and threw down a fourth shot. With the back of his hand, he wiped the vodka that ran down his chin. Looking up, he straightened his face and said, "Oh yes, of course. You would like to purchase some armaments so you can blow up this 'Gimli' whatever. And you would like me to be your provider." He puffed up like a peacock. Popov poured yet another shot.

"No, Admiral," Dravenskey shot back. "That is not what I want of you." He paused, rose from his sofa, and walked behind Popov. In a soft voice, he ventured, "I understand that a new class of submarines is on the same timeline as the Gimli platform … four years. Is that not correct?"

Dravenskey knew that by standing behind him, Popov was too rotund to turn and make eye contact. He heard the nervousness in Popov's voice when he replied, "Uh, yes … that would be the Borei class."

The mogul knew it was time to position his bishop for checkmate.

"I want the Gimli and Troll platforms to go away at the same time, Admiral. Your new Borei submarine will do the damage on its maiden voyage. And, this is important, my dear Admiral, it must look like a terrorist attack. That way, Mother Russia will never be blamed, and we will not start a war."

"But how could we accomplish such a thing? In the first place, it would be necessary to have the support of our government for our submarine to enter the Norwegian Economic Exclusion Zone. As we both know, our navy has been doing many provocative maneuvers to pressure the Norwegians over our disputed oil rights in the Arctic shelf. But that activity has been centered in the Barents Sea off Norway's northwestern coastline. I'm not sure our politicians have the balls to interfere in the North Sea gas fields. Second, it is still our submarine. How could we blame it on terrorists?"

This was the moment for Dravenskey to move his queen in for the kill. "Controlling politicians requires money. Of that we have an endless supply. The American capitalists taught us this fine art of persuasion. We learned well and added our own peculiar dimension of coercion. And our corruption makes them look like school children. It is they who have much to learn from us.

"My colleagues and I will work out the rest of the details. You can use your cruise missiles or conventional torpedoes to blow them out of the water. Either way, I don't care … because it will look like a terrorist act. Please understand, we are the best at what we do, and we will hold up our end of the bargain. Your end is to render the platforms useless long enough for me to make billions in international trading. If the wells are gone, I make more, which means you make more. But then again, I am a reasonable man. And as I have always said, 'Know when enough is enough.'"

He watched Popov expose a wide, toothy grin and pour himself another shot. "I see a perfectly corrupt marriage of business and military might. I think I like you, my friend. Yes, I think I like you very much."

Dravenskey's face assumed a sinister appearance. He raised his glass without speaking a word. He nodded in acknowledgment. The edges of his mouth crept upward and formed a sardonic smile. He stared at the eager fool, thinking, Checkmate!

***

WASHINGTON, D.C.

The paneled walls of the living room were dark and dingy from age, typical of the capital's turn-of-the-century rental housing held by absentee landlords. These brownstones were not part of the city's ghetto; their distinction was that of serving the needs of lesser governmental employees. The mantel clock was pushing midnight and a flickering street lamp cast an eerie pall over the living room. Shadows from partially open venetian blinds lent an even more dangerous feeling to what was already the worst night Tim Daniels had experienced in his ten years of service to the CIA.

He had an old-fashioned morality coupled with a deep sense of ethics. Friends didn't come easy, so to him, a true friendship was not disposable. However, he knew that this friendship was causing him an enormous amount of heat, and the pot was beginning to boil.

"Devon, for God's sake, get it through your head—you don't exist anymore!" He said into the phone. "I don't know what I can do to make it clearer. It's as if you've fallen off the face of the earth!"

Tim knew the risk of having this conversation on his home telephone. God, he wished Devon had prearranged this call at some out-of-the-way payphone. Both of them knew better, damn it; they were not rookies. Working for the CIA had taught Tim that every obscure object and every dark crevice had ears. And they were ears that belonged to cold, sinister people who could snuff out your life with the ease of blowing out a candle. He knew people were watching, and that their eyes would turn to him. His fear was real and he wanted to hang up and call Devon back. But Devon was a true friend—a friend for whom Tim was willing to sacrifice his life.

With sweat dripping down his forehead, Tim gritted his teeth and took a deep breath through his nostrils. Chills ran down the hairs of his neck as he heard a faint creaking from another room. With caution, he lowered his head and looked left, behind himself, and right. What was that noise … a water pipe, an air conditioning duct, normal shrinkage in the wood floors? He couldn't tell. He was trained to discern subtle differences. His life depended on that acute ability.

Tim hesitated, turning his options in his head. He knew he should get up and check the sound, but he shrugged it off. As the palm of his free hand slid up and made a conical covering of the phone's speaker to lower his voice, he whispered, "Listen. Flat out, no electronic record of you comes up, not anywhere! Honest to God, I've never seen the beat of this shit. I've checked and cross-checked every available file I could possibly access ... down to the lousy DMV. Every single aspect of your and Cathy's lives has been sanitized. And I mean everything!"

Tim pulled the phone from his ear as he heard Devon shout, "That can't be! What about those credit card numbers I gave you? Cathy's name is on them and the charges she's making are still being accepted! We have banking, a telephone—"

"...Nothing!" Tim said, cutting him off. He felt his body sag as a sense of helplessness came into his voice. "I can't figure it out. Somehow, the charges are being rerouted, but I keep hitting an electronic roadblock every way I try to chase them down. When it comes to a computer, Devon, you know I'm as good as there is; but even I'm locked out. There's some kind of heavy shit coming down here, and I can't connect the dots. And anything I can't figure out scares the hell out of me."

Tim heard Devon's voice trail off in resignation when Devon asked, "What about those Swiss bank account numbers I gave you? Were you able to make any kind of connection there?"

"No. Look, you're trying to connect two of the heaviest hitters in the CIA with the Russian Mafia. Stealing the components of a small nuclear device and selling them on the black market for profit means we're talking an astronomical amount of money. If you want to have any chance of making something stick, you're going to have to get more proof. The truth is we don't know jack shit about the Russian Mafia. The players are more than enigmatic—they're sinister, murky, and morphing. Hell, they bump themselves off so fast we don't know from day to day who they are or where they are, let alone whom they influence or whom they've bought. You know how far the corruption goes ... it goes right to the highest levels of the military and the Russian government itself."

"What the hell are you saying, Tim? You and everyone else at Langley know how long I've been undercover with this filth!"

"Come on Devon ... the corruption's on both sides. Last year alone, over five hundred million dollars in The Agency's budget was unaccounted for. It disappeared into some black hole. Congress brought it up in a hearing; cameras were rolling, lots of press coverage, a three-ring, fucking media circus. And what did those pompous assholes on The Hill do? Nothing!

They shoveled a lot of shit, preened like a bunch of peacocks in front of a brain-dead media, and shut the door on it. Our puffed-up Senators took turns looking good in front of a national camera for five days and that was all they cared about. They and their media minions know damn well that unless it's a Hollywood-type murder, one week is the public's maximum attention span."

"Tim, we both know that Carey and Grayson are guilty ... maybe even guilty of treason. There has to be a way to out them, there has to be!"

Nestling the phone between his ear and shoulder, Tim opened his desk drawer and pulled out a small pad of paper. "Alright, I'll give it one more shot. I've given copies of everything you've sent me to a friend of mine to cross-check. She's as good with a computer as there is, maybe better than me. And don't worry, she can be trusted ... even with my life."

Tim leaned to pick up his pen when his body jolted forward. In one violent motion, he tipped over and landed on the floor. The phone went with him, breaking the connection. Blood pooled from the single shot to the back of his head.

"Tim? Tim!" Devon shouted. The last sounds he heard were the unmistakable muffled sound from the silenced pistol and his friend crashing to the floor.

Devon sat stunned. His eyes were fixed on the wall opposite him, yet he saw nothing. In his heart he was certain ... he and his wife Cathy would be next. They were coming.

CHAPTER 2

THE FIRST RAYS OF A BUDDING SUNRISE BROKE THE CRISP horizon, casting a bluish, diamond-like sparkle to the previous evening's fallen snow. Feeling the familiar, arthritic pain in his stiff shoulder, Devon McKenzie rolled over and forced one crusted-over eye to open. He squinted to catch a glimpse of the clock on the wooden crate next to his bed. Seven fifteen. He forced his other eye to open. His gravelly voice murmured to no one, "Hell, the day's half gone, you jerk."

The stench of his damp clothes and leather boots lying in a heap on the wood floor wafted across his nose. His eyes rolled backward and he feigned passing out. Doesn't anything ever dry out in this stinking state? He thought. Wrinkling his brow, he shook his head as if the raunchy smell would disappear. Cupping his chapped hands together, he rubbed the tips of his fingers across his bloodshot eyes, cleaning the night's crust. His hands slid down and scratched the scaly skin under his scruffy beard.

The solitude of living alone in the wilderness brought its own anxiety, but the ever-present fear of when "they" would come taxed his stamina. The rustling of bears or wolves in the bushes, the hoot of an owl, even the sound of wind in the trees caused him to act in defense. Every time he rose to a new day, every step he took outdoors, or every night he drank himself to sleep, was filled with terror. They would never leave him alive … he knew too much.

His life was upside down. It had imploded, becoming small and confining. His stage was no longer the world's power centers, Washington, Moscow, and London. Rental cars had been replaced by an old snowmobile, luxury hotels by a neglected one-room log cabin that hadn't seen an occupant in twenty years. There were no embassies, no intrigues, no missions, and worst of all, there was no one.

A tingling chill ran up his spine and spread across his knotted back as he crawled from under his woolen blankets, his bare feet touching the cold planks of the floor. Turning his head, he scanned three of the four dreary walls of his cabin. They appeared closer in than they had the day before, and the day before, and the day before that. Laden with ash from the smoke of his fireplace, only the mortar chinking between the logs changed with the evolving spider webs that covered its crevices.

He ran his fingers through his shaggy hair and did his best to shake the fog from his pounding head. Each morning, coherent thinking was a daunting task. Lying on its side, an empty bottle of single malt Scotch presented an ugly message. Was it three-quarters full when I began drinking last night? If it was ... does anybody give a rat's ass?

Dragging his feet to a rusted sink filled with unwashed metal dishes, he tried to stretch, tugging to straighten his red, long underwear. He looked around, raised one eyebrow, and feigned a look of disgust at his dog, Oscar, who had refused to acknowledge him, let alone budge an inch. The dog was in no hurry to share another grouchy morning with his hungover master. Devon's toothbrush was hidden behind the un-washed frying pan, and didn't show itself till he picked up the coffee pot and drained its day-old contents. Humph, he thought, his lips pursing, how pathetic am I? ... My only pleasures in life— coffee, scotch and a lazy-ass dog with a Great Dane head on a Boxer body. He snickered and shook his head in disgust. But what would I do without him? He thought.

It didn't take long for Devon to plan his day. After all, it would be no different than any other day in his life. He had wood to split, elk and mountain goat meat to dig out of the ice, and his mutt to feed. He needed to track and kill an elk, or sneak into Otter Creek and purchase another three months of provisions. Each morning he turned on his short wave radio. If it wasn't for the occasional relief it offered, there were times when he thought he would put the barrel of his rifle into his mouth and join his beloved wife. Therein lay the problem ... the religion of his youth no longer gave him the comfort and peace he craved, yet the beliefs that defined his existence still ruled out suicide as an entry into Heaven. And if he didn't believe that he would see his wife in Heaven, the pain of living without her would have no meaning.

"Where's that damned toothpaste?" He growled, pushing the crusty plates apart. He discovered it curled up in the corner of the small countertop, where he had thrown it the previous day in another fit of lonely rage.

As Devon spit toothpaste into the sink, his head snapped to attention. A garbled distress call broke the chilly cabin air. "Mayday... Mayday! This is Piper 0622 ... Mayday! Engine stalled ... making emergency landing ... south of Black Pigeon Ridge, east of Tyner's Pass ... Mayday!"

"Shit!" Devon said, his toothbrush dropping into the sink. He bolted across the room for his radio. He tried to dial the plane's frequency. His fingers fumbled. "Piper 0622 ... Piper 0622 ... do you copy? Piper 0622 ... do you read me?"

The muffled sound of a crash in the distance was his answer. Within seconds, Devon was dressed. He pulled the supply sled up and hooked it to the back of his snowmobile. Another chill ran up his spine. This time, it wasn't the freezing cold. The warning was crystal clear. He paused and looked back at the cabin that was also his prison. Was this the day he had feared? Was a chain reaction being set into motion that he would have little or no control over? Was this the opening that would allow the dreaded shadow world of his past to sneak back into his life?

"Damn!" He mumbled, climbing onto the machine. He remembered he had left the blankets and first-aid kit. When he had the gear stowed under a tarp and had hooked the last bungee cord, he cranked up the engine and raced off in what was the general direction of the crash. Crisp, freezing wind burned his face between his goggles and beard, but he didn't care ... someone needed his help, and that was all that mattered. As if on autopilot, the snowmobile raced across the rolling hills of gleaming white, negotiating the snow-laden pine trees. Devon stared straight ahead at the wispy black smoke rising into the gray sky above the horizon.

Watching the smoke waft upward, Devon noticed that it curled outward like the soft delicate strands of a woman's hair. A warm feeling overtook him ... a woman's hair. His mind drifted to a happier time.

***

It had been twelve years, but his graduate school days at Stanford were vivid. They weren't the hell-raising days of the University of Michigan, where he had majored in computer science with a minor in Russian. But, obtaining a doctorate in computer science wasn't conducive to late night parties.

During his summer breaks he took a job as a lifeguard at a beach facility along the shores of Lake Michigan. He stayed at his roommate's house. Tim Daniels was more than a roommate … he too was a lifeguard and shared Devon's fascination for computers and the world of espionage.

Devon first saw Cathy Sullivan at one of an endless row of dark walnut tables in the main library. He preferred the library in the Computer Science building. It was quiet, void of the hustling masses of students that frequented the main facility. Hitting a mental block in his research, he yawned and his eyes drifted down the long table. His world came to an abrupt halt. She was drop-dead beautiful and he couldn't pull his eyes off her. But it wasn't just her beauty. Devon McKenzie knew in an instant that this was the woman he would marry. He had the strong conviction that God kept an eye on him, and he was certain that divine intervention had placed them at that table at that moment in time.

After a while, she rose to check out her books. He threw his papers into his leather briefcase and stepped into line behind her. It required great stealth and a limber neck to read the student ID card she passed to the librarian. Weeks passed before he manipulated a friend of a friend of a friend to line up a blind date. She was out of his league in every way, but he was confident that guile and sheer determination would win her over.

Stanford was also where Devon took his first bite of the CIA's forbidden fruit when Tim suggested they attend the CIA's Career Day symposium. He was in love with Catherine Sullivan and considered himself the luckiest man in the world when she agreed to marry him. But the private recruitment by two Agency honchos stirred a passion in him that ran on parallel tracks with his love for Cathy. She was the true focus of his quest, but the CIA's pursuit was relentless. In the growing world of computers and its exploding technology, he displayed signs of pure genius.

With his deep love of country, and his craving for heroes, Devon developed a fascination of the adventurous life of a James Bond styled agent. Long before the CIA courted him, he had lusted for a hero's life in undercover intelligence.

Upon receiving his doctorate, he received The Agency's offer. It was heady and the adventurous picture they painted stroked his ego more than he wanted to admit. But the pay that the private sector offered was astronomical in comparison. The prospect of a normal life being married to Cathy and working as a senior analyst for a growing tech company carried the day.

CHAPTER 3

DEVON MCKENZIE HAD WORKED IN THE PRIVATE SECTOR for two years and married life wore well with him and Cathy. But, without warning or provocation, the catastrophic events of 9/11 altered the world geo-political equation. The paradigm changed and the United States homeland became vulnerable in every way. The United States was not some empty name, an isolated world power protected by two oceans and operating within its own bubble. Its sacred soil, and more importantly, its people had been attacked. Any American city, stadium, or mall was open to a terrorist attack— even its seat of government— and these attacks could come on the cheap. All that was needed was a small cadre of fanatical sleeper cells willing to die for a cause. The world waited, wondering not whether these terrorist cells could lay their filthy hands on a WMD, but when and where they would. The U.S. government turned up the heat and labeled its efforts a "War on Terror," and increased its dependence on its enigmatic covert intelligence.

The CIA at Langley, Virginia continued to loom in the far corners of Devon's mind. Its call appealed to a sense of revenge for the 9/11 attacks and became the cause of his discontent. His fantasy grew until myth replaced reality. His love of the endless possibilities of computer application drifted to an obsession with its military use—specifically covert counter-espionage. Devon's flights of computer fantasy became the dominant topic of water cooler whispers, and his ideas eventually found their way back to The Agency. His musings piqued the interest of the computer wonks at Langley, and their pursuit began again in earnest. The courtship steamed up, this time stroking his ego to his yielding point.

He began feeling "stuck" in his job and was soon openly complaining that the work was unimportant and no longer interested him. He couldn't imagine himself doing it for the rest of his life. He would look at Cathy and kick himself for having these thoughts. His love was deep and he believed that she made him the luckiest person in the world. How could he not sacrifice this small piece of *his* life for the sake of *their* comfortable life? This day-after-day scenario soon turned into year after year.

Agent Tim Daniels came out to California for a visit. His stories of working at The Agency displayed a contentment and satisfaction that Devon could never realize. Jealousy reared its ugly head. His restlessness became inflamed to the point of obsession. Over and over, he tried discussing it with Cathy, but to her, the thought of him working undercover in some foreign country for months on end was unacceptable. The thought of giving up her career as a marketing executive in Silicon Valley and moving to the hot and humid suburbs of Washington didn't help either. The argument continued unabated until it was Cathy who made the sacrifice.

At age thirty, Devon yielded to his dream and became Agent McKenzie. He requested and received extensive training in sophisticated demolition. He was everything the CIA believed he would be. He was quick on the uptake, and proved his complete grasp of the integration of computer micro-circuitry with high tech explosives. At the end of his training, fate again played a major role in his life.

CHAPTER 4

A LOW BRANCH FROM A SNOW-LADEN PINE BRUSHED Devon's head, dropping a heavy layer of snow against his face. He snapped out of his long reverie and once again became aware of his frigid surroundings. The rising smoke was no longer distant. It loomed close, past the next hill. Glistening white snow again washed upon his face as the snowmobile dipped into a soft recess, sending clouds of powder spraying to each side. He cranked up the accelerator when the motor began to lug under the steep ascent of the last hill. There it is! This doesn't look good, he thought.

Like a wounded duck that had been shot from the sky, the plane lay in a crumpled mass. Its tail was sitting high in the air with its nose buried in the snow at the base of a large tree that held its ground and became its final barrier. One of its wings was raised at an angle and the other lay vertical against another pine that had sheared it from the fuselage. The rising band of smoke that had been his beacon was emanating from the torn cowling on the left.

Making his final descent, Devon detected a small flame that burst into the open below the base of the smoke. He knew that every second counted. If the gas line ruptured, he could be hurling himself into a ball of fire. Running on instinct and pure adrenaline, he brought the snowmobile around to the plane's side with a skidding turn that drenched the fuselage with a cloud of snow. His maneuver had no effect on the flame that was becoming a growing fire. He climbed the plane's ski strut, brushed away the snowy debris of brown bark and green needles the crash had caked upon the side window and peered inside. The pilot was slumped over against the opposite door. Smashed suitcases, clothes and gear were strewn everywhere. Devon grabbed the latch and gave it a quick twist. It wouldn't budge. He yanked harder; still it would not yield.

Time was crucial. He spotted a broken piece of the landing gear. He grabbed it and smashed the Plexiglas window. Reaching in he grabbed the inside latch and forced open the crumpled door. Pulling one glove off, he reached in again and stretched to place two fingers on the pilot's warm neck. In spite of the freezing temperature, a faint pulse could still be felt.

The wind shifted, causing black, noxious smoke to fill the cockpit and burn Devon's eyes. With his lungs heaving and coughing violently from the noxious smoke, he pulled his knife out of its sheath and cut the pilot's harness belt free. It took all of Devon's strength to hoist the pilot's limp body up and out of the plane.

The engine fire was raging out of control. He knew he was out of time. What few seconds he had left were slipping away. He wrapped a blanket around the body. He noticed blood coming through the sweater above the abdomen. He slid his fingers under the sweater and felt a gaping hole that flowed with warm blood.

"I don't know if I can save you, friend," Devon's gravelly voice whispered. He wadded a towel over the open gash. He cinched a rope over the blanketed body, making sure to keep tight pressure on the wound.

Jumping on the seat of the snowmobile, he turned its skis away from the plane and gave it full throttle. As if a powerful and invisible hand had swooshed it forward, the machine roared away up the slope. Reaching the peak, Devon felt the heat of the blast. He heard the massive explosion. He breathed a sigh of relief and pulled his goggles down over his burning, swollen eyes.

The trip back seemed infinitely longer than the trek to the downed plane. A thousand questions raced through his mind. Could he save the pilot? What would he do to stop the bleeding? Should he attempt to close the wounds with stitches? He tried to keep his composure, but someone's life was on the line, and even as an ex-CIA field man, he still felt that the wound was beyond his capabilities.

When they reached his cabin, Devon eased his grip on the steering bar and felt a burning pain race over his fingertips. As he began to untie the rope, he squeezed his fingers down—they felt as if they would fall off. Were they frostbitten? He didn't know and didn't have time to care. Snow was falling hard and the wind whipped to a furious pace. He staggered back under the pain of picking up the pilot and almost fell to the ground, but managed the few steps to his cabin and kicked open the door. As he set his bundle down on the bed, a low, guttural groan told him his human cargo had survived the ride. Devon pulled his hood back, shut the door and dropped his parka all in one motion. Grabbing a fresh bottle of Scotch, he pulled the cork off with his teeth and spit it on the floor. The large gulp warmed every inch of his insides as it trickled its way down. He took one more swig for strength, knowing he had to examine the wounds of the injured pilot.

Devon was gentle as he pulled the parka's drawstring and eased the fur lining back. Startled, he blinked as the image of his wife Cathy flashed in front of him. Sliding the zipper down, he made sure he avoided the bloody circle of the wadded towel. Shock came over him as he eased the coat back.

"A woman!" He whispered. His whole body froze, as if he were doing something wrong. Her eyes eased open and stared at Devon for several seconds, trying to comprehend where she was and what had happened. They closed again as her consciousness slipped away.

He knew what had to be done. Reaching down and slipping his hunting knife out of its sheath, his other hand gripped her sweater and he cut it upward toward her neck. As he peeled back the sides of the sweater, his eyes confirmed what he had suspected … the wound was far more than he could handle or even know how to care for. Devon was convinced he had to get her to the nearest medical center in Otter Creek—immediately. At least there was a doctor there who could give her the emergency care she needed. The question was: Could Devon do it without being exposed, without someone spotting him? "They" still wanted him, and "they" were everywhere, like some festering cancer that wouldn't go away. It could mean his death … or it could even mean hers. A petrifying chill ran down his neck as he stared out the window, gathering his thoughts.

A low, rasping cough and weak groan broke his trance. He looked over to see her head roll to its side, a slow drool of pale red blood spewing from the side of her mouth. She was bleeding internally and he felt his body sink. He knew the decision had already been made for him. It would be risky and the ride would take three hours, but there was no other way. She was going to die if he waited for another bush pilot. As he turned her head back upward and wiped the blood away, he brushed the soft, pale brown hair from her face. It was an innocent face … one that pulled at him, as if from a distance. It wasn't that the feeling was new. It just had not been felt for a time longer than he could remember.

In a flash, he could see himself and Cathy driving in her Alfa Romeo on the Pacific Coast Highway with the balmy wind blowing her long chestnut hair and the mild California sun warming their serene faces. They knew this was more than a getaway. It was their freedom. A freedom that promised they could start their lives over, and no matter what they faced, they would see it through … together. Life could begin again. He looked into her strong emerald eyes, the blinking rays of the sun that broke with every tree they passed made her eyes dazzle like a sparkling ring. For him, he knew this was the right move and it felt good. Neither could have known this moment was to be their last moment of happiness.

The memory faded and his focus shifted to the oil heater thermostat. When he had wrapped the last of his blankets around the sinking pilot, his fingers bumped up against a small, hard object in her coat pocket. Reaching in, he found a cellular phone. Comforted with his find, he filled the gas tank and prayed that he would make it in time to save this woman.

CHAPTER 5

MOSCOW

FOUR YEARS AGO

BATU SIGUA MAY HAVE BEEN A "RUSSIAN" MISSILE SCIENTIST, but in his heart, he was a pure Georgian patriot. When Georgia became "independent," Batu was already one of Russia's dissident scientists. His job was to oversee the writing of all computer programs that controlled the guidance systems of the missiles on the latest Borei class submarines.

Batu was never overt, for living in the Soviet Union required watching your mouth and your backside. He had seen too many friends hauled off for being what the state called "lunatic dissident scum." It never took much … one statement could gain you that label, and its owner could be put on a twenty-four-hour watch list. One day those friends were gone … off to a gulag in Siberia, or remanded to an asylum for rehabilitation. The ones who went for rehab came back a year later, but were never the same. They were withdrawn and introverted. Worse, they never talked to anyone again. They performed their jobs, but friendship was out of the question. It was as if they were mindless robots—and they were the lucky ones. Batu Sigua bit his tongue and watched … everyone and everything.

In 2004, the Rose Revolution took place in Georgia and Saakasvili became its first freely elected president. Saakasvili was dedicated to reuniting his country and bringing the breakaway republics of Abkhazia and South Ossetia back under full Georgian control. Moreover, he pledged Georgia to joining NATO. Batu was ecstatic. For the first time, life had real meaning, and he saw light at the end of his personal tunnel.

His depression returned when the Russians began making life hell for Saakasvili and the Georgian nation. The new Russia began acting like the old Soviet Union. They funneled money into the breakaway states of Abkhazia and South Ossetia, and inflamed their interest in rejoining a Russian commonwealth. Flyovers erupted like a plague of locusts over Georgia. Batu made up his mind to do anything he could to seek revenge on his Russian overlords.

In spite of his efforts to keep his views private, the CIA uncovered his dissidence. After receiving subtle overtures, Batu responded to a CIA contact working the U.S. Embassy in Moscow.

Langley wasted no time, and its profiles pointed to one person. Its newest Near-East agent was fluent in the Russian language and also happened to have a doctorate in computer language. The CIA questioned the validity of the Georgian scientist and the inexperience of Devon McKenzie. They wanted more time, but the clandestine meetings were put on the fast track. They deemed the prize worth the risk.

CHAPTER 6

DEVON MCKENZIE WAS THROWN INTO A CRASH COURSE TO polish his Moscow street dialect. His accelerated courses in Borei submarine design and Bulava Submarine Launched Ballistic Missiles (SLBM) were strenuous and tested his scientific mettle, but he was up to the formidable task, and finished ahead of the time his superiors had allotted. He felt a sense of accomplishment and pride that he hadn't felt before. He glossed over the new tremor that was rumbling through the foundation of his marriage.

McKenzie was given a straightforward mission. He was to assuage Batu's conscience while showing him how to install an encrypted program that would cause every Bark missile to misfire and shut down. This would force the Russian armament scientists to shelve the Bark program and move forward with the research and development of the next generation SS-N-15 Bulava missiles, thus further delaying the deployment of their Borei submarines. It would also force them to commit to a smaller, odd-sized SLBM which would cause another alteration of the sub fleet. Devon's program would cause the first eleven Baluvas to misfire when tested, but the subsequent thirteen would fire in order. Sheer pandemonium and frustration would develop in the psyche of the Russian admiralty. What the Russian Navy would not know was that every Bulava fired after the thirteen would revert to malfunction. The trick for Devon was not in the installation of his program, but in its encryption. Deep cloaking and the subsequent impossibility of dismantling the virus, even if discovered, were paramount. This was why Devon McKenzie was chosen.

At his final meeting with the scientist, Batu Sigua, Devon's ability to smother his misgivings came to a halt. The dissident Russian confirmed that the program they had installed in the newest Borei sub was working, and he had tested it for cloaking and portability, but he was growing nervous and feared for his own life, and for those of his wife and children. Shadows were everywhere—and these shadows had eyes! They were outside his apartment, they tailed his car, and they were at his laboratory. He told Devon knew that he had become despondent over what he had done, and that maybe he had made a grave mistake. Maybe he needed to undo what he had done. Devon had neither the experience nor the wisdom that was needed to finesse and diffuse the psychological crisis.

Devon reassured Batu that no one could detect what he had done, and told him not to do anything until he could talk to his people at the CIA. They would know what to do and how to protect him and his family. Two days later, Devon saw the byline in the morning paper:

SCIENTIST COMMITS SUICIDE … DISTRAUGHT OVER FAMILY KILLED IN AUTOMOBILE ACCIDENT.

The young agent was stunned. He had made the mistake of befriending Batu Sigua. He had listened to his stories and felt empathy for the man's plight … stories of being a Georgian patriot living in fear under Soviet Communism, then to see a chance that he and his family might live in a free and independent Georgia … only to have those hopes dashed. For Devon, the conflict wasn't about the mission, but of placing the scientist and his family in jeopardy.

Devon raced to their contact place in the wooded park bordering Moscow. Finding nothing on or by the bench they had so often used as a drop, anger welled up. He kicked the closest tree, savaging it. Was he responsible for the death of four innocent people? Was this the price of being in the CIA … did women and children have to die? The playing field had become a killing field, and that field included innocent people. Cathy had known this, but he had been blinded by a juvenile image of James Bond without any of the consequences. He thought he could play in this game, but be in the background … some techno-wonk that could have it both ways.

In total resignation, Devon leaned his shoulder and forehead onto the tree behind the park bench and questioned the direction his life had taken. He thought again of Batu and his family. The dissident had had the family life Devon couldn't attain.

After staring at the ground, he turned and faced the gnarly barked tree. Gripping its trunk with both hands, he leaned his head backward to smash his forehead against it in anger, but a small white patch caught his eye. He raised his fingers and pulled a folded piece of paper out from behind a loose piece of bark. His jaw dropped as he unfolded the paper. The handwritten note was short, yet ominous:

I WILL BE AVENGED!

Devon had never experienced anything like this. His training at The Agency had dealt with the collateral death of innocent women and children, but that was death as a result of terrorism ... someone else's terrorism. I'm supposed to be the good guy trying to prevent that. Out of the blue, his job had become personal and ugly. Was Batu's threat of revenge directed against him? ... The CIA? ... Or the Russian secret police?

He contacted his superior, Thomas Grayson, but the response from his boss was terse and right out of the manual. Four years later, Devon McKenzie had wearied of his time in The Agency. He had been transferred to the American embassy in Tbilisi, Georgia and survived the turmoil of Batu Sigua. He knew that he could no longer stay in its employ. His tipoff came with the arrival of a new administration following the recent presidential election. This brought change in the directorship of one its most critical agencies ... the CIA.

CHAPTER 7

THE PRESIDENT'S CHOICE TO STRAIGHTEN UP THE MESS WAS Ernest Hatcher, a former naval intelligence officer and four-term congressman from Tennessee. Hatcher accepted the appointment and was grateful. But he thought the newly elected president was weak by nature and chose him because he was a bulldog and would "clean up" the CIA. After the attacks on the U.S. Embassies in Kenya, Tanzania and the Cole, the bombing of the New York subway, 9/11 and the subsequent "weapons of mass destruction" debacle, he agreed the once proud name of the Central Intelligence Agency was beginning to look more like a worn-out oxymoron.

While U.S. policy hunted al-Qaeda forces in Afghanistan and Iraq, Hatcher came to the CIA pledging full transparency to his Commander-in-Chief and to Congress. He also made a firm commitment to rebuild The Agency's morale. That he was Crusader Rabbit couldn't have been stated better. At Hatcher's first meeting, with all department heads in attendance, he was quoted as saying, "Let's all just get along, shall we?" The rolling of eyeballs was as embarrassing as it was comedic. Even the department heads that were total suck-ups checked their watches, begging for the meeting to be shortened, or to find a reason to be excused.

After the initial "kumbaya" moment, the discussion focused on the Russian Mafia and its tentacles reaching into the armaments black market and taking it to far more sinister heights. And this complete inability to stem the flow of WMDs was not just Langley's, but the entire world's. Not one to risk initiating a program or idea, Hatcher asked for an open brainstorming session on this subject. It was here that a plot was born to infiltrate the morphing black market and intercept the flow of WMDs. While interception and confiscation were agreed upon to be the preferred method, it was also agreed that it was impossible to shut off the spigot. That could only be accomplished inside Russia by an uncorrupted and diligent government. And because the corruption had penetrated the highest levels of the Russian government, the consensus became that the spigot would continue to flow in everyone's lifetime and possibly beyond that. Some kind of plan had to be initiated, if for no other reason than to show the president that Hatcher was doing something.

Sitting next to Hatcher was a department head named Dennis Carey. He shared the DCI's belief that a third element had to be added to the goal of interception and confiscation. That element was diversion. The theory was that if terrorists could never get their hands on any WMDs, they would nonetheless continue to spend a bottomless amount of money and time creating more and varied methods to accomplish their procurement. And more often than not, they would be successful, thus causing untold terror worldwide. This method of diversion was a way to stay ahead of the curve and maintain some semblance of control. If some weapons were allowed to get into the hands of terrorists, they would continue to use that source. The problem was that even one WMD in the filthy hands of terrorists was a prescription for disaster. The remedy, as suggested by Carey, was to intercept and render useless the WMDs and pass them along to terrorists as if unimpeded. In spite of its inherent conflict of interest, Hatcher liked the idea. He wouldn't have to own it if it failed, but he could take all the credit if it proved successful.

He kept his finger in the loop by personally choosing the agent to run the black operation. Devon was chosen for the mission. Under the guise of procuring these devises for terrorist clients, the agent was to secure and alter these weapons before they ended in the hands of the enemies of the West. It was a precarious line to walk. Through a network of closely held Middle East operatives, a pipeline was set up—one that could be monitored and controlled. Monitored so that the enemy would still receive weapons, and controlled because the weapons would be altered, rending them useless. If not, the flow of materiel would be outside the control of the West. The arms smugglers inside Russia would supply al-Qaeda, and its Wahhabi financiers would pay. But neither would know that the minutest of key components had been modified or diverted back to the United States. Well known for its ubiquitous lack of quality and performance, an inept Russia would be the ultimate bogeyman to blame. Careful *control* became the CIA watchword of this risky, yet morally convoluted policy.

CHAPTER 8

THE LENGTH OF DEVON'S ASSIGNMENT IN GEORGIA AND Chechnya had strained his marriage and the penalty was being paid. The couple had discussed his getting out of the CIA or them going their separate ways. Devon was torn. He had told Cathy that Dagestan would be his last assignment, and after its completion he would be home to stay ... their lives could begin again. But it was this mission in which he would discover the one small piece of incriminating evidence that would forever alter their lives, changing it into a living hell on earth. The evidence pointed to his direct bosses and he was convinced that their hands were dirty.

Never comfortable with the expanding role that he played in these wretched countries, Devon longed for the days when he was designing complex computer-assisted explosive devices—it was his passion. It was also the bait which had lured him to The Agency in the first place. Training people in the use of these explosives to obtain their freedom sat well with his deep-seated sense of justice. Especially when the intended target was the nemesis society he had learned from youth to despise.

The old Soviet Union had disintegrated and the new Russia was its mutant offspring. But the devolution process was ongoing, spiraling out of control. No one in the West knew what this morphing by-product would end up being. As the second most powerful army in the history of the world began to unravel, it was inevitable that the ease of stealing stockpiles of its war materiel would grow in the same proportion as the amount of money available for procurement. Even after the "Evil Empire" had collapsed under its own bloated weight, there was a satisfying sense of irony in the CIA as another of their plots was hatched. This plot would turn the table and allow a portion of the intercepted arms to be used by terrorists back against Russia, thus insuring that this twisted aberration of history, called Russia, would never again rear its ugly head in a civilized world.

Dealing with the newly formed "Russian Mafia" and a host of Muslim financiers, including the Saudi Royal Family with its perverse love/hate relationship with the Wahabi cult, Devon found that his role had expanded far beyond his original assignment of teaching the art of using and hiding the smallest, yet most powerful explosives. Bit by bit, his procurement list from Langley grew as it became apparent that there was no form of weaponry outside the reach of the brazen, yet enigmatic Russian Mafia, which, like a stench-laden sewer, was blind to what was flushed into it. But the weapons were no longer being used against Russia. The Muslim jihad had become a worldwide scourge and turned its anger against any and all countries that were considered "infidels" to Wahabism.

Devon had come to the uncomfortable realization that he was nothing more than a Middle East arms whore. He saw firsthand how the Muslim religion had been hijacked by an insidious form of Wahabism that was bent on nothing short of the complete destruction of the United States, and all of Western civilization. It galled him whenever he heard someone refer to the terrorists as part of a "peaceful religion," as if this hijacked version of faith had anything to do with any rational person's notion of what a religion should be. "We *think* we are manipulating these Islamo-fascists, but they are the ones who are manipulating us!" He would shout to no one.

His ethics overcame his ability to suppress his conscience when he saw that the targets of his explosives were redirected against innocent people, not military or inanimate objects. It was one thing to blow up a communication system or a munitions depot, but the bombings had become targeted against innocent human beings, the bulk of which were Muslim. In spite of his growing inner struggle, he continued to smother the last vestiges of a crumbling conscience. That is, until his superiors redefined his mission once again.

CHAPTER 9

THE CIA HAD LONG HEARD THE RUMORS THAT AN EXTENsive array of small, suitcase-sized nuclear explosives had been developed by the old Soviet Union. But because swarthy, Middle Eastern types carrying heavy suitcases could be ferreted out at any customs checkpoint in the world, the Russian FSB knew they had to alter the dynamic. Replacing the old KGB, it set its path on the art of separating and disguising the bombs' components, allowing for the subsequent ease of their reassembly. These parts could come to the U.S. through shipping containers on boats or, depending on their size and configuration, could be shipped through any overnight carrier from anywhere in the world. The reassembly would require neither an extensive laboratory nor a nuclear scientist. All that was needed was a bench in any small warehouse and a computer-savvy jihadist willing to risk his life for seventy-two virgins in the hereafter.

Devon became immersed in his new assignment in Chechnya. His mission was clear and without ambiguity. He was to contact the Chechen underground, procure the newest designer demolitions from his contacts in the Russian Mafia, and teach the local rebels how to defend themselves against an aggressive Russia bent with imperial designs. The United States was in a global war against terrorism and Chechnya was to be used as a pawn to curb the new Russian appetite. In spite of official statements to the contrary, a blind eye toward terrorists was once again being turned. The CIA assured its young agent that "America doesn't have friends, only interests."

Devon succeeded well in the first part of his mission. Struggling at first with the guttural Nakh dialect, the spoken tongue of Chechnya and Ingushetia, he was able to get through most meetings with the help of a few rebels fluent in Russian. His larger problem was containing the number of contacts that kept flooding his way. Faced with annihilation, the rebel cause had splintered into numerous tribal groups vying to receive any outside help that might be available. Exposing themselves to the Russian FSB meant little to a people who had already lost their families and homes.

The second part of his mission was also successful. His passion to delve into the hybrid microtechnology produced, little by little, the most sophisticated explosives that could be hidden in a small, shoulder-carried duffel bag. Devon hit pay dirt … he was told a nuclear device had become available.

His boss Grayson tried to remain calm when Devon reached him on a secure line, but a stuttering in his voice betrayed him. He told his agent to go ahead and make arrangements to secure the WMD. Devon handled the transaction like a veteran of many years. He thought it strange, however, when his next instructions were to sit tight, secure the weapon, and wait a few days until further arrangements could be made. Devon was uneasy, not just because of the personal danger of possessing the WMD, but by the sudden lack of urgency on The Agency's part. This weapon needed to be moved—and moved now. Why wasn't a cohesive plan already in place? Shouldn't he already be rendering the weapon harmless?

When the instructions came three days later, Devon was even further confused. He was instructed to deliver the unit to a terrorist camp in Afghanistan, receive a valise in return and proceed to Geneva. Something in his analytical mind came to a roaring halt—but what? Was he getting paranoid? That comes with the job—but this was different. This arrangement of receiving money for the exchange sickened him. With no second guessing, he had trusted orders from above during his whole career with the CIA. But his mission in Moscow had changed him. The death of Batu Sigua had forever taken its toll on Devon. It became clear. There was no direction given for him to disable the WMD prior to its delivery. This course of action wasn't part of his or any other mission.

The customary transactions were always the same. He made sure the altered components were delivered on time, with an agent for al-Qaeda giving him a sealed briefcase as payment. He handcuffed the valise to his wrist and left to deliver it in person to the assigned address in Switzerland. This transaction caused his world to stumble and come to a screeching halt.

CHAPTER 10

ZURICH, SWITZERLAND
FIVE YEARS EARLIER

A DRIZZLE STARTED TO FALL, SO DEVON LIFTED THE VALISE over his head and began a slow run to the rental car parked in its usual spot—three places in, from the end of Row K. He opened the door and reached under the seat to grab the keys, left in their prearranged hiding place. A prick to his finger caused him to retract his hand and bring it close to his face for inspection. He applied pressure with his thumb against his middle finger and a small droplet of blood rose from the point of pain. Assuming he had caught it on a sharp piece of the seat rail, he bent over again, stuck his finger in his mouth, and sucked the droplet off. Sliding his hand under the seat once more, the blood seemed to drain from his head. He became light-headed, felt the world spin, and his legs buckled out from under him. Devon knew he was in trouble. He staggered back, trying to stand erect, but stumbled as he backed into an immovable body behind him. An arm, strong as a vise, lodged under his chin, choking off all but the last of his fading consciousness.

Devon struggled to release the lock of the arm, but in his drugged state his strength was diminished, and the death grip held firm. In desperation, his fingers ripped into his shirt pocket, grabbed his pen, and thrust it downward into his assailant's thigh. The arm lock on his throat slackened enough to allow Devon to twist himself free. Like a drunken sailor being thrown out of a wharf bar, he tried to run, but his legs wouldn't respond. He felt his body list to one side as his eyelids began to close. As he slid downward to one knee, his hand caught the coat pocket of the doubled over attacker, ripping it off. His consciousness drained. This time, total blackness came as he went face down into the grass.

An hour later, the gentle drizzle turned into a steady downpour. Heavy droplets pounded the side of his face and woke him from his altered state. My wrist! He brought it up, but the case was gone—half of the handcuff remained. As he rolled over, Devon opened his clenched hand while trying to push himself up. A small pack of matches fell to the ground. Its cover gave him the lead he needed. L'Hotel Darcon was a known safe house for the Israeli Mossad. The fact that he was still alive made sense. How did they know? Had they followed him without his knowing? Was he getting sloppy or have they planted a mole in The Agency? The questions were coming fast, but Devon had no time for answers. He turned his wrist again and noted the time. He knew they had an hour lead and time was fleeting. Devon had one hope … the wounded Israeli would go to the hotel and dress the stab wound before returning to Israel.

The desk clerk had his suspicions. L'Hotel Darcon didn't do enough of a street trade to survive without its Israeli connections, but the clerk's reaction still wasn't swift enough to parry the lighting-like strike to his head by the Berretta that appeared from nowhere. He looked past the slumped-over clerk to the pigeonhole cabinet that held the keys to the rooms. Devon saw that Room 21 was the only slot without a key. He climbed the stairs to the second floor and made his way down the dimly lit corridor. The door to Room 21 was typical of most nineteenth century hotels. It was made of solid wood plank, but no stronger than the antique lockset that time and lack of funds ignored. He knew that one kick in the right place would resolve any problem of entry. Reaching into his pocket and pulling out a silencer, he screwed it onto the barrel of his Beretta. He pressed his ear to the door, but there was no sound. Was he too late? The clerk told him they had checked out, but his face told Devon a different story. Was it the blurring effects of the drug, or were his basic instincts wrong? The incident at the rental car had taken its toll on his confidence.

In one violent motion, he stepped back, raised his foot, and slammed it into the outdated lockset. The door burst open. A Mossad agent spun to reach his coat draped on the arm of a chair. Devon's aim was clear and on target. The Israeli bolted backward from the shot that entered his shoulder. Devon moved toward the wounded man. His knees bowed, his steps were slow and deliberate. His aim never left the forehead of the field agent. Scanning the room, he looked for the valise. It sat upright along the side of a small table. He moved toward the briefcase. He kicked the agent's gun away from him—under the bed. Like a computer, his mind processed the table's contents—one open beer, one cigarette in the ashtray. The bathroom door stood to the right of the table. It was ajar. The mirror reflected the opposite wall. The room appeared clear—towels hanging. He was limited to a partial view of the back of the door. His eyes returned to the agent, who was barely conscious. Devon eased himself down on one knee. He gripped the handle of the valise.

A sudden movement came from the bathroom. There were two! The second agent slammed into Devon's back. The case flew from his hand. The two bodies fell tangled onto the table. The edge of a lampshade caught Devon's open eye. It caused his vision to blur. He felt the second agent pull his arm, making a desperate attempt to take his gun. Devon grabbed the second assailant's hair. He snapped the man's head backward. He loosened his grip on Devon's arm. He slammed the gun butt into the man's temple. The agent slumped over. Devon pushed the lifeless body off and reached to cover his blurry eye. The valise came crashing down upon his shoulders and head. He twisted as he headed for the floor. He squeezed off a shot into the first agent's chest, dropping him to the floor.

Devon lay motionless, trying to clear his foggy head. The valise was to his left—one latch broken, its lid bent and ajar.

***

Devon was racing out into the rising countryside of Geneva. He hadn't paid attention to the direction he was traveling. His only thought was to get out, into the open spaces where he knew he would have a chance to regain control and make sure that no more Mossad agents were trailing him.

He drove his rental car about an hour before finding a pull-off on the high mountain road that gave him a full circular view. He hadn't been followed, of this he was sure, but the events of the last three hours had shaken him. As his mind cleared, he remembered several close encounters he'd had before, but none that brought him this near to death. The two dead Israelis bothered him, but he knew from the moment he kicked in the door that only one side would come out alive. Clearing his thoughts, Devon looked down at the valise sitting on the passenger seat. He knew its contents were off limits and out of his classification, but the oddness of an attack by so-called "friendly" Israeli agents caused him to pull the sealed envelope out to examine its contents. The money transfer that he pulled out was clean, with depository account numbers as the method of transaction. As he slid the papers back into the envelope, resistance was encountered from a small, crumpled piece of paper in the lower corner of the manila envelope. Pulling it out, Devon read a short note written in Arabic. It was intended for the eyes of the mysterious terrorist Khattab. Assuring the Jordanian fanatic that, in the name of Allah, any and all means justified the end, bin Laden bemoaned this contemptible arrangement of having to put money into the personal accounts of two devils of the CIA. But receiving a small, disguisable, nuclear devise would advance their cause twenty years and bring the Great Satan to its knees. The names of the devils were those of his immediate superiors—Grayson and Carey.

Devon McKenzie's world unraveled; it lay forever broken and shattered. The razor-sharp lines that separated right from wrong and good from evil blurred beyond recognition. Had he become an integral part of some "off your rocker" equation that perpetuated human misery and death? Worse ... is it in the name of graft and corruption? He looked down again at the piece of paper—his eyes must be betraying him. Following the names of Grayson and Carey, the next line confused his tired mind even more. It showed the Arabic figure for the Saudi Royal Family. What did that mean? He leaned back into the seat of his car—his senses were numb. With a tightening grip that would not ease, the small paper in his hand crumpled further. His chest felt heavy and his head pounded. Sleep overtook him as his anger turned to utter disillusionment.

The lugging sound of an approaching truck woke Devon from his sleep. He struggled to a sitting position and wiped the palms of his hands over his sore eyes. As his hands drew down, the truck's headlights reflected in his eyes from the side view mirror, startling Devon into a sharp focus. How long had he been asleep? The paper in his hand caught his attention and his head eased back against the headrest. He had been deceived and decided he could no longer be part of the lie that had become his life. He had to expose Grayson and Casey. But who could he trust at The Agency? There was only one person he trusted to give the information to: his longtime friend at Langley, Timothy Daniels.

CHAPTER 11

THIS TIME, THE MEETING WAS AT A RATHER SMALL AND unassuming country dacha, not much different from a multitude of others that former mid-level Communist bureaucrats owned and enjoyed prior to the fall of the old Soviet Union. It was chosen because it was plain and inconspicuous. The exterior walls were unpainted and the rustic wood siding had weathered to a bleached, grey patina. On the outside of the dacha the real beauty was its natural surrounding: A lush, wooded landscape that even in the winter months displayed a twinkling icy beauty that could match any scene from the movie Doctor Zhivago. But most important of all, it was away from the radar of governmental eyes.

Inside the borrowed dacha were the people that counted the most: Rear Admiral Popov and Admiral Vedeyev were seated together on their side of the round, wooden table. On the opposite side were seated their "business" counterparts. In Russian tradition, the table was festooned with Vodka bottles—some full, but most empty and lying on their sides. The table was soaked with Vodka that spilled over with every zealous pouring of new rounds. Their speech was loud, vulgar, and boisterous; but like most Russian men, they were veterans at drinking and had the stamina to consume massive amounts of alcohol without the downside of slurring their words.

The man that controlled eighty percent of Russia's natural gas fields pulled his crossed legs off the table and allowed his chair to rest again on four legs. Leaning forward, Igor Dravenskey placed his elbows on the table and joined his hands together in front of his chin. He focused in on Rear Admiral Popov and queried again, "I want to be sure, Dmitri. Tell me again why we went ahead outfitting the Borei submarine with the Bulava missiles after one successful firing on top of eleven failures."

"As I told you six months ago, timing is everything. The Dutch combine, Norske Shell, advanced the moving schedule of its newest platform to the Gimli Fields. We felt the need to take the steam out of Europe's euphoria when the new platform would be put in place." Popov raised another shot glass in the air, waiting for the others to join in. "We wanted to be there to 'share' in their happiness," he said. He slammed the shot down. The other admiral laughed and threw his down as well. The glasses of the businessmen remained on the table. They took their cue from the gas magnate who sat with his arms folded. A chilling pall hung in the heavy, smoke-filled air. The smiling faces of the admirals sagged and went sour.

"But with all due respect, Admiral, how can we know that these missiles will work?" The magnate queried. "Please remember that we have already laid down millions of dollars on this project to date and we do demand a sizeable return on that investment."

Dravenskey remained stoic when Vice Admiral Vedeyev clenched a fist and pounded it on the table in contempt. "We have put our careers and pensions at risk, and our lives if we are caught. Need I remind you that this would be considered treason?" He thundered.

Dravenskey nodded, giving the third businessman his cue. He half raised himself from his chair, grabbed a bottle of Stoli by its neck, and refilled all shot glasses. He stood with his arm raised, shot in hand. "Gentlemen, gentlemen … please. I think it is time for one more toast. To the Yuri Dolgoruki … let it sail to success in calm waters!"

This time all members repeated the toast and threw their shots down. The civilians of the meeting were nervous over the investigation that had been opened up by Russia's Military Industrial Commission (VPK). The inquiry was targeted at the debacle surrounding the Bulava R-30 missiles. Dravenskey looked across to the naval men and asked, "Is there reasonable assurance that the missiles will fire? After all, we are all in this together and all sides need to be sure that the Federal Security Service (FSB) worms won't be crawling up our asses."

"Better them than the old KGB," said Admiral Popov. "They were worse than worms!"

Rear Admiral Popov's feelings were still on edge. He leaned his chair back on two legs and gave a smile large enough to expose his yellowed, nicotine-stained teeth. He had already been given the results of the yet unpublished findings.

"First, let me assure our respectable partners that the report of the VPK inquiry is to be released within days, and its findings are as we directed it to be. It is another exhaustive study that ran into a brick wall and came up with no conclusions." Popov raised his palms upward. "Oh well, such is life in our new Russia. Next, you ask, will they fire? Of course they will. You see, our information comes from deep inside the American CIA. We know it is accurate, because we threatened our contact there with leakage of past dealings if he did not tell us the truth. Gentlemen, it was the CIA that was responsible for the misfiring of our Barks and the first eleven of the Bulavas … *with* our approval, of course."

"But, how was this possible?" Asked Dravenskey.

"May I remind you that over four years ago it was you who came to us with a proposal that was of the highest magnitude as well as personal risk? We took that proposal with much risk and came up with a long-term plan to match. The details of how we handled this are not important at this time." Said Popov, putting his arm around Vedeyev for emphasis. "Suffice it to say that the world of high tech armaments and intelligence is similar to a large family. One brother may want this and another brother may want that. There may be rivalry and even bickering among siblings, but the family stays together because there are few ways to split the pie. It is in everyone's best financial interest to keep harmony. But rest assured, gentlemen, you will be briefed and will be given the whole picture in due course."

"But what do we know of the other Bulavas … the other sixteen on the Dolgoruki?"

Popov smiled and gestured with a shrug of his shoulders. "The Americans have encrypted a virus in our system that is set to allow the next twelve missiles to fire. After that it's back to permanent failure. That is why we lobbied hard and certified the decision to go with the Bulavas … so the idiot scientists wouldn't fire off another twelve missiles."

"Does the CIA have any idea of what we are up to?"

"No, not even a clue … we are sure of that," said Popov.

"But that gives us a mere twelve missiles to work with!" The gas magnate replied. "The last four will be as worthless as tits on a boar hog."

Popov reached forward and refilled the glasses. As he raised his chin in Mussolini-styled defiance, his eyes focused back on the gas magnate, and through a warped sardonic smile he hissed, "One is all we need to accomplish our mission."

"And we are confident that this will come down as an outside ter-rorist act … our dear Mother Russia will be exonerated?"

"We control the Admiralty and the Admiralty has 'friends' in the VPK, whom you have purchased through your generosity. Again, we will control the investigation. Trust us, we know what we are doing and our plan is fail-safe."

CHAPTER 12

YURI DOLGORUKI

DREARY, LOW-LYING CLOUDS DOMINATED THE FOREBODING Arctic sky as the Russian Borei class submarine churned the frigid, ice-filled waters at Arkhangelsk Oblast. Its dark metallic skin created an image of a malevolent, gigantic killer whale stalking its prey.

Passing the towering, pale red construction cranes that stood as lonely sentinels against a somber skyline, Captain Andrei Illanov turned his face into the freezing wind, pulled the collar of his naval greatcoat up around his neck, and took one more heartening look at the receding naval base facility. As he scanned the bay, he fixed on the white flag with the pale blue diagonal cross that signified the Russian Navy. Gone was the old red flag with the hammer and sickle. It fluttered near to tattering in the stiff wind and gave him a sense of pride that brought tears to his eyes. This, he thought, is no longer the navy of a failed communist system that stifled initiative and hard work. At long last, our country is on its way back to respectability. A disgusted sense of embarrassment overtook him as he reminisced of the abandoned buildings of the once powerful bases that had fallen into wretched disrepair by the budgetary axe of a dysfunctional economy. The oft heard sarcasm, "third world nation with missiles," ran through his mind, causing him to snicker in disgust and grit his teeth. "But I guess that was then, and this is now," he whispered.

Nearing the age when most commanders burned out and chose to ride a desk for the remainder of their careers, Illanov had called in his years of accumulated markers and was given command of the latest Borei class nuclear sub, Yuri Dolgoruki, named after the founder of Moscow. Being the youngest in a long line of stealth submarines, her construction was started in 1996. It was a time when the Soviet economy was reeling like a punch drunk boxer, staggering to regain his footing after taking a nine-count. Its construction was begun several years ago, but its finish was hampered by one delay after another ... until now.

To Captain Illanov, it had seemed that the project would never end. He knew time was not on his side and he had feared that the countless delays would cause him to never get another boat. First the sub was designed to carry the new Bark R-39UTTH submarine launched ballistic missiles (SLBM). Then, because of continuous failures in their test launches, that missile line was abandoned. Engineering was started on a new Bulava SLBM design. This of course, threw everything into chaos as the new Bulava missiles were smaller than the Bark missiles, thus causing another redesign in the missile compartment of the Yuri Dolgoruki. Andrei was old enough to relate the mess to the old American Three Stooges movies he remembered from his childhood. The difference was that those movies were comic relief based in the absurd. This clumsy project was seeded in the hangover of communist reality.

Reducing the once vaunted Soviet Navy to a collection of outdated and deteriorating garbage scows that took a Russian with too many shots of Vodka to call submarines, the arms race, fostered by the technology crazed Americans and their "cowboy" president, had taken a painful and bitter toll on an empire that appeared to be no longer relevant.

God! How his feelings toward those bastard Americans ran the gamut. On the one hand, he admired their creativity ... their gritty ability to overcome any and all adversities. Even the devastation of their Twin Towers in New York City proved to be nothing more than a short hiccup in their timeline of history. Yet their phony attitude and condescending sense of moral superiority made his Russian skin crawl. How could any of his ancestors have immigrated to that whore nation?

He remembered how galling it was after the United States had finished bombing the Serbian people into submission, they moved NATO Alliance ground troops into the city of Pristina without even the slightest acknowledgement to his government. Serbia, after all, was one of Russia's best trading partners and was "under our sphere of influence." In a swift and brazen countermove, the Kremlin placed a small, but effective cadre of troops at the heart of Pristina—its airport. The NATO advance stopped dead in its tracks as stunned Western politicians scurried to weigh the risks of using force to engage and dislodge the troops of a nuclear hanger-on. No major nation has since had the temerity to pull off such a brilliant stratagem. He was proud of that move.

Emboldened by its success at remaining some sort of player in the game of global politics, the Kremlin was convinced it couldn't afford to compete with a "Star Wars"-type missile defense. Picking up on the "Pristina Stratagem," as it came to be known, Moscow believed that the threat of a couple of stealth submarines patrolling the waters of the Atlantic Ocean with sixteen ballistic missiles would generate enough fear to be their perpetual ace in the hole. A modernized fleet of fifteen Borei subs would continue to be that ace.

Illanov was proud that he commanded the first Russian sub to have the use of pump-jet propulsion. Because of the breakthrough development of its integrated hydro-dynamically efficient hull, broadband noises were so reduced, that it could be almost undetectable by sonar while cruising. A recent gain in stealing the American satellite coordinates and their own latest cloaking technology buoyed the admirals and politicians to giddy heights. The potential for a premature deployment of the Yuri Dolgoruki presented a risk of reputation, but was nonetheless a risk worth taking—a risk born of desperation ... of trying to again become a player on the world stage. Russia needed the world to understand that Russia was still an equal in every way.

As another biting wind buffeted his body and caused a shiver to run up his back, the submarine captain longed for the warmer waters of the Atlantic Ocean. Knowing full well this cruise would include a two-week layover in Havana, Illanov's chill disappeared. One more dying communist rat hole, he thought, but at least it's a warm one. Getting there was the drawback. A considerable amount of time would be first spent in the icy North Sea.

"I hope the decision to race ahead with the Bulavas after one successful firing was correct," he said to his executive officer standing next to him. "I tell you, something doesn't sit well with me. Why is it, Anton, that we have sent men into space over and over again, we have built ICBMs by the thousands, and yet we had to abandon the Bark missiles because they kept misfiring? Then we switch over to the Bulavas and the first eleven misfire. And out of nowhere comes the decision by our Admiralty that after one successful firing, all the misfiring problems have disappeared. I swear ... life keeps getting stranger and stranger. And after all this delay, what do we get? We get *smaller* missiles."

"They may be smaller missiles, Captain, but we do have four more of them at sixteen, rather than the twelve Barks. And don't forget, we can fire them *all* within a split second. There is no other salvo system in the world capable of doing this ... not even the American Ohio class. I mean, we can fire them all and they should work ... shouldn't they?"

"One would think, Anton, but let's not forget that they're not American made." He paused for emphasis, snickered, and let out a horse laugh. "Ha! I remember how proud I was when I left the Naval Academy and I received my first Russian Army watch." He looked over to his exec and nudged him with his elbow to emphasize that this was going to be good. "It ran fine for the first year, and then it started running backwards. I mean it ran ... but backwards!" Illanov began laughing again so hard that his eyes squinted shut. When it became apparent that his exec was silent, he opened his eyes and felt embarrassed. He stopped his laughing and wiped a tear from his cheek.

"Oh well, it looks like it will be once more into the breach, eh Anton?" Illanov said, as he stiffened up and slapped his executive officer on the back.

With an unusually stoic face, Anton looked down and away, and with a foreboding tone of finality in his voice said, "Yes, Captain, one last time."

CHAPTER 13

DEVON MCKENZIE SHIFTED DOWN THE GEARS OF HIS SNOW-
mobile and brought it to a halt. Looking out over a continuous sea of white,
the first glimpses of Otter Creek appeared on the horizon. Reaching into
his coat pocket, he pulled out the cellular phone he found in the pocket of
the pilot. He knew by this time of day the streets would have been plowed
and salted and his snowmobile would be rendered useless. However, even
Otter Creek was big enough to have a paramedic unit that would be able
to meet him at the outskirts of town.

***

It was midday, and the sudden ring of the telephone set all five members
of Otter Creek's fire department into an excited frenzy. They hadn't received an incoming call in three days, and all present hoped it would
be a welcomed respite from their stretch of boredom. Included was Josh
Abrams, the newest reporter at *The Times-Dispatch,* who had sauntered
through the door.

"Anything big?" He asked as his ears picked up on the tail end of
the call.

"Huge," the lead paramedic replied, trying to hide his effort at teasing
the rookie, "at least twenty people injured in a massive tanker explosion
... better get your dead ass in gear and follow us."

Josh was off and running out the door before the last words of the
paramedic closed his sentence.

"Don't you just love 'em when they're young and dumb?"

***

Devon looked at his watch and calculated that the paramedics would take
less than twelve minutes to reach them. His instincts told him to wait ten
minutes before taking off for the woods, but he couldn't walk away from

the strange feeling he had for this woman. He reached down and pulled the blanket off her face. There was a soft, honest innocence about her face, so similar to Cathy's. He pulled off his left glove, and with feelings of trepidation, he reached forward and ran his fingers down her warm cheek. He watched her eyelids crack open and blink as she focused on her rescuer. The blurred image clarified before her. She was overtaken with a strange bewilderment. "Trojan," she muttered … "You're Trojan Horse."

"I'm afraid I don't know what you're talking about," he said. He felt the heat of his blood rise from his neck up into his face. The name, the heat of his face ... the scene of a bomb blast flashed through his mind. It was Dagestan two years earlier. People were pouring out of a smoke-filled, crumbling governmental building, screaming in pain, with blood, body parts and debris everywhere. Not civilians, goddamn you! I trained you to blow up military targets, not civilians!

His focus returned when her hand rose up and touched the long scar that ran from the outer corner of his left eye to the bottom of his ear lobe. "I ... I know you," she whispered. Her eyelids began to blink—her hand paused and fell back to her side as she slipped once more into unconsciousness.

Within seconds of his estimated time, Devon heard the rhythmic blaring of the emergency vehicle's siren begin to cut the crisp, quiet air. He hadn't cut and run, of this he felt good, but he also sensed approaching danger and knew he should go. There would be questions asked, forms to be filled out, and worst of all; locations would have to be given. His stomach churned as the approaching vehicle ground to a halt in front of him. He didn't know why, but it seemed right to make sure everything was okay. Taking another risk seemed to be the thing to do. Maybe it was time to finally reenter the outside world … no matter the consequences.

As the paramedics jumped out of the emergency vehicle, Devon cautiously moved forward and began recounting his story of the crash. "Hey! Be careful there," his gravelly voice said, interrupting himself as the lead paramedic began to unleash the ropes of the sled, "... she's got protruding ribs, left side." Another vehicle pulled up and distracted Devon for a moment. The door opened and Josh Abrams bailed out of his car with camera and notepad in tow. Before Devon could even begin to react in defense, a sudden flash of light blinded him. It was the dreaded flash of a camera—a camera that could expose him to the shadow world that stalked him—a world that needed him to die and disappear.

Devon was swift to react. As if a demon were exploding from his body, his two fists gripped the coat of the young reporter and had him thrown up against the side of the emergency vehicle, his piercing eyes inches away. Josh felt the heat of his assailant's breath as his own body went limp in fear. "You *can't* take my picture!" Hissed Devon through his clenched teeth. "Do I make myself clear?"

"Hey! Hey! What the hell's going on?" He asked. "Is there some kind of problem here?"

As Devon's grip on the kid's shirt began to relax, he turned his head and saw the other paramedics lifting the injured pilot onto the wheeled stretcher. He knew his role was finished for the moment. It was what was to come that turned his insides. His fists let the reporter go. He gave the kid an apologetic look and bolted for the snowmobile. Within seconds, all that could be seen of the mysterious man was a diminishing cloud of snow on the white horizon as he melted into the hazy distance.

CHAPTER 14

AS ADMIRAL POPOV HAD STATED, THE BUILDING OF NOR-way's deep-water gas platform, Gimli, was indeed ahead of schedule. For the most part, it was because Norske Shell had placed the construction of the behemoth in the steady hands of its project manager, Peter Jorgesen. Like its previous platform, dubbed The Troll, Gimli got its name from a mythical character in the J.R.R. Tolkien trilogy, Lord of the Rings. To most under him, it was hard to separate Peter Jorgesen from the crusty, but lovable, literary character. Reality and fiction seemed to blur.

As the gate to the open-caged elevator swung back toward him, Peter Jorgesen hesitated before entering the cage that would take him on a nine minute ride to the top of the longest elevator shaft in the world. The first and longest phase of his job was drawing to a close, and though he felt the exuberance of the task that lie ahead, he couldn't help the melancholy that came with the completion of such a monumental undertaking. He touched the gate's well-worn, yellow-painted frame and a flood of warm memories came over him.

Had it been six years since the energy combine Norske Shell discovered a vast new natural gas field equal to Norway's original "Troll" reserves? And did the find have to be yet a little further out into the North Sea? Was he still the same person? It had been a long stint for a man who could turn his face into any blowing wind and feel the haunting seduction of a distant siren call. The blood of his Viking ancestors flowed strong and passionate through his Nordic veins. A man at peace with himself, Peter knew that the sedate life of a structural engineer sitting behind some desk in an office was not the life that would satisfy his sense of adventure and wanderlust.

He recalled the first time he had entered this fjord on a small ferry lazily making its way up the glacial valley. The crisp, azure sky with its puffy, white clouds was reflected in its still, pristine waters. Cutting a narrow passage between majestic, green covered mountains that rose from the water like giant, cupped hands, the fjord drew his eyes forward to a more distant mountain, draped in varying shades of green and blue, with the sun highlighting its snowy peak like icing on a cake. Far at its base, a slight glimpse of bright colors—red, yellow, green and white—began to form the outline of his destination, the small town of Vats rising at the fjord's end.

Peter was flooded with those deep, genetic memories of his heralded Viking ancestors making their triumphant return home laden with glittering plunder from some distant Celtic land. In his mind he could hear the huge, deep-throated horns blaring from the mountain lookouts, announcing their long-awaited arrival. The glistening sun danced on sets of long oars, rhythmically cutting the glass-like water. It was as if he could reach right out and touch the fierce, intimidating dragon that adorned its sleek wooden hull.

He shook his head and exhaled a long sigh of relief as his hand pulled the steel gate closed, for he knew this would be his last ride up the elevator. The conical foundations were complete and his work would be confined to merging his foundation with the upper structure. Funny, he thought, I had grown to hate this ride. It scares the living bejeebers out of me, and for a long time! Peter's eyes moved away from the control panel to the tiny spot of light at the top of the shaft. The thought of this small cage dropping eleven hundred feet ... he shook his head again and cleared his mind. "Last time," he muttered. Now the hard part begins, he thought, but can we float this monstrosity out into one of the roughest bodies of water in the world, the North Sea, let alone the serene protected waters of the fjord? Deep, in the pit of his stomach, he knew the odds were stacked against them. Still, its predecessor had made the trip without failure and he couldn't back away from the monumental challenge. Like some cosmic black hole, the enormity of the task drew him in, and the risk consumed every fiber of his being.

He took his hands and rubbed his sore eyes. He slid them down his ruddy, weather-beaten cheeks as he thought through the procedure of the tasks that still had to be conquered. The platform was completed and waited the merging with its top structure. First, the dry coffered construction site had to be flooded with water from the fjord. But would four hollow concrete tubes whose collective base was the size of three soccer fields be able to withstand the mammoth pressure of the water and float? For God's sake, he thought, together they weigh more than ten super aircraft carriers! And with four hundred of its eleven hundred feet of height sticking above water, I've got to tow this base out into the middle of the fjord, all the while keeping it stable to prevent it from tipping over and sinking.

The pencil-neck geeks in engineering say it will work, but they're not the ones who'll have to do it ... that task falls to me. What if we snag any one of the shafts on a glacial boulder at the bottom of the fjord? The whole thing would tumble down like some flimsy house of cards. Hmph! When I voiced my concern, that young smart-ass engineer with his crisp, white shirt and tie cut me off and said not to worry, it would be as easy as towing an iceberg. I took that as an insult. Towing an iceberg ... I wanted to roll up that set of plans and shove them right up his pimple-faced ass. Peter drew a long breath of air for strength and questioned his own sensitivity. He's not the enemy ... I guess when you turn forty your accumulated wisdom renders you less tolerant of the young and brash.

A sudden jolt in the elevator car broke his train of thought. His eyes scanned the cage, left, right, and back to the control panel. The cab was still rising. Peter looked over the edge of the gate and saw the floor of the shaft reducing in size to that of a postage stamp. "Damn! I've *never* liked this ride," he whispered.

Within seconds, his fear abated and the long ride let his mind wander into another remembrance: the pride he felt when he was selected by the Norwegian military to test pilot the new deep sea rescue vehicle, SRDRS-RCS, developed by the Americans. This new vehicle was touted to be the world's most advanced and technically capable rescue system for stranded submarines. Because of his extensive experience on the old DSRV units that had been the world's gold standard for forty years, Peter was the logical choice to be Norway's representative in NATO's Bold Monarch submarine rescue exercise in the deep waters of Norway. Peter and the unit passed with flying colors and demonstrated its total effectiveness as a more reliable rescue system.

The notoriety he received when the Norwegian Navy called his employer, Norwegian Contractors, and requested he take a three-week leave of absence to serve his country, was all that was needed to award Peter complete control of the largest moving project in the history of the world. That was six months ago, but seemed an eternity. The enormity of the task ahead weighed on him and he again returned to the work that had to be done before they would head out to sea. And that schedule was crystal clear in his mind.

Once we get the base structure out into the fjord, he thought, we've got to pump water into the shafts and make them sink three hundred feet further into the water and hold them steady while some thirty-two-year-old female engineer floats a 350-foot-tall drilling platform over it. Then, pump the water out of them and let them rise up and connect to it. And that platform is the size of three soccer fields, has a helicopter pad, two cranes and a ten-story hotel sitting on its top! That monster weighs twenty-two thousand tons itself, and I'm supposed to bob it up and down like some kind of a yo-yo. What kind of clearance did she say we'd have when she slides it over my shafts ... one meter? Three lousy feet! I guess they think I must be some kind of miracle worker. One small stinking mistake, anywhere, and the whole thing comes down like a house of cards ... and takes a lot of good people with it. "Damn!" He whispered. "They ask one hell of a lot."

CHAPTER 15

SWISHING THE ACTIVATING CHEMICAL ONE MORE TIME with his tongs, Josh Abrams watched the image in the photograph rise from a haze and come into view. He could make out the rugged face of the mysterious man that was soon to become both local hero and enigma. But why was he so adamant that his picture *not* be taken? He thought. A variety of emotions ran through him as he swished the picture one more time, picked it up and pinned it on the overhead line to dry. He knew he had a responsibility to his editor to run the picture along with the story he had pieced together, yet a strange sense of fear nagged at him. Not just fear for him. After all, he did get body-slammed against the emergency vehicle, but the man appeared to be in some sort of danger. It was as if he were begging me not to print it, he thought, even while he was threatening me. Or was it a threat? He wondered.

Josh's head turned as he reacted to the knock on the door behind him. His hand pulled the photograph off the line and laid it face down on the table. "It's okay, c'mon in," he replied. Josh was nervous and he knew what the question would be before it was asked.

"You ready to go with that plane crash story?" His editor queried. "We're gettin' our asses right down to the deadline."

"Uh, yeah ... I uh, I need a few more minutes."

"How'd the shot turn out?"

"I'm ... not sure. I'll let you know in a couple." He knew it was a lie. His face flushed beet red, even in the dim light of a dark room.

"Listen, Josh," his editor said, his years of experience telling him something wasn't right. "If you want to make it in the news business, deadlines are an essential part of the game—you make them or you don't. People who make news happen; even when there isn't any real news, survive in this industry. Good reporters make their own stories, they make something from nothing. 'News' is whatever you tell the public is

— 49 —

'news.' It's as simple as that." The craggy editor paused, leaned his face in to about twelve inches from Josh's face, and added for emphasis, "Do you understand what I'm saying?"

"Yes sir," he replied.

As the door shut behind his editor, Josh stood with his head down, staring at the trays on the worktable. Something didn't sit right with him, but he couldn't put his finger on it. His hand made its way to the overturned photograph and turned it face up. The eyes of the wilderness enigma had a haunting, pleading look that wouldn't go away. Was his conscience beginning to rise up like the photograph in the activator? "Damn!" He whispered. Shaking his head, he looked downward at the floor, as if in shame. He squared the typed papers of his story, grabbed the photo, and exited down the hall.

CHAPTER 16

THE WHITE WALLS AND CEILING OF THE HOSPITAL ROOM drifted from a blurry haze and came into focus. Looking for protection, Julie Weston shrank back within her outer shell. A dull pain emanated from her lower abdomen and she raised her arm to see the IV drip taped to her wrist and hand. As her foggy mind grappled to put the pieces together, an image arose that carried her away. She was looking at the instrument panel of her Piper aircraft, desperate to figure out why her engine had failed. Her hand lunged at the switch for the carburetor heat. Her fingers twisted the ignition key—nothing. The nose of the single engine plane plunged earthward. She pulled the wheel back, easing its sudden descent. Her eyes darted back and forth, looking for a spot to land—there! Off to the left ... looks like a small, flat area between two jagged foothills ... should be able to put down there. The wind! Her eyes darted to the instrument panel. What's the direction? Can't tell ... gotta guess. She fumbled with the radio frequency. Where is it? There! Her hand snapped the radio mike out of its holder and held it to her mouth.

Mayday! Mayday!

Julie Weston closed her sleepy eyes as tears began to well up. The memory of the crash was too painful to relive. Taking a deep breath, her thoughts turned to her refuge, her father. She could picture him sitting alone in their rustic Alaskan house, waiting, anxious to see the daughter he had raised by himself since she was twelve. From that tender and impressionable age, he had taught her to ride a horse, hunt wild game, and fly an airplane. With their kennel of assorted Huskies, her father had even trained her for the Iditarod, where she came in a close second. But it was more than life skills that her father had imparted to her. He gave her strength ... a deep inner strength that gave her the courage to know who she was, what she was about, and the ability to discern that fine line that separates what is right and what is wrong. Not some mental copy of the Ten Commandments, but a true sense of the role that God, love, and respect played in life. She loved him, but over the years she had come to the slow and painful realization that there wasn't a life for her in the outstretched backwoods of Fairbanks, Alaska. The time had come to make the break, and graduation day at the university proved to be the saddest day of her life—the day she told her father she would be leaving soon to take a job in McLean, Virginia ... for the CIA.

The image of a bearded man with a scar from his eye to his ear came into her reverie. She squeezed her eyelids shut, trying in desperation to make the image reappear. Fear entered her emotions—fears for, not fears of. A quiet sense of trust came over her. I know that face, I've seen it before, she thought. But she could not make the image return.

The floor nurse came through the door for what seemed to be the tenth time in the last hour to check her blood pressure. Julie Weston's irritated frown changed to a smile as she noticed a staff worker following behind with a tray full of food. It was morning, that she knew, but she wasn't sure of the day, or even how she had gotten there. The crash was vivid in her confused mind, but what had happened after was still a mystery, blurred and sketchy at best. The face! There! It flashed again.

"So, how's our little barnstormer doing this morning?" The nurse asked.

"Good morning. I'm groggy, but famished."

"Give me a minute to check your blood pressure. Then you can go ahead and eat, but take your time. I don't want you pushing it too fast."

"Can you tell me how I got here? I mean ... I remember the plane crashing. But after that, I get nothing. It's like I'm in some kind of a mental fog."

"Well, I don't know too much, just that you were piloting a small plane that went down about a couple hours from here and someone brought you in on a snowmobile to the emergency facility in Otter Creek."

Snowmobile! The bearded image jumped in front of her once more ... gone. "Where is here? I mean, where am I?"

"Here, is Fairbanks, honey, at the regional hospital. You were brought in here by a Medi-Vac chopper. It's a good thing we have an excellent surgeon that was up to putting you back together again." The nurse smiled, patting Julie's tender abdomen.

As she shifted on one elbow to look, a sharp wrenching pain shot up her side, causing her to lie back down. "Am I going to be alright? I mean, how bad is my injury?"

"Oh yeah, it looks like part of the steering wheel column pierced your abdomen. The bleeding was severe, but it was fortunate your bushman hero knew what he was doing, packed it well, and Doc here sewed you up. No problem. Don't worry, though, it missed hitting anything vital. My guess is you'll be out of here in about three days, but we still need to monitor your vital signs. You're gonna be sore, but you'll be fine. You know, you're a lucky girl. It could have been a whole lot worse. Not many people survive a crash in the bush, but I'm sure you already know that. That's 'cause most of 'em are never found."

"Did they tell you who it was that rescued me?" Julie asked.

"Sorry," she said as she was halfway out the door, "all I got was that he was some backwoods recluse. But what I *can* tell you about him is that he saved your life. You go ahead and eat and I'll check on you in a little bit."

"Please, could you tell me how I dial an outside line on the telephone? I need to let my father know where I am. He'll be in a panic that I never arrived … oh, and could I get a newspaper?"

"Sure," the nurse said, walking back to the side of her bed. "I'll put the phone right here next to your hand. Dial nine and wait for the dial tone." She bent over the side of the pushcart and pulled a thin newspaper from the stack on the bottom shelf. "I happen to have one newspaper … hot off the press. Be careful opening it up and stretching your arms, though," she said as she slid the paper under the food tray while sliding the stand across Julie's lap.

CHAPTER 17

THE DRIZZLE THAT FELL FROM THE DREARY SKY TAPPED against the chiseled face of the long distance runner. As he turned the last corner leading to his apartment building, he looked down at his sport watch to gauge his time. Come on, he thought, gotta make up fifteen seconds! He was in the final half mile of his daily, eight-mile run. The muscles in his well-developed thighs were on fire, but Gregor Polnich would not yield one single second to the aging effects of a thirty-four-year-old body. Abs feel good, he thought, better push the sit-ups past two hundred, though. He kicked hard and the inside of his lungs burned beyond belief. Can't lose a second ... aagh! He strained even harder as he approached his entrance. Just ... a ... little ... more—there! His wrist came up and his thumb jammed the stop button of the watch. He raised the watch up and took a quick glance. "Still got it," he whispered.

As Gregor's aching legs began to slow, he pulled his open hand down across his face, wiping the drenching mix of drizzle and sweat. Slowing to a rubbery walk, he ran both hands through his blonde, brush-cut hair and saw an elderly lady approach him with a small, yapping Schnauzer. Gregor felt good about the time of his run, but his attitude soured when he saw the annoying little rat on a leash. When the dog passed, it made the mistake of jumping and nipping at the steeled man's shin. Gregor stopped, curled the side of his upper lip at the woman, looked back down, and drop kicked the dog under its chin, sending it airborne till it reached the end of its leash, yanking its startled master to the ground. The elderly woman screamed in tears as she knelt, wiping the bloodied fur from her precious dog's mouth. The whimpering and crying that emanated from the crouching figures turned his stomach and with a sinister sneer of disgust, Gregor cleaned his mouth with his tongue and spat the residue in their direction. He stared a moment longer, debating whether he would kick the dog again, then turned on his heels and walked to the entry door of his building. "If this was Moscow, I could have kicked you as well," he muttered.

Exiting a steam-filled shower, the hard-bodied Russian took one more look in the mirror at his sinewy profile and felt the satisfaction of completing yet one more of his difficult regimens. With the towel tucked around his muscular waist, Gregor walked past the opening to the kitchen, grabbed his waiting cup of coffee, and sat down at his breakfast table where the morning edition of the Seattle Dispatch lay neatly folded and tucked.

Gregor Polnich was not unhappy with his new assignment in the United States, yet he longed for the more intense missions in the Muslim-dominated, breakaway republics. Every aspect of his duties there were clear-cut. The enemy was real and his assignments were straightforward—kill this vermin terrorist, eliminate that one. What he liked most, however, was the thrill of the hunt. He was told who to kill and when. How he accomplished his sanction was left up to him. This gave him the twisted latitude he enjoyed. He could plan, he could stalk, he could make the kill clean and swift, or he could inflict any amount of brutal pain that met his cruel fancy at any given moment. Sadism had found a comfortable home in Gregor's warped idea of patriotic duty. Kill, and do it on time. Simple, yet satisfying. Life had meaning.

With a quick snap of his two wrists, Gregor shook the newspaper out and laid it flat on the table in front of him. Scanning the front page, there was nothing of particular interest to him, the customary police blotter and a few local political stories. As he took his first sip of the steaming coffee, his other hand turned the page over. His fingertips had not left the corner of the page when his eyes riveted in on the picture in the center. "What?" He said, his mouth gaped open. The image before him was too incredible to believe. "It can't be, he's dead ... I killed the filthy bastard! No one could have survived that crash."

With his eyes still locked on the picture, Gregor slid his arm downward to place his coffee on the table. The misplaced cup tipped over the edge and spilled to the floor, splashing the scalding brew up the side of his naked leg.

"What?" He yelled, as he raised his whole body up, his thighs sprawling the table on its side. It didn't matter. Nothing mattered—only the picture that went over with the table. He grabbed the chair to the left and flung it out of his way, sending it slamming into the wall. Like an unfed, caged animal searching for food, Gregor tore at his surroundings till the paper was secure in his grip. Focusing in on the scar that ran from the man's eye to his ear, a deep rage began boiling up inside him. His fingers crumpled the newsprint under the strain of his clenching fists. Anger-filled images flooded his being.

***

It was Dagestan, four years ago. Polnich could feel the dampness of the frozen, rocky ground penetrate his camouflaged field jacket as the cold worked its way inward through his sweater to his body. This kind of cold-ness was overwhelming, making his concentration a Herculean effort. His exposed fingertips felt numb holding the infrared night glasses that had scanned its objective for over two hours. It was a known Chechen rebel camp, housing some of the most passionate insurgents that the Russians had dealt with since the war in Afghanistan. The minions were milling about, and Gregor fantasized picking them off, one by one. But *they* were not the focus of his weapon. His assignment was Akhmad Kadyrov, a Chechen warlord who had been trained in Afghanistan by the American CIA in the '80s. Gregor had another reason to persevere. His hopes had been buoyed by the rumor that the mysterious Amir Khattab, the Jordanian-born, Islamic fanatic who had become the most dreaded terrorist in Russia, was to make an appearance at the camp after dark.

Standard field orders dictated that he pass this information upward to his superiors, but Gregor was not going to allow some boneheaded bureaucrat to screw up an opportunity to bag two major trophies at the same time. His bullets were custom made, hollowed and loaded by hand with the exact weight of powder. Closing his eyes, he enjoyed the image of heads exploding like ripe melons. To Gregor Polnich, the feeling rose to near sexual arousal.

As time dragged on, his exhaustion began to reach its peak. Gregor held the night glasses with one hand and reached over his shoulder, massaging his neck with the other. The cold stiffness had begun to loosen when a moving image broke from the right side of the camp. It was him! The cold-blooded killer, he knew it. Whereas most Chechen men wore the traditional Keffiyeh, no other Muslim wore a black, Che Guevara style beret pulled down over his long, scraggly, black hair. His dark beard, coupled with the recognizable Cohiba cigar scrunched in the corner of his mouth, gave Gregor reason to pause. It was as if the Cuban revolutionary had been transported in time. He moved the glasses to the left and identified the Chechen warlord, Kadyrov, walking two feet away to the side of Khattab.

Laying his night glasses down in front of him, Gregor reached to his side and slid his rifle up into position. Like a smooth robotic machine, the scope of the gun swung around till it found the unsuspecting targets, its crosshairs zeroing in on the forehead of Kadyrov, then that of Khattab's. Gregor took a slow, deep breath and licked his dry lower lip. Khattab continued to walk at a slow, but sure pace, and the crosshairs followed, never leaving the center of his head. Be patient, Gregor assured himself, they're both yours. All he needed was for them to stop, to pause long enough for this killing machine to get both shots off. No other covert ops assassin in the world would top this feat. These trophies would be his. In an instant, they would be lying in a pool of blood, half of their heads exploded into grisly pieces over a five-meter radius. His lust for blood, his craving for the hunt had converged into one orgasmic moment. He could end his days as a hired gun and Mother Russia would embrace him as a hero till the day he died. His heart was pounding. Like a stalking cheetah, he could taste and even smell their warm blood spewing forth. His finger massaged the trigger, his breathing continued, but slow, deep, and deliberate. Seconds, mere seconds were all he needed and they would be his.

As if it were some twisted turn of fate, another terrorist came out of a tent. His pace was quick and his arms opened to greet the two dignitaries. They paused. This was it! There would be no better chance. Gregor slowly and purposely inhaled and held his index finger on the hair trigger. The crosshairs split the center of Khattab's eyes. Without warning, a heavy knee between his shoulder blades forced the air from his lungs. The cold barrel of a gun pressed into the back of his neck.

"Don't move," a hissing voice whispered in Russian. "Don't even breathe ... take your finger off the trigger and put the rifle down—now!"

Gregor felt the silencer press deeper into the muscles of his neck for emphasis. He eased the weapon to the ground and stretched his arms and hands out in front of him. As he turned the empty palms of his hands over, he twisted his head to catch a glimpse of the assailant that had thwarted his kill. Out of the corner of his eye he caught a glimpse of a man wearing the traditional black and white checked Keffiyeh. But this man was different. His skin wasn't swarthy—it was white. Within the opening of the headdress, a scar ran from his eye to his ear.

"Not now, my friend," his assailant again whispered. "Not until I receive what *I* need first." They were the last words Gregor heard before the gun slammed into the side of his head.

***

Gregor's focus returned to the present, his eyes returning once more to the black and white newsprint photo stretched in his hands. Once again his rage began to spill over. As his fingers slowly and deliberately crushed the newsprint again, he closed his eyes and a sinister snicker was formed by his curling upper lip. He savored every second of the image that came into view. It was the watering, bulging eyes of Devon McKenzie as Gregor's hands gripped the neck of his hated nemesis and choked every last ounce of life from his body. His eyes were locked on Devon's, three inches from his face. It was the final triumph, and in his sick, twisted mind, it was what gave his life meaning. He slammed his fists together. His eyes opened and looked upward as he tried to make sense of this scarred face that had come back into his life.

He had assignments that were scheduled for the next three days; but he would alter his schedule, for they paled in comparison to the burning urgency he felt to even this old, festering score. Once again, he opened the crumpled paper and read the dateline of the story. Yes, Fairbanks was where he would be going. His superiors would have to wait. Alaska was his destination and it consumed his every thought.

CHAPTER 18

YURI DOLGORUKI

EVENING HAD ARRIVED, BUT ANY CONVENTIONAL SENSE of a spatial timeline meant little to the crew of the Russian nuclear submarine. In the black, frigid depths of the icy waters below the arctic mass, time had no particular relevance beyond the tedious hours that must be tolerated to pull its crewmen through another long, monotonous shift. By design, the sub's huge size allowed for unheard-of comfort aboard the Borei, featuring a gymnasium, a solarium, and a sauna among an assortment of other recreational centers. But in spite of its enhanced habitability, the day-to-day life on any nuclear submarine could only be measured by the ticking hands of a seamen's watch.

With coffee in hand, Fyodor Strivnych negotiated the narrow passage that led to the missile compartment. As if moving along on human autopilot, his eyes were focused on his coffee mug, trying not to spill the steaming Russian brew. Stepping through a bulkhead door, his startled body jumped back as he almost bumped head-on with another sailor coming through on the opposite side. A large portion of his coffee flew onto the chest of the equally surprised crewman, yet the nervous man's eyes darted down and away as he wormed his way past without even a whimper of pain, let alone any form of protest. Fyodor stood befuddled. I've seen him before, he thought, but he's not part of this section. He's that brooding loner ... never talks with anyone during mess ... probably why he's a stinking torpedo rat. Looks like a Chechen, too … could even be a Dagestani. Anyway, who gives a damn? They're all the same. The navy shouldn't be letting those darkie bastards in—too many problems with them. He'll say he's Russian, probably passed a rigid clearance ... but I know better than that. I can smell 'em. Still, what the hell's he doing here near the missile compartment? He's got no business here. Fyodor looked down at the remains in his cup and decided that what was left was still enough to get him juiced. Looking up, he paused and turned his head back down the passage. The man had disappeared, but the encounter had left him with one of those nagging, uneasy feelings. Fyodor stood staring at the empty corridor, his gut instincts telling him he should take this to his captain. But kicking it upstairs meant confrontation. Instead, he frowned and shrugged his shoulders. Reluctantly, he threw it off and moved on to his work station.

CHAPTER 19

THE SKIES ABOVE THE FJORD WERE AZURE AND CLEAR. NOT a cloud could be seen and the wind was still. The only drawback was the temperature. It was bone-chilling cold. "Why does it have to be so damn cold?" Exclaimed Peter Jorgesen. After six years of managing the construction of the underwater substructure, this day had arrived. It was time to float in the massive upper deck of the gas rig and connect it above the support system he had finished.

Peter was standing on the deck of one of the tugs that would take the entire platform out to its destination in the North Sea. Standing next to him was Stellan Emanuelsen, skipper of Alpha tug and the man who would command the other seven seagoing tugboats. With his left hand, Peter slid the back of his trademark sailing cap down tight to his head and gave one last pull on its elongated bill. Shielding his eyes from the harsh glare of the morning sun, Peter was in awe of the approaching platform. The beige sailing cap was worn and rugged, like its owner, matching well with the trim, full reddish beard that covered his handsome ruddy features. "Damn!" He mumbled to Stellan, his left fingers rubbing the palm of his right hand. "Well, what do you say we get this friggin' show on the road?" Stellan reluctantly nodded. He wasn't as nervous about this maneuver as Peter was. It was the arduous journey that came next that sent a chill up Stellan's backside.

Although connecting the two massive components of Gimli was in the still waters of the fjord, Peter well knew that any unexpected gust of wind could raise the level of the fjord at least a half-meter. Even though the fjords were protected by the surrounding mountains, errant gusts were a problem. These sudden wind gusts were not an everyday occurrence, but they did happen, and always when you least expected them. Over and over he had prepared himself like Thor about to enter a battle. One small error, any momentary lapse in his attention or judgment could cause human lives to be lost, corporate profits to go down the toilet, and the entire project to be scuttled. In spite of his irritability, he was mentally ready for the hardest part of the connecting maneuver.

One damn meter! He thought. You think they could've spared maybe another? Hell, I could sink the shafts another meter on my own! Or why the hell couldn't they have floated the above-water platform in at one meter higher? "This is such garbage!" He bellowed, startling the already tense crew around him.

They all knew Peter was an overstuffed teddy bear and his bark was far worse than his bite. It was his way of relieving the tension that was knotting up the muscles of his shoulders. Nonetheless, after passing glances amongst themselves, it was agreed upon by all to ignore the growling Norwegian bear. Peter was not the easiest person to work with … he was a perfectionist in every detail, but not one single person in the small control cab that cantilevered out over the icy water would trade him for any other, bar none. When it came to performing this kind of maneuver, he was considered to have the mind and skills of the finest heart surgeon in the world, but could he and his army of computers and technicians control every possible variable that might come their way?

The monstrous gas-drilling platform was towed around the greenish-blue escarpment of the twisting fjord. A slow rumble grew to deafening heights, as one by one, the oversized seagoing tugboats were the first to break the pastoral scene of tranquility. But even these monstrous, churning beasts became dwarfed in size as the platform's tower turned the first bend in the fjord.

In his mind, Peter knew full well how big the platform was, so he shouldn't have been surprised. But even he was taken aback at the enormity of the behemoth when his perspective was from the surface of the water and not overhead in a company chopper. The tension in his back seemed to ratchet up proportionately with each meter as the floating city lumbered closer and closer to them.

"Bjorn, I want a continuous readout on the wind speed near the surface!" Peter barked out, his eyes never leaving the approaching platform.

"Three knots, but it seems to be holding steady."

"Remember, I want to know if even a passing seagull farts! And I'm dead serious," Peter added.

"Skipper, we've been through this a —"

"Don't give me any of your damn lip, Bjorn!" He thundered. "I don't want to have to call your wife and tell her how three quarters of a million tons of iron and concrete took her husband to the bottom of the fjord ... along with a lot of other good people. So stay focused—and that goes for all of you!"

Greta, who was in charge of monitoring the pace and position of the tugboats, looked over at Bjorn. She caught his quick grimace as he raised his hands, palms upward. Bjorn bit his lip, shook his head, and again returned his attention to the screen in front of him. His feelings were bruised and a little pouting would have helped his fragile ego, but Bjorn was still a professional and smart enough to know that his role was supportive, and the weight of the world rested on the shoulders of Peter Jorgesen. If something were to happen, he thought, I'd rather be on the platform above, than down here.

As the team of tugboats began to pass left and right of the submerged support towers, the disaster that happened to the project that preceded, "The Troll," played out in his mind. Its platform towers had been filled to three-quarters capacity, but were crushed under the extreme pressure of the water as they were lowered to a depth of one thousand feet. Free falling another five hundred feet, the support towers hit the bottom of the fjord with such massive impact, an earthquake tremor was set off that measured 3.8 on the Richter scale. Thank God no one was killed in that fiasco, he thought, and if I have any say in the matter, nobody is going to die here today either. He tugged the bill of his cap once more again, this time for emphasis.

But like his predecessor, "The Troll," his towers had also held; the engineers having learned from their disastrous mistakes. Three days prior, the submerged shafts of his Gimli had been lowered to a depth of fifteen hundred feet and inspected by several teams of divers. No stress cracks had appeared. All the computer models showed a favorable connection would be had, all systems were GO, and the barges carrying the upper platform were cutting the calm water like a warmed knife through butter. So why was his gut still wrenching? All Peter had to do was to direct the tugs to place the plumb bob over the bull's-eye and have the computers pump the water out of the shafts. They would rise to meet the platform and the connection would be made. Sweat began to stream down his forehead, interfering with his eyesight. What if one of the pumps failed and the towers bolted up lopsided? What if the still waters swelled, or one of the taught lines to any one of the tugs snapped? Dozens of questions fought for his attention and bombarded his senses like the blaring horns of rush hour in an inner city traffic jam. All the computers in the world still couldn't replace the eye contact judgment that had to be made by one person.

"…Now!" Peter bellowed into his microphone. "Begin pumping now!"

The partially drained shafts groaned and creaked under their own weight and began to rise above the water, as triumphant as the resurrection of Lazurus, making a loud, deafening thud, announcing to all that the long-awaited connection had been made. Amid the blaring foghorns of the tugs, the completed gas platform began to majestically rise, towering above the water in all her magnificence. With her legs connected to her body, she could wear the name "Gimli" proud, for she was ready for sea.

With his eyes tearing up, Peter Jorgesen smiled like an awaiting father who had just been told that his child was born and his wife was fine. His fully connected platform, his Gimli, was ready for its arduous journey. Consumed by all the back slapping and hoopla of his crew, the blood of his Norwegian ancestors fought for dominance and to calm his external emotions. For inward, he knew that his newborn child faced danger … somewhere out in the fury of the North Sea.

CHAPTER 20

IT WAS AN HOUR TO MIDDAY WHEN THE CALL TO JULIE Weston's department head came in. The pained response of Thomas Grayson let Mrs. Franks know that his shorts were in a serious wad at having to take the call from someone he considered too far down the food chain to merit his time or effort. He was having an otherwise uneventful day and it chapped his ass that he might have to get involved in some obvious petty matter with a female underling.

Thirty years of riding someone else's coattails at the CIA had left him with an arrogant attitude that could only be born of a small, petty person in a tenured, high governmental position. Presidents would come and go, as would their appointed Directors of Central Intelligence (DCI), but the true bureaucrat knew how to transcend these periodic, inconvenient interlopers, for they were viewed as nothing more than political hacks whose power base was made of shifting sand, mere straw blowing through the halls of Washington. No, the real power was not in the hands of these glad-handing politicians with their fake, toothy smiles. It was hidden deep within the twisting maze of their own bureaucratic departments ... labyrinths that were like frozen glaciers, functioning and creeping forward, but in a direction that the insiders knew and guarded. As long as the required numbers of years were put in, a pension would be there in the waiting—modest, yet comfortable. Unless, of course, someone with a keen eye and a sharp ear took advantage of the various "opportunities" that availed themselves to these privileged gatekeepers of the maze. Hell, why not? There wasn't an elected official on either side of the political aisle that wasn't lining their own pockets. Twenty years into his otherwise uneventful career, Thomas Grayson had found such an opportunity.

Was it a midlife crisis that had caused him to turn dark? Was it his nasty divorce, the settlement that had wiped him out? Or was it a combination of the three? He had asked himself these questions time and again without satisfying the questions of his weak immoral character. When his colleague, Dennis Carey, approached him, Grayson was sure that he needed cash—and lots of it. Had he been that obvious, or had Carey seen him as one of *his* own "opportunities"? It mattered little, for when Grayson learned the Russian Mafia had weapons to sell, in his mind it became crystal clear that even the most miniscule cut of the pie could grow into something substantial. And why shouldn't he cash in? What he had ordered to be done over the years in the name of "National Security" had already compromised any sense of ethical standards he may have had in the beginning. To Dennis Carey, people were nothing but pawns in a global power game of national interests. Individual lives lost their value and became expendable to any justifiable end. Over the years, those justifiable ends became twisted and blurred.

"Who ... who did you say you've just seen?" Grayson asked, his response to Julie Weston lowering to a whisper of astonishment.

"He was one of ours, a former mid-eastern operative who—"

"His code name, dammit, give me his code name!"

"It's Trojan Horse, sir. I ... I'm positive I've seen the former agent called 'Trojan Horse.' Here—right here in Alaska."

Grayson's face blanched. The temperature of his blood went into freefall. His mind tried to comprehend the danger that was threatening to unravel his carefully covered trails. His fingers clenched into a knot around the telephone. He closed his eyes and felt his breathing become heavy. It was as if his office had become the size of a small closet. The walls were moving in to crush the life out of him.

"Mr. Grayson, I know I'm on vacation, but I feel ... I feel compelled to find him. He did save my life ... as long as I have your approval, of course."

The conversation fell awkwardly silent. Julie's face frowned as she questioned whether she still had a connection. Grayson's confusion faded and he formulated a plan.

"Yes, yes you have my permission to track him down," he said. "But you must keep me informed of what you have found prior to making contact with him. Have I made myself clear? You will not make contact until you have talked to me," he repeated for emphasis. "And you'll be talking to only me ... on a secure line."

"Yes sir. All clear, sir."

Grayson laid the phone down in its carriage as if it would erase the fact that he had been on the line at all. He stared at the wall across from his desk. The pictures faded into white nothingness. His thoughts became coherent.

He's supposed to be dead. We paid the stinking Russian to kill him! We can't let some little bitch ruin what we've done. My God, we could be tried for murder—treason! He felt the ground beneath him move. It became rubbery. His whole world seemed to be collapsing—from one phone call. An image of him wearing an orange jumpsuit and hobbling in leg irons flashed before him.

His focus returned. He reached for the intercom to buzz his secretary. "Mrs. Franks, get in touch with Dennis Carey. Have him meet me at O'Malley's—twelve sharp."

CHAPTER 21

THE EMOTIONAL ROLLER-COASTER RIDE OF THE PAST SEVEN days had taken a heavy toll on Devon. His days were again filled with anxiety and it was now a Glock semi-automatic pistol that carried him through the night instead of his usual single malt scotch. But the nights were even longer, with fear and painful memories filling the sleepless hours.

Her warm smile was the last image he saw before drifting off to sleep in his refuge—a refuge, however, that had been breached. His hand, still holding the Glock, slid down the side of his thigh and came to a rest on the blanket.

A long groaning crack followed by a crashing thud caused Devon to bolt upright, the Glock gripped with two hands, scanning the door and the windows. Realizing the security of the small cabin had not been breached, his mind processed the sound and recognized it as a long row of icicles breaking off en masse and crashing onto the blue vinyl that covered his woodpile. A quick look out the window gave him the verification he sought. Lying back down, he saw the bottle of Scotch on the counter and yearned for a nerve-settling swig. Pushing down with his right hand to get up, the cold steel of the semi-automatic weapon reminded him that danger was on its way. His days with The Agency had taught him well, so he nixed the Scotch. There were those who could not leave him alive and would not stop until they were certain he was dead. How had it come to this? Devon released a sigh of weariness and closed his tired eyes. Sleep came, but with it, the same dreams.

He was back in Dagestan and the weight of trying to save his marriage and yet salvage his career at The Agency had become a balancing act he could no longer perform. Petition after petition to be relocated back to Langley for a desk job were denied by his superior, Tom Grayson. His pleadings to Tim Daniels for help in rediscovering his and Cathy's identity had run into an electronic dead end. He was on a skiff without oars, its moorings cut loose, drifting in a desolate sea with no land in sight.

Once more, he was given a change in assignment. He was ordered to the consulate in Kabul, Afghanistan. This time, however, there would be no flying into Afghanistan or any other Near-East rat hole. Devon remembered hearing the heavy sound of Tim Daniels' lifeless body hitting the wood floor.

Devon bolted out of his sleep. His nightshirt was dripping wet. "Dear God, let me have peace!" He cried out as he ran his fingers through his damp hair. He looked around at his cabin walls, and in frustration, threw himself backwards onto his bed. One night, please, no dreams, he begged, as he fell asleep again. Soon, however, the dreams started once more.

Devon and Cathy were fifty miles out of Napa Valley when a long, black Mercedes began to tailgate them. Devon was in no hurry. He felt as if he had come out of some dark, blinding cloud and a huge weight had been lifted from his shoulders. Yet, it was more than the liberation from a painful burden. He felt as if his friend, Tim, had made the ultimate sacrifice in order to wash him of his sins. Consummate shame and sorrow had been replaced by instinct for survival. From deep within, his gut told him he must grab his wife and go into hiding. There would be no chance of exposing Grayson and Carey. The wilderness of Alaska might not have been their best long-term solution, but it seemed their only short-term hope. But would she go? Devon wasn't sure. He would have to share with her every ugly aspect of his life at the CIA. That was the risk. If he told her everything, would she even want to be with the monster that he perceived he had become?

He slowed the Alfa Romeo down to allow the obnoxious tailgater time to pass his car. The opportunity was there for a long stretch, but the driver made no move. Annoyed, Devon stuck his arm out to the side and motioned for the Mercedes to pass—nothing. The Mercedes remained ten feet off his bumper. He looked over at Cathy and gave her a face of growing irritation. As he turned the radio volume down, he looked ahead for a break in the guardrails, hoping to find a scenic pull off to let the jerk pass. Through the floorboards, he heard the faint muffled sound of a small explosion beneath the car. He felt a vibration run up his leg. Instinct told him what happened. The payback had begun. The brakes! His foot slammed onto the pedal. It fell with no resistance to the floor. His hands tightened on the steering wheel. His mind tore at what to do. All of a sudden, their heads snapped backward. The car behind them slammed into their bumper. Devon's heartbeat became explosive. His hand gripped the gearshift and his eyes fixed on the rear-view mirror. What the—it's him! It can't be! He saw the chiseled face of Gregor Polnich—ex-KGB assassin that worked both sides. There was no time. He downshifted, swung the car hard to the left. He skinned the side of the mountain to slow the car down. Massive sparks spewed forth. Jagged rock screeched against metal. The Mercedes slammed into them again, pushing them into the guardrail. Devon held control and swerved to the left. An oncoming truck appeared as they approached the next curve. Its huge bumper magnified in size. The blaring sound of its horn panicked him. He over-steered the car to the right. They hit the guardrail hard. His Alfa crashed through. His arm stretched out to hold Cathy against her seat. All he could see were the rocks rising up to meet them. Cathy's terrified screams were the last thing he remembered.

Devon McKenzie awoke with a start. His pillow was soaked from sweat, and his blankets had been kicked off to the side. The devils in his head wouldn't allow him the respite of peace he needed. Too many images continued to flood his worn-out mind. He felt as if he was at wits' end and wondered if there was some purpose to his torture, some divine plan in which he was a bit player. Or was he just a bit player? Maybe his role was larger than he comprehended. Devon pushed himself up into a sitting position with his legs hanging over the bed. He placed his elbows on his knees and rested his chin in the palms of his cupped hands, his fingertips massaging his eyes. The vision of the dissident scientist, Batu Sigua, broke through the cobwebs and again came fresh to his mind. He looked upward and said, "God! What else are you going to torment me with?"

The logs in the metal grate had dwindled to ash and the temperature in his cabin had dropped to about 40 degrees. As he raised his hand to pull the hair off his forehead, he felt the Glock still in his clutch. He turned his hand and his eyes studied the sinister weapon. It disgusted him and he let it fall from his fingers onto the blanket. In his primal fear he wanted to run again. But to where, to what purpose? Was running and hiding in fear like a hunted animal all that remained in life for him, another cooped-up stinking armpit in the wilderness of Alaska? Having to booze himself into a stupor every night to be able to forget all the death that surrounded him? Devon was worse than mentally worn-out, he was bone-deep exhausted and sleep deprived. Down deep he knew he couldn't continue on this way.

Now there was this other woman. Saving her had given him a glint of purpose and optimism that he hadn't felt in years, but his situation had put her at risk. In coming after him, would they go through her first? Use her to find him? Could he run again and cause the death of another woman?

Cathy's haunting face, that last glimpse of terror he saw in her eyes as they plunged through the guardrail, flashed in his mind again. He couldn't escape. It came in his sleep—it came in his waking hours. It was relentless. He vowed he wouldn't let this happen again. He couldn't let this happen one more time. Devon's eyes lowered to the Glock sitting on the bed next to him. Trembling, his hand picked up the gun and raised it toward his temple. Would this last act end the pain … for everyone? Because he would be saving someone else's life, would God forgive this last desperate act?

CHAPTER 22

SITUATED AROUND THE CORNER AND DOWN THE STREET from the FBI building, O'Malley's Irish Grill was a safe spot to meet. As all sorts of governmental employees ate their lunches there, two department heads meeting for lunch would raise no real suspicions. Tom Grayson was the first to arrive, and secured the end booth along the front wall of glass. Short, green curtains hung on a polished brass rail, covering the lower half of the windows—perfect for privacy from the outside, yet high enough so as not to obscure those who passed by on the sidewalk. He positioned himself on a bench with his back to the booth preceding him.

Knowing full well that he would piss the hell out of Grayson, Dennis Carey came in, as usual, ten minutes late. During this time, Grayson fidgeted as his displeasure mounted. Carey felt the need to remind Grayson who had the senior position—especially when the message from Grayson's secretary demanded he be there at twelve sharp.

"What seems to be your little sense of urgency?" Carey mocked as he slid into the booth. Grayson hated Carey's flippant attitude and produced a snarling sneer.

"Trojan Horse," he whispered through gritted teeth. "Need I say anything else?"

"What did you say?" A look of perplexity filled Carey's face.

"I said 'Trojan Horse!' Did you think I would call you here to talk about my Aunt Harriet?"

Carey's face blanched as his eyes locked straight onto the fidgeting bureaucrat. "Why the hell are you bringing that name up? The man is dead!" He whispered.

"Yeah, well he isn't," Grayson growled back. "I got a call this morning from someone named Weston ... a Julie Weston. She's a stinking nobody in I don't even know what stinking, nothing department," his raspy voice hissed. "The little bitch was in Alaska on holiday and crashed her plane outside of Fairbanks. Would you like to take a guess at whom she was rescued by?"

"Wait a damn minute. Weston …? Who in the hell is she?"

"Hello … Julie Weston … CIA … Langley … that's us," he snarled, dripping with impatience at Carey's apparent slow uptake.

"Are you saying she belongs to us … that she's part of 'the community?'"

"Yes and no. She's nothing but a mid-level analyst. She was assigned to analyzing the breakup of the Soviet Union … said she recognized his face from one of our files. Anyway, she claims it was Trojan Horse who pulled her out of the burning wreck and took her by snowmobile to a medical facility in some bung hole town called Otter Creek. From there, they flew her by chopper to a hospital in Fairbanks. But here's the kicker … his picture was taken by a reporter when he met the ambulance."

"Have *you* seen the picture?"

Grayson paused to turn his head left and right, trying to scan one hundred and eighty degrees behind him. His hand slipped into his suit jacket pocket, pulling it out as if it were toxic and slid the paper across the table to Carey. "The answer to your stupid question is: 'What do you think?' She told me the name of the newspaper, so I pulled it up."

As Carey unfolded the piece of paper, his lower jaw dropped as he drew a long, slow breath. "It's him all right," he said. "I'd recognize that turncoat bastard anywhere."

"What are we going to do?" Grayson asked in a pitiful tone.

It was Carey's turn to look around before he whispered, "Simple … we kill him again. He can't be left out there, unless you're interested in going to prison and becoming some badman's nighttime squeeze."

Grayson had hit his boiling point. "We're talking high treason and murder here, Carey. Prison orange won't be an option for us. What about using Polnich again?"

Carey's eyes were focused on the curtain to his left. His brow furrowed at the thought of the Russian, but his trance remained unbroken. When his thoughts gelled, his head snapped around. "And give him one more chance to mess it up? If he couldn't finish the job the first time, what in the hell makes you think he could do it now? No, we'll use Stringer for this one … that way it keeps the circle tight. Get hold of him immediately … I'm pretty sure he's in San Diego. Have him get up to Fairbanks and await further instructions. When this Weston bitch contacts us again, he can take them both out."

CHAPTER 23

OTTER CREEK, ALASKA

JOSH ABRAMS OPENED THE DOOR OF HIS SALT-COVERED Jeep and swung his left leg out into the freezing evening air. When his foot hit the ground, he paused for a moment, thinking once more of the difficult choices he had made. Not the choices of this particular day, for it had been an uneventful day, one more in a string of ten since he had released his news story with its lead photo of the wilderness hero. Never one to be bashful, the young reporter was comfortable that it was a good story. Obviously not Pulitzer material, but a story that was nonetheless his own … and well written, if he didn't mind saying so himself. But his conscience kept gnawing at him till it took little to set off the festering irritant. He couldn't shake the nagging feeling that ate at him. Coming in and out of his memory when least expected were the man's words. Questioning his intentions for what seemed to be the hundredth time, Josh resigned himself to the fact that he had sold his soul to the devil. But the final question remained: For what, one lousy story that his boss pressured him into?

Perhaps a follow-up story on the hermit would salve over his conscience, or at least some information on his status might help, but Josh didn't know where to find him and hadn't had enough years under his belt to even know where to begin looking. Still, what if his story had done something to the man, or set some harmful action in motion? God knows he went ballistic over the photo. In any case, Josh figured he would shower up, head to the local watering hole, and who knows, maybe even get lucky tonight.

As he backed the key out of the lock and turned the handle to open the door, something didn't seem right. Where's Maggie? He thought. His door had a well-worn gouge, under the inside handle, where his dog would scratch with her paws, anxiously waiting for her master to come home and serve up her customary treat of two biscuits. Josh eased the door open and called out for his faithful friend. No response. Frowning, he hollered out a little louder "Come on, Maggie!" …Nothing. The small bungalow seemed lifeless, as if the dog had gotten out, or worse off, had choked on a bone. Josh's angst increased with each step he took and each turn of his head that produced nothing, not a sign or even a whimper. Stepping into the small kitchen, he reached across his body and flicked the light switch on.

"Maggie!" He screamed in horror.

The German Sheppard lay lifeless on the floor—her head in a pool of blood that had spewed from her throat. His body froze and he went into shock. He wanted to drop to his knees and gather his dog into his arms. He couldn't budge. Scorching pain came over his head. His scalp felt as if it were being ripped from his skull. His head snapped back under the force of the hand knotted in his hair. A razor sharp knife was thrust up under his chin. Josh's body went rigid in terror. He lifted himself up on his toes, as if it would make the knife go away.

"Relax," the hardened voice hissed. "You'll get through this—if I get what I want."

Josh Abrams was a young man of words, not action. He weighed his options and made his choice. "Wha..." He started to say, but stopped. He realized the need to keep his throat steady. "What is it you want?" He whispered. "I … I don't have any money ... no drugs." His voice quivered. The youth in him wanted to cry, but his mind suppressed it. He feared the assailant would punish him for that alone.

"I want information on the hermit. I want the vermin that brought that pilot in from the bush. I want to know where he is—right now."

"But, I don't have that information. I swear to God. I don't know."

Cold steel pressed harder against his throat. He felt a slow warm trickle move down his skin. He wanted to tell the assailant anything he wanted to hear, but he couldn't. Tears welled up in his eyes and ran down his cheeks.

"I swear to you—I don't know."

CHAPTER 24

YURI DOLGORUKI

THE PURRING VIBRATION OF THE RUSSIAN SUBMARINE HAD helped computer man Feodor Strivnych to drift off into a deep, meaningful sleep. He had learned from his early days as a Soviet sub-mariner that regulated, consistent sleep, even if short, was the key to passing your watch alert and attentive. Working submarines had never been a job to Feodor. No, to him it was a life's mission. He was unabashed. He loved his life at sea. He took his job more than serious and centered his whole existence on the proper functioning of his boat's nuclear missiles. Unmarried and no spring chicken, Feodor recognized that changes in technology came faster than he was aging and had a ripple effect that encompassed every aspect of his work. He kept pace with the ever-changing times, and along the way, the spawning ground for many of the advances in Russian technology had come from the mind of this peasant from the collective farms of Ukraine. This night's sleep, however, was different.

Feodor's mind wouldn't shut down and he tossed and turned in what seemed to be a night from hell. Because of his need for all things to have their place and time, it was the series of disordered events of the day that ricocheted off the inner walls of his head. The cunning eyes of the Chechen crewman rolled in and out of his dreams. Again and again this swarthy face came at him as some sort of enigma, close enough to touch, but never able to grasp. The puzzle came together … the eyes became a head and the head was on a full body. That's it! The body was in a corridor … coming out of *his* compartment door! Feodor bolted upright, his sweat-soaked sheets clinging to his body. His hands covered his face, trying to clear the cobwebs. He remembered. He had been looking downward while carrying his coffee, trying not to spill it. Prior to bumping into the torpedo man, he had looked up, catching a long glimpse down the corridor. He spotted a man leaving his work station. He had assumed it was his assistant Alex, but Alex had hurried in *after* he sat back down at his station. His excuse was lame … had to go to the bathroom, couldn't wait. In twelve years of working with Alex, neither man had left their compartment unattended—that was forbidden. Why was a torpedo man coming out of my compartment? And worse, why had Alex abandoned our station? He thought.

Feodor's mind was made up. Alex may be his best friend, but a cloud of suspicion and distrust hung over his head. He and that Chechen would be watched close and yes, the captain would be informed—about them both.

CHAPTER 25

CREEPING AT THREE NAUTICAL MILES PER HOUR, THE LONG arduous journey down the fjord to the North Sea was short in terms of lateral miles, but to Peter Jorgesen, it might as well have been to the other side of the moon. His crew was exasperated and the jokes about being able to walk at a faster pace grew old … and the grousing never stopped. Complete boredom had set in. Peter had to stifle his yawns, even after slugging down a mug of bitter black coffee. Sitting in the control bridge that cantilevered out over the side deck, the thirty-meter distance to the calm waters of the fjord distorted his perception of moving at all. But the haunting thought of one of the underwater tower legs snagging a jagged rock forced Peter to keep his attention focused and on edge.

The protected inlet, with the lone Spruce that forced itself through a natural jetty of glacial rock, appeared as they turned another bend in the fjord. Peter not recognized the conifer and related to it. He admired its long, bent trunk, leaning forward toward the North Sea, defying the intimidation of its cold, biting wind. He was sure that his Viking ancestors, coming in on longboats laden with plunder from Celtic lands, would have shared a similar view. As a slight snicker broke out on his face, Peter thought, God speed old tough.

"One more kilometer and we hit the rough waters of the North Sea," he warned his crew. Would have been nice to have had several more weeks, he didn't say. "Stay alert and remember, praying is not above any of us. It soothes the soul and toughens our mettle."

CHAPTER 26

OUTSIDE OF FAIRBANKS, ALASKA

JACK WESTON SAT IN HIS CHAIR WATCHING THE DAUGHTER he had raised by himself since she was twelve years old. The corners of his mouth turned upward as the comforting feelings of pride drifted to that strong love that parents feel. Her face was the mirror image of the wife and mother that was denied to both of them. He wondered, as his smile faded to a blank stare, should he have married again? Did he have an obligation to see that his daughter have a mother to get her through the complexities of the teenage years? His loneliness was overwhelming, but in Alaska, the options and opportunities available to a single man with a half-grown child were slim and next to nil. Men were in the lopsided majority and women came at a high premium. Good-looking women cost you your soul. Still, should he have moved to a larger city to increase his chances? Would a new mother have helped or would there have been further problems? The questions and the subsequent guilt never changed. He masked them with constant activity.

For the last two weeks, he had been watching her recuperate from her wounds. It caused him the customary pain that all loving parents feel when they consider the loss that might have been. He also felt a little embarrassed. Behind the façade, he was relieved to have his daughter back at home. Floods of warm memories cascaded over him as he alternated between seeing the daughter he missed, and remembering the child that never left his side. He also knew the time would come when she would leave him again, returning him to the emptiness that had become his life since her first departure. She told him at breakfast she felt recovered enough to go out for a visit, and asked if he would be willing to drive her. Jack sensed that this day would be the start of her second leaving.

The front door opened to the log-beamed canopy where his vehicle was parked. His Yukon may not have been the easiest vehicle for someone recovering from an abdominal wound to climb into, but it was all he had.

Maybe I should have rented a lower sedan, he thought, as he watched her grimace in pain as she stepped off the running board and climbed onto the passenger seat. She saw the look on his face and read his thoughts.

"Dad, relax … the SUV is okay. Being here with you is all I need to feel better and heal up fine. If you don't mind, on the way to the store I would like to make a short stop in Otter Creek. There's a reporter there that I need to see to get some information on my plane crash."

"That information … is it on somebody you want to find … a bush hero maybe?" He queried. A wink of his eye gave approval. He prayed that the bushman might be a reason for her to stay a while longer in Alaska.

"Well it's more than that, Dad. I think I need your advice."

"I'm not sure what I can offer, but you know I'll sure give it my best shot."

"It isn't just to thank him. Something's troubling me … something at The Agency," she said, turning her head and staring out the side window. With the first turn of the vehicle, the dull pain in her gut brought her attention back. "It has a lot to do with my job, Dad, not the usual problems, its CIA spook crap. I called my boss at Langley and told him that I thought the man that rescued me was a former agent of ours. His reaction didn't sit right with me … something doesn't seem to fit."

Jack Weston knew his daughter too well. Something was the matter. He waited, hoping that there wasn't a problem and she would be able to settle it in her own mind.

"A few years ago," she said, lowering her voice, "I had a close friend at The Agency … his name was Tim Daniels. I never told you, but we were more than friends. I think it may have …" Her voice trailed off as she turned her head and stared out the side window; she wanted to mask the tears welling up in her eyes. "Anyway, he had asked me to run some checks for him on an agent of ours that worked the Middle East and the Northern Caucasus. He was Tim's best friend and I wasn't running a criminal check on him. I was checking why his identity had disappeared. I mean, we have double agents everywhere and their identities are super secret, but if you've got inside access and know computers inside and out, you can track them down with the equipment at The Agency. But not this one! His and his wife's identities went into a black hole that I couldn't access any which way I tried. This wasn't normal. Then Tim

… Tim was killed …" Julie's voice broke. She covered her face with her hands and began to cry.

Jack pulled the Yukon off onto the shoulder of the road, leaned over, and gave her an assuring hug. Wiping the tears away, she paused and took a deep breath.

"Dad, I believe he was murdered in cold blood! His throat was cut and the D.C. police wrote it up as another drug-related slaying. Dad, he never touched drugs—not ever! Anyway, it was the last thing Tim asked me to do. The agent's code name was Trojan Horse, and I know that the person who rescued me is this man. I was shocked to see his face because he died … four years ago!"

Jack was bewildered and searched for something to say. "Sweetheart, why ...?"

Julie turned her head back to her father and cut him off. "Why and what are the key words, Dad. Why would my boss use the term 'track him down,' but tell me not to make contact with him? I'm to inform him, no one else, of where the agent is … on a secure line. If he's a former agent, why are they afraid of him? And what are they planning to do to him?"

Jack began to feel uneasy; he could sense a looming danger approaching. "Could he be some sort of rogue agent, I mean, maybe he somehow crossed The Agency? Maybe he was involved in something … say criminal? He could have some sort of a past for all you know."

"Dad, I believe Tim died because he was trying to help this man and now this same man has saved my life. I don't know if he has a past or not, but I think the answer starts with the reporter that did the story of my rescue. Oh—turn left at the next light, he lives out on that road."

CHAPTER 27

GREGOR POLNICH TOOK A DEEP BREATH AS HE WALKED UP to the information desk of the hospital. He wanted to appear to be in no hurry, interested in the health of 'his cousin.' Disappointment was written all over his face as the receptionist indicated she had checked out five days earlier. "I'm sorry, but who did you say picked her up?" He asked.

"I didn't, but there's no harm; it was her father, Jack Weston. I'm sure you can reach her at his house."

"And that would be where?" He asked, reaching to turn the discharge file around. He had overstepped.

"Uh, excuse me!" The receptionist said, as she retrieved the discharge booklet from Polnich's grasp. "That is covered under the HIPAA privacy laws, but I'm sure you can find him in the phone book."

As Gregor turned in the lobby to make his exit, his trained eye caught the site of a man doubled over and coughing, covering his mouth with his fist as Gregor passed him by. Where had he seen that face? He tried jogging his memory, but came up blank. Then it hit him.

***

The man with the cough was a CIA operative nicknamed "Stringer," and he knew who Gregor Polnich was. He also knew the Russian would be his ticket to ride. I'll let that stupid bastard do all the work, he thought, and I'll put him out with the morning trash.

Continuing to fake his cough, Stringer walked bent over until he reached the back side of the reception desk. Out of the corner of his eyes, he noticed Gregor Polnich had exited the hospital doors. As he stood erect again, his hawk-like eyes never left the retreating figure of the Russian assassin.

"Can I help you find a patient, sir?" The receptionist at the information desk queried.

"Uh yes, Weston, Julie Weston," he said, his eyes still locked on the Russian getting into his car.

"Sorry, she checked out five days ago. Are you also a relative?" She said with a tinge of sarcasm.

As her computer screen brought up the file again, she said, "You can reach her at her—" But as she looked up, there was no one to finish her sentence to.

Stringer had reached his car and caught sight of the rental car speeding away. The sight of the Russian made his skin crawl. Why didn't Grayson tell me this scum was going to be here? He thought. What the hell is he trying to do, make me look like I'm some piece of trash? Polnich is the idiot who screwed up taking that agent out in the first place. I'll show them—I'll dog this bastard till he finds them. I'll take control of this three-ring circus.

CHAPTER 28

THE GRAVEL OF THE SNOW-COVERED DRIVE CRUNCHED under the weight of the slowing SUV. "This is it, Dad; pull in here. There it is—number 23."

As the vehicle came to a stop, Julie put a hand on her father's wrist. Her tight grip conveyed caution and fear. Her training at the CIA was kicking back in. The cabin loomed in front of them. It was an old structure, deep brown batten on board siding covered by a rusted tin roof that had the look of a lost war with nature. The temperature outside was twenty-five degrees, but no smoke was coming out of the stone chimney. Her eyes scanned over to the furnace's crooked vent pipe that rose from the roof like a dislocated finger. It stood cold and lifeless. Something, she wasn't sure what, but something seemed wrong to her. As she stepped onto the front stoop, she noticed the door was ajar. It wasn't ajar because it was rickety from age—the door had been retrofitted. Should be closed, she thought. The feeling caused goose bumps on her arm and a chill ran down her spine. It was eleven o'clock in the morning, but the curtains were drawn tight. Through the sun-rotted fabric, she saw a light was still on inside—not right.

She turned, looking into her father's eyes, paused, and gained the reassuring strength she needed. She rapped her knuckles on the door. The door yielded its semi-closed position and with a drawn-out, painful cry, creaked its way open. The odor of death wafted across her as she eased her way into the small cabin—her father following close behind. Julie was the first to see the blood-soaked remains of the dog lying on the floor. She froze, knowing that this was an omen. Jack Weston clutched his daughter and pulled her in with a hug as he spotted the lifeless body of Josh Abrams also on the floor. His parka muffled her shriek as she caught sight of the dead reporter in a pool of blood.

With his arm still around her shoulders, Jack Weston helped a shaking Julie back into his vehicle. On the drive back to his house, nothing was said between them. There was nothing either could have said that would have helped. As they arrived under the covered front canopy of his house, he slammed his SUV to a halt, grinding the frozen gravel. He looked over at Julie—it was one of those moments frozen in time. Someone had been brutally murdered and he felt like a boxer that had taken a punch square in his face. The questions flooded in: Who could have done such a sadistic thing? And worse, how could his daughter be involved in such a sick, criminal act?

Fear guided his next move. He slammed the vehicle back into drive and pulled around the rear of the house. Jack was a strong man, but the sight of the young reporter lying in a pool of blood had shattered his placid rural world. His mind grasped for a plan of action, yet his instincts told him to take his daughter and run. The how and the where were not the issues. He knew that this danger was coming to them. "We've got to go!" He blurted out. "We've got to get you to safety, maybe the police in Fairbanks. We can tell them there about the murdered reporter."

"Dad, hold on a minute!" Julie responded, pausing long enough to gather her thoughts. "I need to go in and contact my superiors. I don't know if it's the right move, but I have a hunch it may give us the clues we need."

CHAPTER 29

GRAYSON WAS NERVOUS. HE SAT DRUM ROLLING HIS FINGERS on the arm of his chair. He may have been leaning back with his feet crossed on the top of his desk, but he was tensed, contemplating the cage he had been backed into. The door to his office was shut, as it had been since his first contact with the minor subordinate who had become a serious cancer. He could no longer concentrate on the tasks of his daily job. The inner workings of the CIA were akin to a painting by Dali. The Agency was America's eyes on the world, but those eyes looked inward as well as outward. Trust was not a household word. Every plan, every relationship, every alliance had a contingency; an alternative route that in most cases doubled as an escape route. People used people for advantage, and that advantage was enhanced by any knowledge that could be gathered. Words and action had meaning, however small and insignificant. Why did someone say that, what did they mean by that, and how does that affect me? The people who succeeded were the ones that understood the game, connected the dots, and turned it to their own strategic advantage.

With his eyes still glazed over, Grayson leaned forward in his leather chair and began swirling his middle right finger on his desk, tracing the meandering grain of its mahogany veneer. The desk was old, but of high quality with deep mottled tones of brown, red, and orange. The color of orange, not the subtle orange of his desk … prison orange to be exact, was all his mind could conjure. Prison life dominated his every passing thought. Short, clumsy steps, ankles bound by restraining chains, wrists low, bound by handcuffs. Would he be protected from the other inmates, or would the guards loathe him for his treasonous acts and turn a blind eye to aggression, even sexual assault? He knew full well that many criminals have an odd compass. They have no problem with theft, fraud, or even murder; but to many, patriotism remained a singular guiding light. To them, screwing over one's country was an act of abomination and their peculiar sense of justice knew how to deal with it. Grayson could handle being executed for his crimes, as long as it was by lethal injection. Even long years of isolation didn't bother him. But it was the specter of being beaten and sodomized that he couldn't deal with. The mere thought of this sent him into a depression that was hard to climb out of, let alone disguise.

Mrs. Franks noticed the change in her boss and covered for him as best she could, but she sensed deep-seated trouble. Not the usual in-house bureaucratic turf war type of squabbling, but something sinister and foreboding. Twenty years of working for the same man gave her a clear and succinct read. Her love of country urged her to take her suspicions to a higher level, but Dennis Carey was the next level and she loathed the arrogant little prig. Worse, she didn't trust him. But she had no comfort level navigating her way through the layered mine fields beyond him. She decided to wait and move if Grayson's situation worsened and became indefensible.

Grayson jumped out of his skin as the vibrating pager went off, spinning his cell phone on the hard surface of his desk. "Damn it!" He blurted out, grabbing the invader in his hand and snapping it open. The caller ID showed it to be Jack Weston. "Ms. Weston, hold on one second," he said.

His hand covered the mouthpiece to reduce his whispered voice. "Have you found the location of Trojan Horse?"

"No sir, I called to tell you that I went to the house of the reporter that wrote his story and he was lying in a pool of blood. His throat was slit and I don't know what to do." Julie paused to let the message sink in, and said, "Should I call the local police or—?"

"No!" Grayson shouted.

Julie was startled at his aggression, but kept her mouth closed as her suspicions began to come together.

"Listen to me," he said, his composure regained. "Trojan Horse has killed that reporter to protect himself. He will do anything and every-thing to cover his trail. And that means he will come after you, Ms. Weston. Remember, you are not experienced in these matters."

The knocking on his door broke his composure. "Damn it, this is personal!" He snapped, waving his hand in a dismissive fashion at Mrs. Franks, leaving the mouthpiece uncovered. He paused, waiting for her head to disappear with the closing of the door. He paused to calm his nerves. "As I was saying, Ms. Weston, you're an analyst and you are in way over your head. I'm trying my best to protect you. Believe me, Devon McKenzie is a cold-blooded killer who is coming after you as we speak. I hope that the man I have sent to clean up this mess will get to you in time to save your life."

Julie's eyes met her father's and held firm. Jack knew his daughter was rattled. "What should I do?" She queried, suspecting what the answer already was.

"You are calling from your father's house. Stay there until one of our agents reaches you. And Ms. Weston, do not call anyone else but me—no one. Am I clear on this?"

She hesitated while thinking. "Yes sir, I'll wait right here at my father's house."

The phone went dead in her hand. As if she were in slow motion, she placed the phone back in its receiver. That was enough time to put her thoughts in order. Her eyes rose once more to meet her father's. "It's dirty, Dad. I know it as sure as I'm standing here. I don't know how and I don't know why, but Grayson is behind this and the son-of-a bitch has sent someone to kill us. He knows we're at your house through caller ID. Our only hope is to find the man who saved me from the plane crash. Quick, go pack, Dad. I don't think we have a minute to spare. Oh, and better grab some of your firepower too; in fact, get whatever you've got. It's possible we may need every damn bit of it."

Jack Weston moved upon his daughter's orders. He smiled to himself and said, "I was worried about *you*, Julie. Hah! You're fine. In fact, you're more than fine."

CHAPTER 30

YURI DOLGORUKI

EVERYTHING WAS RUNNING WELL AND ON SCHEDULE, BUT Captain Andrei Illanov sat in his commander's chair with a feeling that he was sitting on a keg of dynamite with a short fuse running. The sub itself was drop-dead state of the art and seemed to hum like no other submarine he had captained. This is good technology, he mused … must've stolen it from the Americans. Andrei loved Mother Russia, but he was aware that his country could never match the United States in the overall sophistication and quality of their weaponry. Even if the Yanks became frozen in a bottle, it would take Russia twenty years to equal their existing achievements. Once in my life, I would love to command an Ohio class American submarine, he thought. He needed the escape—his mind had been troubled since Feodor had come to him with his misgivings and concern.

His exec tapped him on the shoulder. "Captain, you told me to remind you when it was 1500 hours," he said.

"Oh … yes, thank you, Anton. The helm is yours." He frowned and looked up at his exec. "What time tomorrow do we make the turn south?"

"Zero five hundred hours, Captain."

Andrei Illanov motioned for his exec to meet him at the mapping table. As he rose from his chair, he pulled a sealed envelope from the inner pocket of his uniform jacket and handed it to his second in command. "These are the coordinates you are to program, Anton, and there has been a slight modification."

The exec read the orders and feigned surprise. "Sir, these coordinates will take us within the restricted waters of the Norwegian gas fields! Captain, you must be testing me, or it is a mistake by Central Command?"

Illanov paused for a moment. He saw it in the shifting of his exec's eyes and how his words rang hollow and insincere. How did he know the location before he even glanced at the map panel? The coordinates of this mission were known by Illanov and no one else. "You are correct, Anton, but only about the first of your statements, not the second. Nonetheless, it is a small deviation designed to test our cloaking. And if the arrogant noses of NATO get tweaked in the process, well, so much the better. May I remind you that Norway's territorial waters extend twelve miles out, not the sixty-four of the gas fields? And we do not have a signed treaty that gives Norway exclusive control over passage of these waters."

Anton Kashnikov didn't want to overplay his hand, but felt one more protest would strengthen it. "But in the past—"

The captain was becoming weary of the discussion and cut the exec off in mid-sentence. "Perhaps Mother Russia has been too agreeable in the past, Anton. This little sojourn may be a small statement, but our politicians feel it is appropriate to 'display our renewed military strength'... their words, not mine." Andrei Illanov stared into his exec's eyes and said, "Then again, you might like to argue with our admiralty?" With a cracking of a smile, he said, "May I remind you, Anton, that this submarine was not built to be hidden under a bushel basket?"

"But Captain ..." the exec said with a feigned sense of resignation.

"There are no buts, Mr. Kashnikov. We have our orders and they stand. The rest is up to the politicians. Zero five hundred hours ... no deviation."

"Affirmative, Captain, but we still have to contend with Norway's air force. What are your plans to evade the RNAF's Orion surveillance aircraft?"

"In case you may not have paid attention, there is a gale coming our way. We will wait until the storm is upon us. That way, the RNAF will be grounded. That is the strategic moment when we make our dash for the gas fields. Once we have arrived, we will have accomplished our mission. We will see the West's reaction—lame as it may be ... zero five hundred hours," Illanov repeated with a cold stare for emphasis.

Anton Kashnikov was well satisfied with his performance. He was sure that it was good enough to keep his captain's suspicions at bay.

Dreading what he knew he had to do, the captain turned and exited the conning tower. Twenty-five years in the Russian Navy and never once had he even thought of searching a crewman's quarters. He was old school, authoritative and aristocratic. His father was Navy, as was his grandfather and great-grandfather, their unbroken chain of influence dating back to the Czars. What he was about to do would have been dealt with by a subordinate at any other time, but Andrei Illanov had a gut feeling that something catastrophic was underfoot. He sensed the lives of every man on board depended on him and his trusted computer man, Feodor Strivnych.

Illanov was a proud man and it took all his resolve to do what he knew he must do. He took one last look down both lengths of the corridor before he entered the quarters of Alex Sigua. He abhorred subterfuge as it made him feel petty and small like some smarmy ferret. He would rather face a hundred battles than to be caught in this unseemly situation. Drawing the curtain behind him, he held his breath and listened for footsteps before he turned the light on. He wasn't worried about Alex barging in because Feodor assured him he would create a situation to keep him long enough at his station. It was the other crew members that concerned him most. If they saw me, would they think I would go into their quarters? Stop worrying, he thought, Feodor said he would take care of them as well.

As his eyes scanned the small cubical that allowed for few personal effects, nothing seemed out of the ordinary. The walls were a dreary light gray with no sense that a man would call this his home. Then again, a submariner was not encouraged to spend any quality time in the confines of his small quarters. His closet measured 18" in width and contained two pair of dungarees, three shirts, and his dress uniform. On the shelf above were the usual toiletries: shaving accessories, toothbrush and paste, and a hairbrush with a comb stuck upright inside, all in proper order. Illanov lifted the lid of the small footlocker at the foot of the bed. It contained his undershorts, socks, and tee shirts. In the lid, held in by an elastic cloth was a picture of a family—a man, a woman, and two small children. Turning it over in his hands, he saw it was addressed:

To Alex, a most wonderful brother, and signed: With all our love, Batu, Helena, Alexei, and Ivan.

Behind the picture, folded in the same flap were two newspaper articles—one describing an automobile accident that had killed Helena and the children, the other the suicide of Batu. Illanov sifted his hands through the underwear until he came across a small folded letter. His hands trembled as he began reading the letter from Batu. He wrote Alex of the depths of his despair over the death of his family, for he believed they had died because of his involvement with an American agent named Trojan Horse. He begged forgiveness from Alex for using his connection to gain access to the onboard computer of Alex's submarine. He meant no harm to Alex or any other Russian. Batu also told Alex of his plans to kill himself and begged him to avenge the loss of his family. Andrei turned the paper over and read a name with a St. Petersburg address. The name was Ruslan Petrova, the forward torpedo man.

CHAPTER 31

PETER JORGESEN WAS SPENT. HAVING LOOKED AT THE clock every hour on the hour, it was obvious he hadn't slept well. Sure, he knew he had slept, but he was positive that if his sleep had totaled three hours, that would be an overstatement.

At forty-two, he was no stranger to adventure and extreme stress, but the enormous danger of this storm gave him a rush of adrenaline like nothing else. This was to be the most monumental moving project in the history of mankind. Destined for the new Gimli gas fields, this natural gas drilling platform would be the largest and tallest structure to be moved across the face of the earth. There had never been anything comparable since glaciers cut the very fjord he had used as its pathway. The pinpoint coordination between the super-tugs that had to be orchestrated tried and strained his every fiber. Seventeen million man-hours of work had been put to task in the construction of the drilling platform's base alone. More steel was in the four supporting shafts than in fifteen Eiffel Towers. Each hollow shaft was eleven hundred feet tall with concrete walls six feet thick. A modern aircraft carrier stood on end could not rise to its soaring height. These four connected shafts supported a platform that would tap into a field so vast that it would supply natural gas to thirty million homes in Europe for the next fifty years.

This modern-day Viking was commanding eight of the most powerful seagoing tugboats built, and towing, in a half-moon formation, the equivalent of the Empire State Building, standing on end, out into the ferocious and unforgiving North Sea. And a major storm was fast approaching!

As he fastened the last button of his fleece-lined coat, he stepped out onto the windswept platform overlooking the fleet of tugs in front of him. The biting wind was cold and bitter—much colder than what had been anticipated. Why was it that he was not surprised? Peter had wanted to wait another month to move out to sea, but the money wonks in charge of the numbers were salivating to get Gimli in place. Time meant money, money to cover the burgeoning cost of overruns in a budget that came from inexperienced pencil pushers in the first place. It didn't matter that the Gimli platform would be producing fantastic profits for fifty or more years. Yet, all that seemed to matter to the green eyeshade types was the money that would begin to stream in the immediate fiscal quarter. "How decisions of this magnitude could be made by bean counters that have never experienced the unpredictable and hellacious fury of the North Sea is unbelievable," he whispered to no one, staring straight ahead. But hell, I guess I'm not the only one in charge, and the insurance rep did sign off on it. The difference is if we go down he loses billions, but I lose the lives of twenty-two of my men.

Belying its fairy tale look, the moon lit an eerie path of light fog ahead of the oceangoing tugs that were beginning a long, rhythmic rolling, buoyed by the swells that were beginning to form. As his hands gripped the railing that surrounded the overhanging command center, Peter couldn't take his eyes off the tugs with their long cables attached to Gimli. He was three hundred feet above the level of the sea and knew that every move of the churning behemoths below was controlled by his computers and crew. He felt their strength and for a few fleeting seconds he felt like a maestro in absolute control of his orchestra. His mind conjured a silly Wagnerian image of The Valkyrie: Magnificent stags champing at their bits and he in his ornate chariot controlling their reigns as he soared through the heavens.

Bjorn came up beside him and broke the spell. "Peter, Harold gave me the latest readout of tomorrow's weather. We have an unexpected trough moving in and it looks like it could be a bad one."

Peter's face flushed in embarrassment as if Bjorn might have been watching the images of his daydream. He took the paper, looked at the data, and whistled while exhaling. "Those tugs are going to have a rough way to go. We should be alright up here, but I feel sorry for those lads down there. It is gonna be one hell of a bumpy ride tomorrow."

"We'd better hope these numbers don't get worse," Bjorn replied. "If a gale forms, the winds could get up to sixty miles an hour with fifty-foot swells."

"Well, let's not get too far ahead of ourselves. When you go to bed,

Bjorn, a long fervent prayer for God's gentle hand would be in order," Peter sighed. As Bjorn opened the door to exit, Peter said, "And Bjorn, please ask the rest of the crew to do likewise. God's providence is powerful and too often overlooked."

CHAPTER 32

AT THE ROYAL NORWEGIAN AIR FORCE'S NORTHERN BASE, the "tracking" data on the Yuri Dolgoruki was continuing to stream in. In the air, the pilot looked again at his fuel gauge, knowing full well that one more look would not change the fact that he was already past time to return to base. He was tired, but like a true hunter, leaving his prey was not in his lexicon. Chafing at the ever-increasing Russian submarine activity in the North Atlantic and in particular, the unflagged activity off Norway's western coast, he would track these bastards 24/7 if his body and his plane would allow it. He knew their activity was nothing more than pure provocation and it rubbed him raw.

Sven Gundersen was good at what he did. In his P3C Orion surveillance aircraft, he had been tracking the Russian sub since it left its base in the White Sea, traveled through the Barents Sea, and passed Norway's North Cape. From the plane's "MAD Boom" tail stinger, magnetic detection of submarines was possible by his nine-man crew. When the sub had passed North Cape, the computer model showed that it should swing a wide arc westward and plot a course southwest between Faeroe Island on the east and Iceland on the west. Instead, it turned south on a course for The Troll gas fields in the North Sea.

After landing, he entered the debriefing room and Sven looked at the man from Norway Armed Forces Military Intelligence Unit (MIU) sitting in a chair waiting for him.

"Looks like you've had another long day," the man said.

"Peasants with nukes," Sven replied. "They've slowed to five knots and are almost in a holding pattern."

"Yeah, but they're holding right off of our coastline. These 'peasants with nukes' could try to make a run for the gas fields and shove their presence right up our ass. I don't get those Ruskies—why the provocation?"

"Don't worry, Anders is in the air and I'll be back up again at zero three hundred. If they're going to make some sort of power statement, Ministry of Defense will hear about it as soon as it happens. ”

"When you are up hunting again tomorrow, if they make even one move toward the fields, I'm going to recommend dispatch to NATO HQ."

CHAPTER 33

OTTER CREEK, ALASKA

THE DRIVE TO THE CITY, ALTHOUGH NOT A HUGE DISTANCE as the crow flies, seemed an eternity for Julie and Jack Weston. Each was preoccupied in their own way. With his two oversized hands clamped on the steering wheel, Jack stared straight forward as if on autopilot. Mile markers and trees passed as if they were a blur. At this moment in time, nothing else mattered to him. He was trying to figure out a plan to save his daughter. He feared for one thing and one thing only … his daughter's life.

Jack Weston had been a man's man, but the ghoulish scene in the reporter's house was something he was neither prepared for nor was up to. He had experienced combat and death in Vietnam and had held his share of wounded comrades with fire coming in from all sides. But that was different. That was war and had purpose. No, the sick, twisted scene that he had witnessed was mindless and diabolical. No one could justify it—for God's sake. The victim was a kid. But no one will do that to my daughter, he promised himself. No matter what came their way, he would protect her, come hell or high water.

Julie's head was turned toward the side window. Trees and an occasional house passed, but she too stared into nothingness. Her thoughts were split between the father she loved and the obligation she felt to the man that had saved her life. She had to find a way to keep her father out of harm's way, yet she couldn't reach the wilderness enigma without him. A plan was needed, but because of the carnage at the reporter's house, getting it to coagulate in her mind was the hardest part. How will she and her father find this Trojan Horse … how will they even know what direction to begin searching?

The fog in her mind lifted and it all became clear. They would rent a plane in Otter Creek and retrace her steps to the crash. They would begin concentric circles, expanding the radius till they spotted his cabin. When they returned to Otter Creek, they would rent a snowmobile and set the coordinates to his cabin. She was sure that her wound would never allow her to do this on her own. That is where her father would have to help. But would he be willing to follow her lead? Was it her place to even ask … to put him in harm's way where his life could be at risk?

Jack's vehicle hit a small pothole in the road and the jolt pulled both out of their trances. As Jack looked at Julie and her at him, they both started to speak at the same time, but stopped as they interrupted each other. Jack started again first. "Julie, maybe we could rent a plane in Otter Creek," he said.

"Dad … that was what I was going to say."

"You know, maybe if we retraced your flight and did some recon in circles, I betcha we could zero in on his hideout."

CHAPTER 34

GREGOR POLNICH WAS PLEASED THAT HE HAD REACHED Jack Weston's house in the short amount of time that had passed. With a self-confidence born of skill and arrogance, the Russian assassin pulled his vehicle right up under the front portico. Having to deal with a CIA analyst and an older civilian caused him no anxiety whatsoever. He exited his vehicle in as calm a manner as possible and walked right up to the front door and rang the bell, all the while his head darting back and forth to look through the sidelights. No one answered. He pulled out his Glock and decided to case the house through the windows. When it became apparent that there was no one inside, the Russian returned to the front door and with his silenced Glock pointed upward, he raised his left foot and with one mighty thrust he kicked the front door in. Creeping in bowlegged, his pistol between both hands, he scanned every inch of the one-story house. Disappointed at finding no clues, he backed his way out and stood under the open porte-cochere. What he didn't see were the eyes that watched him.

***

Stringer lay prone on the wet snow using a low-hanging branch to give him the cover he needed. His high-powered field glasses were keyed in on the Russian thug as he circled the perimeter of Jack Weston's house. Stringer's focus never left the front door, and when the Russian reappeared, he wished he had brought his suppressed M-4 rifle and scope. Killing from a distance or some other method where he could remain detached and out of the direct fray was his preferred MO. He could've moved in closer and taken him out with his Sig, but he had too much respect for Polnich's ability to risk the fight. But with his .223 sniper rifle, one shot and half of the Russian's head and half of his own problems would be gone. But hell, the Ruskie was doing all the heavy lifting in trying to find the Westons' whereabouts, and that suited him fine.

***

Driving off, Gregor Polnich's thoughts returned to McKenzie. The newspaper article confirmed what the kid reporter said while the life was being choked out of him—that the hermit dropped the wounded pilot off outside of Otter Creek. Returning there would be his next destination.

CHAPTER 35

DEVON MCKENZIE WAS RETURNING FROM ANOTHER OF HIS successful hunting trips. His rear sled was towing one of the largest elk he had bagged since first coming to the state. After analyzing the sprawling rack of antlers, he concluded that this one wasn't some old graybeard, just one hell of a huge young buck. He felt good because the meat would be plentiful and tender. When your menu was this limited, that which you ate day after day needed to at least be something you didn't have to gnarl on.

The stag was so heavy that the sled bogged down in a soft snow bank, causing his snowmobile to sputter and drag. Devon turned his head around, looked back, and saw that the elk had shifted on the sled and its antlers were biting into the hard pan snow below. He made the decision to turn the vehicle off and reposition the elk before he would have to reload it all over again. After the pre-dawn hunt, he was too tired to face lifting the behemoth once more. As he got off the snowmobile, Devon was at least pleased that he had the heavy pines that surrounded him to break the cold, biting wind. He was surprised when he heard the distant sound of an approaching small aircraft.

Devon knew trouble was approaching. The sound of a small plane shouldn't be there, not in this neck of the woods. Someone was looking for him, and that spelled trouble. He began gathering snow in his arms and covered the sled and snowmobile. He broke off several low hanging pine boughs and leaned them upside down against the nearest conifer. With little time to spare, he laid snow against them to make them look like branches that had wilted under the weight of the snow. Seconds later he was inside the boughs with his binoculars and rifle scope.

When the plane passed within a hundred and fifty yards or so of his location, he was able to zero in on the cockpit and saw that it was the downed pilot he had saved and another person in the copilot seat.

Devon's heart rate eased at the site of the woman, but his instincts told him that she was searching for his cabin. He was sure they would find his cabin and he was also sure they would be back to make contact. What mattered more was the extension of that thought … that someone would be following *them*. And that someone had designs to kill them all.

***

As the two-seat Cessna's wheels landed on the runway, Jack Weston looked at his daughter and said, "Okay, baby girl, finding his cabin was the easy part, as will be getting a snowmobile. The hard part will be snowmobiling back out to his cabin. That is going to tax your wound. Maybe you should stay at the motel and let me go out alone and find your Daniel Boone, or whoever the hell he is."

"Dad, I love you," she said, "but, he's a man in hiding. He has no way of recognizing you and I have a strong hunch that anyone that comes within a half mile of that cabin may wish they had never been born. But he might let *me* in."

"And what makes you so sure of that?" Jack questioned, not at all comfortable with her plan.

"My gut, Dad; after all, you're the one who taught me to rely on it. Now, how about we go get that snowmobile and have at it? We've still got five hours of daylight and if everything goes alright, the trip should take four."

"I don't have a good feeling about this, Julie. Look, I've got enough money; we could get out of Alaska for a few years and you could tell that CIA of yours to kiss off."

Julie's shoulders sagged and her head dropped in resignation of the stark reality of her situation. "Dad, you don't know The Agency; this won't go away if something is dirty, and I'm not going to spend the rest of my life looking over my shoulder or not sleeping at night." She took a deep breath and forced a smile saying, "C'mon, daylight's burning."

***

Gregor Polnich motioned the bartender to bring him another shot of vodka. As a habit, he would never string four shots of vodka together in a short time frame while he was "on duty." But this was different; he had no idea how far or how long the trip would be to where Trojan Horse was hiding out. The one thing he did know was that it would be long and cold and an extra couple of shots would help.

He tilted his head backward and threw down the last shot. As the shot glass clunked on the bar top, he raised the empty glass and whispered, "Here's to you, scar-face. I hope you die thinking of your dead wife, knowing all too well that it was I who caused you all this misery and that it was I who won the match."

With that, he threw thirty bucks on the counter and took in a quick, deep sniff to clear his nostrils. Feeling like he could handle a long trek in the frigid outlands, he turned and proceeded out the door, heading left to reach the local outfitter and rental store. Maybe it was the vodka, maybe he was in a hurry, but what he missed was the man standing in front of the storefront window across the street. The man's back was to him, but he wasn't looking into the store. His interest was in the reflection of Polnich coming out of the bar. Stringer had guessed right when he bet that Otter Creek would be Polnich's next stop.

CHAPTER 36

TOM GRAYSON SAT AT HIS DESK IN THE LATE HOURS OF another long work day. He looked up at the clock and saw the hands shy of ten o'clock. Stringer had checked in and informed him that Julie Weston and her father had left with their SUV pulling a snowmobile on a trailer. They must have been heading out to find McKenzie's cabin. He stated that he would rent a snowmobile and take off after them. What he didn't tell Grayson was that he would be third in line after the Russian assassin, Polnich.

Grayson drank the last of his single barrel bourbon and decided to have one more before going home. He had already called Carey and apprised him of Stringer trailing Weston. He told Carey that the tension of finding McKenzie and having him killed all over again was putting him on the verge of a nervous breakdown. He didn't want to add to Carey's own load, but he was at the point of breaking.

As his index finger stirred the cubes in his glass, he reminisced to that day when his agent in Chechnya informed him that he had come up with the first duffel bag-sized WMD. Grayson was as giddy as a school girl when he called Carey and told him the good news. Carey, however, told Grayson to keep a lid on the news until they had the time to talk in private. Grayson realized the real value of what the highest bidder would pay. And that highest bidder was al-Qaeda with its endless supply of Saudi petro dollars. This would be their ticket to ride and they also believed that they could score so high that they could shut down their traitorous deeds and life could go back to normal, except that they would never want for anything again. And they had it all pulled off until McKenzie reared his ugly head from the grave.

"Damn it!" He blurted out, throwing his empty glass against the wall. "I don't need this garbage."

As he leaned back in his leather chair, he could have sworn he heard someone in Mrs. Frank's office. His body froze. Is someone listening? Are they watching?

CHAPTER 37

WILDERNESS OF ALASKA

DEVON REACHED HIS CABIN, ELK STILL IN TOW, AND AS-sessed that he had a good five hours to get ready for his "unexpected" company. His first concern was to get Oscar out for a break. He opened the cabin door—there lay the big lug, sprawled on the small rug, one eye open, giving the appearance of, "oh, you again." To Oscar, his master appeared frustrated, but to Devon, this mutt was his only joy in life. "In a world filled with change, you are my constant, Oscar," he said with a dry smile. "Get up and get outside, I don't have a lot of time!"

Five hours may have seemed like a long time, but it wasn't. Devon knew what was coming, but his last four years as a hermit told him to at least get the elk stripped, gutted, and buried in the frozen earth. He had worked too hard to serve up a gourmet meal for a grizzly, or worse, a pack of wolves. He feared and respected grizzlies, but they still came one at a time and were content to leave if they found nothing. Wolves were different. There were too many of them to contend with and they were inherently vicious.

When he was through with the elk, he buried the spoils and innards and threw in the bloodied snow as well. His thoughts turned to a perim-eter warning system. He paced out a hundred yards around his cabin, stringing taught, low-gauge bailing wire level with the top of the snow from tree to tree. To each section of wire was attached a rusted cowbell or a pair of tin cans with a handful of pebbles inside. Devon's hope was that an intruder would trip the wire and the noise would give him at least a chance to grab his weapons and ready himself.

Never one to believe in fortified shelters as the best defense, Devon replicated the same blind that he used four hours earlier when he first heard the plane approaching. He decided that a point halfway between the perimeter and the cabin would be most effective. Once Julie and her escort arrived, they would attempt to go inside, but his place would be in the confines of the small blind he had set up.

With dusk approaching, Devon felt comfortable that all that could be done outside was done. He took one last trip around the perimeter wire and used a bough off a pine tree to brush away his tracks on either side of the wire. Whistling to Oscar, he summoned the gangly mutt and went inside the cabin to wait. Pulling off his parka, he looked at his watch and figured he still had enough time to reheat a small leftover and have one quick swig of scotch to steady his nerves—but no more. Company was coming.

CHAPTER 38

YURI DOLGORUKI

SITTING IN THEIR MISSILE CONTROL WORKSTATION, FEODOR Strivnych looked over at Alex out of the corner of his eye. Outside he had his game face on, giving his subordinate the appearance of situation normal. Inside, the bile in his gut was churning. It was all he could do to restrain himself from confronting Alex straight on. Feodor was a straight up seaman with an old-fashioned commitment to his boat and every crewman on board.

It had been three days since his captain had rifled Alex's quarters. To avoid tipping his hand, Captain Illanov had waited a day before setting up a meeting with Feodor in the captain's quarters. Feodor told him what he had found and how he had spent a sleepless twenty-four hours racking his brain trying to figure out what Alex and the torpedo man were up to and what their ultimate goal could be. All he had come up with was one dead end after another. The captain wanted to discuss it with his exec, Anton, but there was something stiff and rigid about the man that the captain couldn't put his finger on. He considered himself a keen judge of people, and in spite of Anton Kashnikov doing everything by the book, he found something strange and hollow in the man. Illanov didn't like him. He recalled the first day that they set sail from Severodvinsk and how he told the story of his first army watch that ran backwards. Anton never laughed with him, nor did his face crack a smile. Worse, all that was returned was a cold, haunting stare.

Rank was one thing that Captain Andrei Illanov could have cared less about. People, the honest exchange of ideas, and complete loyalty to Mother Russia were what mattered most. Illanov valued Feodor's thoughts and gave him the respect that he deserved as a veteran seaman and a human being. After admitting that he had come up with nothing, he let Feodor have the floor.

"I know I'm a seaman from the missile compartment, Sir, but I don't think Alex is at the center of this. No Sir, it's all about that darkie, the Chechen."

"Which torpedo man is it again? I checked and we don't have any Chechens on board," Illanov replied.

"His name is Ruslan Petrova, but that means nothing. I think that bastard's some kind of a terrorist. He's a Muslim fanatic as sure as I'm standing here. Captain, we've got sleeper cells all over our country—you know we do. What his end game is, I don't know. But you can believe that those Bulava missiles are at the heart of it. Maybe even our payload of cruise missiles."

"That's it," said Illanov, his brow lowering into a concerned frown. "My God, he's going to destroy the new gas platform in the Gimli fields! Maybe even the platforms in The Troll fields! I can't believe this! Why would they do such a thing? Are they trying to provoke a war?"

Feodor didn't need time to peruse all the options. He answered, "Because he's a terrorist, that's why. He doesn't need any other reason. It's all there in that Koran that he carries."

"But he's passed all the security checks and his father is a respected colonel in the army," Illanov said.

"I'm not trying to be disrespectful Captain, but you and I both know this is not the old navy that we were brought up in."

Illanov sat looking with a hollow stare, making Feodor feel perhaps that he had spoken too freely.

"Sir … if I spoke out of turn or offended you with my language, I'm sorry."

Illanov's stare broke, and it was he who looked embarrassed. "No, Feodor, I'm the one who should apologize for not having the basic sense that you did in figuring this thing out. I think you're right on target, but we've got to keep a lid on this. We arrive at the fields in two days and we've got to find out how deep this cancer is in our crew."

"Have you told your exec about this, Sir?"

"No, and I'm not sure that I will."

"You think he might be involved, Captain?"

"Let me ask you this, Feodor, how does a country with an army that was once larger than any army in history end up trying to pull itself off the scrapheap? How do our armaments end up on every third world black market in the world? You don't need to answer because I'm going to tell you. It's all about money. Money is an insidious octopus, Feodor. It has its tentacles into every aspect of our lives. It has corrupted our politicians beyond anything I would have believed. Rumors are circulating that many of our admirals may be going the way of our politicians. I don't know about my EO, but we must speak of this to no one except ourselves for the moment."

CHAPTER 39

JULIE TAPPED HER FATHER ON THE TOP OF HIS SHOULDER. He turned his head to notice that she wanted him to bring the snowmobile to a stop. Pulling her mitten off, she slipped her hand into her parka and pulled out the portable GPS that she had grabbed from her dad's house. With the wind driving the falling snow at about forty-five degrees, it was all she could do to get a good reading. Tapping Jack's shoulder one more time, she pointed to a large stand of trees off to the left at about eleven o'clock. "Over there, Dad! See that long stand of trees? There should be a creek to the left of it that we'll have to cross and his cabin should be on the other side of that next rise."

Jack never said a word; he gave her thumbs up and cranked up the throttle. As they crested the far hill, Jack brought the snowmobile to another halt. Devon's cabin lay at the bottom of the valley, nestled in a stand of pines. Jack flipped up the guard of his helmet and motioned for Julie to do the same. Their eyes met and a long silent pause ensued. Jack's eyes said to turn back. Julie was the first to break the moment. "Well, let's go, Dad, but go slow. I want to make sure that he sees us early on. When we get about two hundred feet out, turn the machine off and we'll go on foot the rest of the way. And let's keep our arms and hands in view, holding nothing."

"Wouldn't you say that's a little bit excessive?" Jack asked.

"This is his world, Dad, not ours."

***

Devon heard the whining motor long before it crossed the creek—sounds carried far in the dead quiet of the wilderness. He was up, watching from his blind when he first heard the snowmobile shut down. As Julie and her dad approached with arms stretched out, Devon drew a bead on them as they neared his hidden trip wire. He recognized who they were and when they came about eight feet away from the wire, he jumped out of his blind and hollered, "Stop right there. Not one step more."

Julie had already told her father that she would handle the initial talking. "Please," she said. "I'm the woman you rescued from the plane, and this is my father. We want to talk, that's all."

Never leaving the chest of Jack, Devon's gun sight said it all, but the desperation in his gravelly voice belied his actions. "I know who you are and you're still not welcome here. You've put me in danger by compromising my location, and in the process, you've put yourselves in danger. There are people who need me dead and now that they know about you, they will need to eliminate the both of you as well. No trails. No loose ends. Is there any part of what I said that you don't understand?"

"Please, I know who you are. Your code name was 'Trojan Horse.'" Julie ventured one step forward.

Devon's rifle switched over to Julie. "I said don't move another step!" He growled.

"Tim Daniels," she blurted out, "he was my fiancé and he was your best friend. He was killed trying to help you. I know it. Please!"

Devon's aim returned to Jack's chest, paused, and dropped toward the ground. "One at a time, take normal steps forward for eight feet, there's a buried trip wire. Don't stop, I'll tell you when to step over it. Be damn careful. Keep walking with the same gait till you get to the cabin."

***

Polnich had followed the trail Weston's snowmobile had left in the snow. He was a natural at tracking and this was like a walk in the park. But he had the disadvantage of not knowing how far McKenzie's cabin was out in the wild. He would have to keep watching for signs that the Westons had stopped. He had to make sure that he would stop well short of where the cabin was, for sound was his Achilles heel. He had no way of knowing how far the sound would travel as he had no idea of the foliage that lay in front of him. What he did know was that he would have to be cautious and hike a long distance. The distance was not a concern—the rapidly dimming daylight was. He didn't have the time to lay out his usual routine for a hit; reconnoiter, set up a blind, and wait for the perfect shot. He had night vision goggles in his backpack, but he still had no idea of how far he had to travel or how far he would have to go on foot.

***

Stringer arrived at where the two vehicles were pulled off of the snow-laden gravel road. Light was still fair, but he estimated he was at least an hour behind Polnich and that left him at an extreme disadvantage. Being third in line was not a strange feeling to the agent. It was, after all, how he got the name "Stringer." It stood for second string. Because he never left the bench, even once, in high school, he was nicknamed "Second-Stringer" Schultz. The name stuck and like all long names, it was shortened to "Stringer." Born Herman Schultz, the nickname "Stringer" became a moniker that he didn't have a problem owning.

He guessed that McKenzie had to be about three to four hours out. This was a pure guess, but he had asked the outfitter that rented the machine if he knew anything about the hermit that brought the pilot in. The man said that he had pulled the pilot in on a sled hitched to his vehicle and that he had left no room for additional gas cans. Max range, eight hours tops, round trip. He looked up at the sky before glancing at his watch. He figured he had two hours of quality light. That meant the last two hours would be in night vision goggles. Hard to make time with snow falling and you're traveling thirty miles an hour with the NOD goggles on.

CHAPTER 40

YURI DOLGORUKI

CAPTAIN ILLANOV DECIDED TO GIVE FEODOR PERMISSION to get Alex alone and question him, even if it meant roughing him up. Time was getting spare and Illanov still didn't know their ultimate mission or how high up the players went. Illanov agreed with Feodor that the new Gimli platform and The Troll fields were the logical targets, but he had a nagging feeling that there could be something even more sinister at work. He wanted to trust his exec—it would make his life so much easier to have Anton working the rest of the commissioned officers for intel. But that was a risk he was not yet prepared to take. For now, he would have to rely on his missile guidance man.

***

After Alex came in with a fresh cup of coffee, Feodor rose from his chair and said, "The smell of that brew has changed my mind, I think I'll go get some for myself."

"I did offer," said Alex.

"I know, but I've changed my mind." He rubbed his eyes for emphasis and continued, "Besides, my eyes are tired today and I could use a short break."

Feodor exited the station compartment and went down the passage and through the bulkhead. As he stepped through the opening, he shifted his body to the left and concealed himself as best he could. Looking back down the hall, he wanted to be sure that no one else had entered his station to confer with Alex. He waited a few minutes, peeking his head around the opening every few seconds—nothing. Feodor moved on to get his coffee. As he approached the next bulkhead, he thought he heard the shuffling of feet. He turned around and looked, again nothing. He wondered if his nerves were starting to get the best of him.

The truth was that Feodor had moved from feelings of brotherly love toward Alex to feelings of anger and revulsion. Feodor could forgive most faults in people, but someone he perceived as betraying him and worse, his country, crossed the line. As he returned down the passage, he cemented his plan of attack. Stopping and bending over, his right hand unsnapped the knife sheath that he wore on his shin. Feodor entered the station, placed the coffee on his desktop and said to Alex, "I trust that the computers didn't go into overload while I was out."

Before Alex could even open his mouth to respond, Feodor had the knife out of its sheath and under Alex's throat. His left hand grabbed the seaman's hair and pulled his head backward.

"Move one millimeter and I swear, you're a dead man. You're nothing but a miserable barnacle. I'd love to send you to the devil," growled Feodor.

"Feodor, please," he said. "What have I done?"

"You know damn well. And you're going tell me everything. What's the mission?" He hissed through his gritted teeth.

"What … what mission? I don't know of what mission you talk," squeaked Alex.

"Who else is in on it with you?" Feodor pressed harder with the blade, forcing a trickle of blood to begin flowing. "I mean to get it out of you, Alex. The captain went through your locker. He found the letters from your brother Batu. Don't even think of lying to me. Tell me what the mission is about—and everyone who's in on it!"

"The letters—they were from four years ago, Feodor. My brother and I are Georgians. Our blood runs deep through our veins. Batu's family was murdered. He begged me to smuggle an American agent in. He wanted to mess up the firing program of the Bark missiles. He was my brother, Feodor. His whole family had been murdered by the FSB … I couldn't deny him."

"That's a lie!" Hissed Feodor.

"No, I swear on Batu's grave. The American had a code name—'Trojan Horse.' He told me it would delay the process of testing the missiles—nothing permanent. I did this to avenge the killing of my brother and his family. I know the FSB killed them, Feodor. You do too," he wept. "You are Ukrainian, Feodor. You know what these Russians did to your people. They starved millions—they were *your* people, Feodor."

"This is crap, Alex, I don't believe you."

"I'm telling you the truth. Let me finish, I beg you," cried Alex. "Then this man came, I don't know who he was. He was Russian. I think part of the Mafia. But he told me that I had to let the American do it again on the Bulavas. I said no, but the man told me his people would expose what I had done. I'm so sorry," he wept. "But I had no choice. I couldn't risk that my family would be killed. Trojan Horse said that after the first eleven missiles misfired, the program would disappear. The rest would work. And … and they do! I swear to you, on my brother's dead family. That was all I did—nothing more." Alex was sniveling. "Please believe me Feodor. Please don't kill me!"

Time was suspended, and the silence in the small compartment was deafening. Feodor let go of Alex who slumped to the floor, ending up on his knees, hunched over and sobbing. Feodor, the hardened salt, was moved to pity and had to look away. The stories his grandmother told of the starvation by Stalin flashed in and out. His people *were* brutalized, and for no other reason than they resisted the Bolsheviks. Men, women … children …

He whispered, "Who else on the boat is involved?"

A puzzled look came over Alex's face. "Involved in what? There is nothing but what I have told you, just me, the altered program … and my own deep shame."

Feodor paused and remembered the Chechen. "What about that torpedo man who was in here a few days ago? What did he want, a lousy game of chess?"

"Not much. He said there was something the matter with the air ventilation in his area. He wanted to know if I could show him the schematics of the system so he could work on it himself. I told him no. I said go to the engineer and get his help. That is ship protocol."

Feodor's head turned in the direction of the door—shuffling of feet— he swore he heard the sound again. He jumped up and raced to the door, looking out into the hall. Again, there was no one to be seen. He walked over and sat back down across from the sniveling Alex. "Did you talk to anyone else about this incident? What about the exec? Did you go to him?"

Alex wiped his nose and eyes with his sleeve. "Yes, the next day I passed the exec near the weight room and I told him what the torpedo man had said to me. That there was a problem in his area with the ventilation system."

"What did he say?"

"Nothing, but … but he acted like he was pissed off with me. I thought it was because I bothered him with trivial matter."

Feodor set his hand down on the shoulder of Alex and gave it a quick squeeze. "You've been a good friend, Alex. Go get your neck bandaged. I'll cover till you get back. We'll deal with the fallout later. And don't speak of this to anyone." His eyes rose to meet his assistant's. "Now leave me!"

When Alex left, the stories of the human misery that Stalin had wrought on the Ukrainian people revisited him. For the first time in his adult life, Feodor Strivnych, the Ukrainian by birth, wept.

CHAPTER 41

AS JULIE CLIMBED THE SNOW-LADEN STEPS AND ENTERED Devon's cabin, she stopped, turned her head, and looked back over her father's shoulder to see Devon resetting his trip wire and adding more camouflage. She couldn't put her finger on it, but in spite of her father's apprehensions, she felt a connection, a gut instinct that gave her a feeling of safety and comfort.

Devon made short work of straightening up his defense, stood back up, and looked toward his cabin. His eyes, though at a distance, locked onto Julie's. A sense of need to protect again streamed through him, as a new omen of fear and imminent danger overtook him. He stepped into and followed Jack's footprints back to the cabin.

Entering the cabin door, Devon was startled by the sudden lack of room with three people and a dog occupying his space. As Devon pulled off his heavy parka, Jack stood up, squared his body, and assumed a confrontational position. "Look, I don't know you and I don't give a rat's ass about your past, but I'm here to protect my daughter and nothing else matters to me. We don't want any trouble, but she's got some things to say. Am I clear?"

Devon stared at Jack for what seemed a long minute and said, "Fair enough, but remember, I didn't invite you or your daughter here and this is still my place, not yours. All I did was pull her out of a burning plane and save her life. So before you start in on me, pal, you might want to take that into account and cut me a little slack. And if not, get out!"

Time froze as the two stared each other down like two stags ready to lock horns. It was Julie that broke the impasse. "Dad, please, he's right—and so are you. Well, in a way." She pulled off her glove and put out her hand for Devon to accept a handshake. "Listen, I forced my dad to come out here with me so I could offer you my heartfelt thanks."

Their eyes met again and the frost melted. Devon eased off and looked around the cabin. With his hand he gestured for them to find a place to sit. He looked over at Jack and asked, "And you are …?"

Jack was grateful for Julie's gesture to ease the tension, knowing he was wrong. "I'm Jack Weston and this is my daughter Julie. We do come in peace and I'm sorry that—"

"You want a shot of scotch?" Devon asked as he reached out with his bottle of single malt clutched at the neck.

Jack smiled, took the bottle, and turned it around to see the label and said, "Ah … Lagavulin, an Isla sweetheart. You know, you do seem to know how to break the ice. It's mighty hard to turn down a 'Laggie.'"

He passed the bottle back to McKenzie who offered it to Julie in turn. She sniffed the bottle's opening, wrinkled her nose and said, "That smells like urine!" She took a swig, grimaced, and shook her head hard to make it go away. "You two need serious help. How 'bout we get down to the second reason we came out here?"

Jack reached out for Devon to give him another swig.

When Jack finished, Devon took the bottle back, pounded the cork down, and tossed the bottle onto the bed, well out of Jack's reach. He looked over and with the smallest hint of a smile, let her know that everything was cool and it was her turn to tell her story.

Julie took the cue from Devon. "I'm not sure where to begin, but maybe your friend, and my love, Tim, is where it all starts. Tim asked me to check on you and your wife. He was running into a total stone wall at the CIA. He had more than enough security clearance to be able to go deep, and I mean very deep. But he couldn't get from A to Z, let alone B. Your file must have been wiped clean because of what you knew, but I never knew what that was. Tim would not tell me. All he said was that it was dirty and his silence was to protect me." She paused for emphasis and looked into his eyes. "You need to know that he died trying to help you. And when he did, I guess I lost interest when it was reported that you and your wife were killed." Julie's eyes began to tear up and Jack put his arm around her for comfort. "I'm so sorry. You see, I called Mr. Grayson to tell him that you were still alive. But his reaction to my call was so odd that I sensed something was wrong, that he meant you harm. So that's why we're here: To warn you, to try to fix the mess that I've made. I think I owe you at least that."

Devon's eyes never left Julie's. He knew what she said was true, and that truth still cut like a dagger. He said, "Grayson and Carey were redirecting Russian WMDs for cash. I know because I found incriminating evidence. I was the dealer for the CIA who was procuring the weapons. I was in charge of redirecting or altering the materiel. I received the cash payments and it was part of my job to direct the money into CIA accounts in Switzerland. The policy may have been convoluted, but it *was* official CIA policy and the Administration had sanctioned it. I found that instead of ending up in the CIA accounts, much of the money was going to Grayson and Carey's little 'honey hole' in Zurich, not to The Agency. We're talking about at least several million dollars—that's why they needed me out of the way—and still do. I'm the only one with concrete evidence."

"I'm so sorry for what I've done," Julie reiterated. "That phone call, well, my training kicked in."

"It's too late to matter. I'll have to go deeper and darker, maybe even to some other country," Devon said.

"No," said Julie, "you don't understand. It may be too late. Grayson told me he was sending someone here—an agent. This agent would be the one to deal with you. I told him that Dad and I had found the reporter dead and he—"

"What did you say?" Devon's voice rose alarmed.

"The reporter, Josh Abrams, we found him in a pool of blood with his throat cut on the floor of his house. Someone also slit his dog's throat."

Devon shot up from his chair. "What did Grayson say when you told him that?"

"He said that you were the one who killed him—to protect yourself. I knew this was a lie. I knew you couldn't do that. That's why he said he was sending someone here to deal with you."

Devon began to pace as Julie told him of the agent. He pounded one fist onto the cabin wall and turned to face her again. "Did he tell you the name of the agent he was sending?"

"I'm not a hundred percent sure, but I think it was something like String. Yeah, that's it—Stringer."

Devon frowned, pursed his lips, and said, "I don't know how much time we have, but we need to get out of here—and get out now."

As Devon finished his sentence, the low rustling sound of pebbles in a can could be heard. He raced to the table and blew out the hurricane lamp. "I knew it!" He snapped in whispered anger. "I should have gone out to the blind. Jack! I'm going to slide my M40 over to you on the floor. Listen for where it stops. Pick it up and release the safety. It's already chambered."

"Got it!"

"Jack, listen up. I'm going out that door. When I do, lay down a sweeping spray of fire—just over my head. Julie, crawl under the bed. There's going to be heavy fire coming in. Do it now!"

Devon slipped his night goggles on. From his crouched position, he raised his arm and moved his hand along till it came to a halt on the latch of the door.

"Jack, slide over here till you feel my backside. Get on your knees. When I say 'Do it,' lay it on. Remember, above me! Get ready."

Devon pulled the latch down. He threw the door wide open. He hollered, "Do it!" He did a summersault out into the snow. Right on cue, Jack laid a sweeping barrage about ninety degrees across. He shut the door and slid to a crouch under the window with the M40 trained on the door. "Stay down, Julie, no matter what. I love you, baby girl."

Crawling on his belly, Devon stayed under Jack's fire-cover. He made it to the wood pile near the right front of the cabin. He got up on his knees. With his Glock following the sweep of his night vision goggles, Devon traced the area between the span of trees—nothing. He saw what he thought was the area where the intruder had disturbed the cans. He saw tracks leading to the left side of the cabin. He's trying to get around the back by the window, he thought.

Devon lay back down in the snow and stuffed his Glock into his parka pocket. He began crawling military style to the side behind him. His hope was to beat the assassin to the rear and take him out when he turned the corner. He reached the corner of the rear and poked his head around to the back. His breathing was hard, slow, and deep. He rose up on one knee and looked again. He realized he had misjudged. His worst fears came true. He heard a heavy burst of fire from another M40 on the front door of the cabin. The noise came from the outside!

Caution was no longer in charge. Devon raced to the front corner. He saw the killer kick in the door and enter. "No!" He screamed in panic. He bolted for the door. Through the opening he saw Jack laying in a crumpled mass on the floor. He saw the assassin drawing a bead on the bed. Devon fired two shots. One went through the intruder's neck. The other hit the left side of the man's head, blowing pieces of bloody brain matter on the cabin wall. The intruder's large body came to a freeze, wavered, and fell over onto Jack's body.

"Julie! Are you all right? Julie …?"

Julie came crawling in slow motion from under the bed. Devon reached for her in the dark and found her shaking body. He put his arms around her and said, "It's over. It's all over."

"…Dad? Where's Dad?" She cried out.

Devon squeezed her tighter, in what became a bear hug. He placed his lips against her ear and whispered, "He didn't make it."

Julie began sobbing. Devon eased his grip and let her go. He fumbled to find the matches. As he lit the hurricane lamp, the gruesome sight of the assassin lying on Jack's lifeless body was too much for her. Blood drained from her head and she slumped to the floor. Devon was able to reach out and grab her elbow, softening her fall. Devon looked down to see if she was okay. He decided to let her lay and instead pulled the killer off Jack's body. As the bloodied body of the assassin rolled over, Devon was stunned. It had happened again. From out of his past, Gregor Polnich had returned to corrupt his life once more. He reached down to Jack and ripped his blood-soaked shirt open. Jack had been hit four times in the chest when the door was shot in.

Devon bent over, picked Julie's limp body up, and placed her on the bed. He picked up an extra blanket and covered Jack's bloodied body and face. He went to the sink, wet a towel, and began applying it to Julie's face. In a confined space that had been filled with violence and death, it was a needed moment of calm and tenderness. For the time being, there was a lull in the carnage.

CHAPTER 42

FEODOR SHIFTED IN HIS CHAIR AS HE SAT ACROSS FROM Illanov in his quarters. It was nothing the Captain said, it was all about Feodor having misgivings over his conduct with Alex. Illanov had given him permission to rough up Alex if necessary, but Feodor wasn't sure that the knife under Alex's neck may have crossed the line for the Captain. The seaman's eyes were fixed on the floor.

As Feodor's story started to unfold, the captain interrupted him, asking his computer man if there was something wrong that he had done to put him in this unusual straight. Feodor said no, and continued on with his story. When he got to the part of the knife at Alex's throat, he looked up and was surprised that Captain Illanov had shown absolutely no emotion at all. He stared straight ahead as if what he had done was what he had expected to happen.

When he finished, Illanov asked, "Down deep, do you truly believe him?"

"I have to say yes, Captain. I mean the man believed that I was going to slit his throat with that knife—and I never let on that I wouldn't. He genuinely didn't seem to know about any subversive use of the missiles."

"Tell me again about his encounter with the exec," he said.

"That's the strange part. You see, Alex said that when he went to the exec to tell him about the torpedo man's ventilation problem, the exec got real upset. Alex thought it was because the exec didn't want to be troubled with trivial engineering problems."

"What were the exec's words to him in response?"

Feodor's eyes looked back down at the floor in shame. "Don't know, I never asked him. You know, Captain, when I was interrogating him … the knife was sort of getting in the way. Maybe if you talked to him you could get more out of him than I did. You know, you being the captain and all."

"I doubt that my position would carry the same respect as a knife at your throat. You did fine, Feodor. Where is Alex?"

"He's on duty in the station, Sir."

Illanov stood up and said, "Lead the way."

As Feodor entered the station, he came to a sharp stop. He was stunned. The Captain bumped into him, causing Feodor to lurch and take an off-balance step forward. For one of the few times in his life, Feodor didn't know how to react and froze.

Illanov took charge. He moved to Alex's slumped body and placed two fingers on Alex's neck. Looking over to Feodor, he shook his head to indicate the seaman was dead. Alex's head lay on its side to the left of the keyboard. There were no external signs of a struggle, let alone an attack. Illanov pulled Alex's collar back and exposed all three sides. There was no sign of trauma; no blood, no bruising, not even any papers askew on his desk. "Go and get the ship's doctor," he said to Feodor. "Tell him there's no need to bring anything with him. Tell him I want to see him—now!"

"Aye, Captain."

Feodor returned within minutes to the computer station, ship's doctor in tow. Captain Illanov had been careful in going through the pockets of Alex. He didn't want the doctor to know that he had been searching for information. The captain wanted everything to appear above board and beyond reproach. He also didn't know whether he could trust that the doctor was not involved. He had told Feodor to trust no one, and that order was meant for him as well.

As the ship's medical officer entered the compartment, he paused and looked at the captain. Illanov gave a slight nod of his head, acknowledging the doctor's astonishment. The doctor moved to the body slumped over the computer keyboard. After checking Alex's neck for a pulse, he put the ends of his stethoscope in his ears, reached under, and slipped the other end over the man's heart for confirmation. He stuck his finger in Alex's mouth and throat and felt around.

Standing back up, he redirected his gaze to Illanov. "Captain, as you already know, the seaman is dead. Without having performed even a crude autopsy, I'd guess he died of asphyxiation."

"And why would you say that, Doctor?"

"The position of the tongue and the tightness of the throat are the evidence. Again, it would take a complete autopsy to determine the final cause of death, but if he had had a heart attack, I don't think his body would be in this position. There is no gun and there are no pills, so I don't think suicide should be considered."

"What is next, Doctor?"

The medical officer looked at Feodor and said, "This seaman will get another crewman and carry the body to sick bay. I'll do my autopsy there."

"Get back to me as quick as you can, Doctor, but I want this labeled a heart attack until your report lands on my desk. Is that understood?"

"Yes, Captain," the medical officer said. "Looks like a heart attack to me."

***

Andrei Illanov sat in his chair in the conning tower, to his left stood his executive officer. Since hearing of the pass-by encounter with Alex, Illanov was convinced the man was in on whatever the renegade mission was. He was determined to keep a close eye on him. I'm going to know when he takes a dump and what comes out, he thought.

The exec looked at his watch and said, "With your permission, Sir, my watch is over. I think I will go and get a little sleep."

"That's a negative, Mr. Kashnikov. I'm feeling a migraine coming on and I would appreciate it if you would extend your watch for another hour. It is I who needs the shut-eye more."

As Illanov passed the EO's quarters, he went about ten feet past to make sure no one was watching. He doubled back and was in the EO's room. Wanting to be quick about it, he opened up the footlocker at the end of the bed. Rifling through it, he was disappointed to find nothing. He made sure everything was put back as he had found it. Standing up, he perused the small room. He was sure he wouldn't leave anything out in the shelf of his closet.

Illanov looked at the perfect military tuck of the bed. With caution, he slipped his hand between the tucked blanket and the bed frame. His fingers brushed up against some papers. Lifting the whole mattress up, he withdrew a stapled stack of papers covered with diagrams. His fingers flipped through them. He needed to see no more. It was a copy of the layout of the ship's ventilation system. Illanov's body went rigid. The thought of Alex's slumped-over body came to mind. He looked at his watch and remembered that the ship's doctor was due in his quarters at 0600 hours. That gave him five minutes to return to his room.

Entering his quarters, Illanov heard the footsteps of the doctor approaching. He sat down at his desk and gave the appearance of having been immersed in paperwork. The doctor knocked and entered. His face had the wearied look of a ship's doctor not accustomed to anything more than a cold or the flu. Reading the doctor's face, Illanov said in a tired voice, "He was murdered, wasn't he?"

CHAPTER 43

THE GALE'S HOWLING WINDS WERE APPROACHING HUR-ricane status. Peter Jorgesen's headset had become a screaming cacophony in his ears. All eight pilots of the super tugs were desperate to talk to him at the same time. The gas platform was more stable than the tug boats, but even this behemoth was rolling and drifting in the storm. The eight tugs looked like bobbing corks in the maelstrom.

Peter pulled off his headset and threw it on the desk. He looked at Bjorn and said, "God rest our souls if this mess gets any worse. What's the read out on the connections of the towers below us?"

Bjorn's eyes never left the monitor. He responded, "The connections are stressed, but they're holding … for now, anyway."

"What about the towers' framework? Are there any signs of fracture?"

"There's a questionable area to the bow port side. But I'm not sure that a fracture is forming. The computer signals are mixed. There's too much input for the computer to verify with certainty."

Greta added, "It would help if the tugs could keep a tighter formation. They are drifting beyond one hundred eighty degrees."

"Lead Tug Alpha, this is Gimli!" Peter said.

"Go ahead Gimli, this is Alpha."

Peter barked out, "Our computer shows your formation is spreading out beyond one eighty—looks closer to two ten. I know the beating you're taking, but you've got to get the boys to tighten back up. The platform's maxed with stress. The wider the formation, the greater the forward stress. You've got to get them back in line, Stellan, one hundred eighty degrees max!"

"Roger, Peter, but I'm not sure we can handle these swells if they get any higher. We're taking on a lot of water. The pumps are going full bore and they're struggling to keep up. Peter, we could lose one of our tugs!"

"That's a copy. Hang tough. We're going to get through this—

God willing."

Stellan hit the button on his mike to reaffirm. The sky lit up as a massive bolt of lightning struck the Gimli platform. The vision of the lighted behemoth was lost in darkness.

Within seconds, Gimli's emergency lights kicked on. Alpha tug was the first to respond to Jorgesen. "Gimli, this is Alpha. I can see your lights again. Are you all right?"

"That's a Roger, Alpha. Looks like the computers all withstood the hit. The electricians are working on the balance of our power. It shouldn't take long."

"Peter, our GPS is showing we're within a half mile of our intended location. Can you confirm?"

Peter looked over at his second monitor and verified the location. The platform pitched to the rear. Papers and pens slid off the front of the long desk top. Bjorn's voice rang out in alarm.

"Skipper, that swell was beyond what we can control! The alarm in the number one tower went off. We may have developed a stress crack … looks like maybe forty feet down … hard to say."

Peter looked out at his tugs. The closest two tugs were on the upside of the swell that just passed. They looked vertical. Peter gripped the arms of his chair, elbows straight out. He grimaced with concern. The two tugs appeared as if they were going to flip over backwards. They crested the swell and disappeared over the down side. Two by two, the next three pairs followed suit. Alpha tug went up to the crest and seemed to suspend, naked, out of the water. It slammed forward and disappeared over the crest.

"Stellan … Stellan!" Peter screamed into the speaker of his headset. The absence of a response was deafening. "Stellan, do you copy?" Peter screamed again. He believed the tug had gone under. As the swell moved forward, all eight tugs came into view.

Bjorn spotted the tugs churning in the raging water. He shouted out, "They're still there!" Peter's grip loosened from his chair and he raised clenched fists into the air. He crossed himself, closed his eyes, and gave a quick thank you for his men.

Bjorn stepped over and placed a reassuring hand on Peter's shoulder. After a moment, the big Norwegian teddy bear lowered his hands from his face. He placed his left hand on top of Bjorn's right hand, a silent thank you.

"God has blessed us one more time, Bjorn, one more time ..." Peter paused. He leaned his head backward and wiped the sweat from his face with the palm of his hand. He contemplated his decision. Ten seconds later, he again leaned forward in his chair, opened his eyes, and said, "Bjorn, notify all hands: We set the platform down here." Peter wiped his eyes and pushed the send button again. He said one more time, "Alpha, this is Gimli. Do you copy?"

Five excruciating seconds later, Stellan answered, "Alpha tug to Gimli. We're okay, Peter. That swell threw us all for a loop in the cabin. My first mate slammed his head into the control panel. He is unconscious, but we're trying to revive him."

"We're going to Step B—confirming Step B. Shut the team down, Stellan; X marks the spot. It's the end of the line. We're going to set her down right here. Do you copy that?"

"But our GPS still shows another half mile."

"The GPS in my head says that we have arrived—and by God, we are going to drop her right here—final word. Stellan! Stop forward progress!"

"Stellan, tell your men to keep minimum pressure on the cables. We're going to start flooding the towers."

"That's a Roger, Peter ... Alpha out."

"Bjorn, begin flooding in 5 ... 4 ... 3 ... 2 ... 1 ... Go!"

Beginning its slow descent to the floor of the North Sea, the Gimli platform gave the few that were onboard an eerie sense of descending into hell. The full crew was scheduled to be flown out by chopper over the next several days, but that of course, was weather permitting. With lightning continuing to flash about them, the swells grew with every foot that the platform dropped. The sea appeared to be an overwhelming vortex that was sucking the platform into its briny clutches.

Peter was the first to feel the slight vibration that emanated from the port bow tower. "What is that vibration, Bjorn? Something is wrong—I can feel it!"

Bjorn scanned his monitors. "Nothing is showing, Skipper—wait! The port bow pump is malfunctioning—it's revving over a thousand rpm too much. It's dumping too much water in!"

"Shut the pump down, Bjorn—shut it down!"

"It's not responding—there must be an electrical short from the lightning strike! I can't override it."

He felt it. The platform began to list to the port bow. Papers and anything that wasn't screwed down began to shift. "Increase the rate of fill in the other three towers!" Screamed Peter.

Greta stepped out from the other side of Bjorn. She took two steps toward him and gripped the edge of the desktop. "Peter—we can't do that! We'll exceed our normal descent rate. We could fracture the bases upon impact."

Bjorn looked at Peter and raised his right eyebrow. He grimaced and nodded as a sign of agreement with Greta. "I'm afraid she's right, Peter. God knows what will happen."

Peter knew the call would have to be his. There was a penalty for leadership. He took a deep breath. He looked Bjorn straight in the eyes and said, "Increase the water flow rate until it reaches parity. If we don't, this mother will go down anyway."

Peter switched on the mike and said in a staccato voice, "Alpha tug—tell your men to let out one hundred meters of cable. Repeat—let out one hundred meters of cable. We're going to have to let her down fast or she's going to take us all down with her."

"Steady, Bjorn ... back it down, back it down! Too much water coming in—we're listing to the starboard side!" Peter Jorgesen was in the fight of his life. Trying to steady a behemoth in a plunging drop in the middle of a raging storm was proving to be impossible. A miracle was needed.

"I've got it, Skipper! They're backed off twenty percent! It should start to balance out in about thirty seconds!" Bjorn wasn't working on instinct or experience. There was no experience for something like this. Years of experiments and calculations could never allow for every contingency in the North Sea. Every move he made on the flow rate of the pumps was pure guesswork. Like everyone else, he was flying by the seat of his pants.

Peter felt the effects first through his feet. He too was running on nothing but pure adrenaline. When the predecessor to The Troll platform started to sink three years earlier, it was already halfway submerged in place—and it wasn't in the middle of a gale. He had no way of knowing if the tower bases would be able to withstand the impact. It was true that all engineers overdesign for safety, but this rate of descent was not in the calculations or even in anyone's wildest dreams. "That's better. Can you keep her there?"

"I'm not sure. That helped a bit, but we still haven't leveled, Skipper. Problem is our rate of descent isn't changing. I don't know what's going to happen when we hit," said Bjorn.

Greta looked out at the tugs and hollered, "The cables on the tugs are coming out of the water! They've got to let out more line!"

Peter pushed the send button and shouted over the howling noise of the gale, "Alpha tug, this is Gimli, let out another fifty meters of cable! Repeat—let out another fifty meters of cable. That's five-zero—all tugs!"

"That's a Roger, Gimli … five-zero!"

Greta shouted to Peter, "That's not enough. Our descent rate indicates they need to let out a hundred! Our fall rate could take them down if they do fifty!"

"That may be, Greta, but I'm going to rely on their collective drag to slow our rate of fall. Alpha tug, this is Gimli. Boost your power by five knots in tugs: Alpha, Bravo, Charlie, and Delta. Repeat—increase your speed by five knots, Alpha, Bravo, Charlie, and Delta."

"Roger that Gimli, up five knots in Alpha, Bravo, Charlie, and Delta."

A few seconds later, Bjorn looked over at him. A smile broke on Bjorn's face. "It's working, Skipper. The rate is slowing! It may not be all that we need, but it's helping one hell of a lot."

"Greta," barked Peter, "I want to know the distance to the arc of the tugs and the distance to the floor!"

"That's two hundred meters out and three hundred meters to hard pan."

"Alpha tug, this is Gimli. Churn another five knots up in Alpha, Bravo, Charlie, and Delta. Repeat—up another five knots in Alpha, Bravo, Charlie, and Delta."

"Roger that Gimli, up five knots—that's zero-five up in Alpha, Bravo, Charlie, and Delta. Do we let out more cable?"

"That's a negative, Alpha. Repeat—that's a negative on the cable."

Within minutes, Bjorn was exuberant. He shouted out, "It's a miracle! We've taken twenty-five percent off our descent rate! We might make it!"

Greta shouted, "Holding at two hundred meters out to tugs and two hundred fifty meters to the floor."

Peter lowered his head and made the sign of the cross. He could see that Bjorn had been watching him before turning his chair away. He also saw him look around and make a quick crossing himself. Peter waited about sixty seconds and without ever looking at Bjorn, a small smile appeared on his face. With a teasing twinge of dry humor he said, "Was that an itch you were scratching on your chest, Bjorn?"

CHAPTER 44

KNOWING THAT STRINGER WOULD NOT BE FAR BEHIND, Devon put the towel down. He pulled Jack Weston's body out of the cabin and buried him deep in the permafrost. He dragged Polnich out to the rear of the cabin and into the stand of trees. Polnich, however, would get no grave. As he turned to go back to the cabin, Devon said with a sneer on his face, "I wish you'd still be alive when the wolves are ripping your face off."

As Devon reentered the cabin, the thought of Oscar came to his mind. Oh no! He thought. He pictured Oscar being shot up like Jack Weston. He looked around but the dog was nowhere to be seen. Devon got on his knees next to the bed, pulled the blanket upward, and forced himself to look under. There was Oscar's face staring straight back at him, his tail flopping on the floor in acknowledgement of his master. "You are one lazy-ass, chicken, piece of do-do!" Devon whispered. "Helen Keller would be a better watchdog than you are."

Devon's voice woke Julie, and he gave her a caring look. He looked into her eyes and with tears welling in his own, he said, "I'm so sorry, I couldn't save him."

Julie broke down sobbing. No words were spoken. Devon, still on his knees, put his arms around her and held her for comfort. They stayed this way until Devon raised his head and pulled away from her. From under the bed, Oscar reported a low, menacing growl. They heard the faint sound of a snowmobile downshifting. Then it shut off.

Devon jumped to his feet and searched for his M40 and Glock pistol. He checked the clips and discarded them both. Slipping in fresh clips, he chambered a round in each. He picked up Polnich's M40 and did the same. Taking Julie's hand, he eased her off the bed, and stood her up. He pulled the bed on the diagonal across the right rear corner. He took her by the shoulders and turned her around to face him, forcing her to look into his eyes. With a deliberate stare, he said, "I want you to crawl over the bed and get on your knees, facing me—now!"

Devon knew she understood the emergency as she obeyed his command. Devon wadded up the pillow and blanket and shoved the balled mass in front of her. He motioned for Oscar to get under the bed. Knowing that her basic training at the CIA included all weaponry, he handed her the M40 and said, "I'm going outside to intercept the piece of garbage that's coming after us. Listen to me. The safety is off, the bullet is chambered. If anybody tries to come in that door or that window and isn't me, I want you to hold the trigger and vaporize him. Remember, I'm the first line of defense. If he gets through me, only you can take him out." He pulled an extra clip out of his jacket and threw it on the bed by her side. He went to the hurricane lamp and before blowing it out, said, "Stay calm and draw on the energy that your dad left you. He died trying to save you. Don't let him down."

Devon closed what was left of the cabin door the best he could. The bottom hinge was shot out, so he kicked it back into place with his boot. He pulled his sleeve back and squinted to see the luminescent dial on his watch. It had been ten minutes since he first heard the snowmobile turn off. All Devon had were his wits and instincts to go on. He knew that Stringer would be forced to stop further away from the cabin than Polnich did. The assassin would not have heard the gun shots from the ordeal with Polnich and would have to assume that he may have to do battle with both of them. Stringer wouldn't know whether Polnich would risk attacking tonight or lay in wait to pick off the targets in the morning. In any case, Devon was sure Stringer wouldn't allow for Polnich to hear his vehicle announce his approach. The problem remained: Stringer didn't know how far away to stop.

This gave Devon more time to prepare, but time was the enemy of his nerves. He pulled his night vision goggles back on and repaired his disrupted trip wire defense. When he was satisfied that the wire was camouflaged as good as it was going to get, he turned around to face the blind. With the same pine bough in hand, he covered his tracks as he made his way to it.

Devon wanted to check on Julie, if for no other reason than he wanted to see her face. But he knew her nerves would be on a razor-thin edge. Creaks on the porch step would send half of a clip his way.

Stringer was winded. At age forty, he wasn't in the peak physical shape that Polnich had regimented for himself. He was still trim and his muscle tone was that of a much younger man, but this was winter in Alaska, and he never was a psycho like Polnich. Stringer's longevity in this business came from his wits, not his brawn. But his wits were confined to his abilities in the field. He longed to get out of the CIA while he was still alive. Due to his finances, however, retirement wasn't an option he could consider.

In spite of the money he had siphoned off from each assignment's "working capital" that every agent was given, Stringer never put a penny away in an exit strategy. He never expected to live a long enough life to become another greybeard agent. Also, the lure of cheap, sleazy women and the fast life that went with them was too much of a temptation for a man whose moral compass was between his legs.

Stringer's gait was a strong military pace, but his lungs were on fire. I guess I need to cut back on the booze, he thought. He traveled light, or at least as light as he deemed necessary. He carried a Glock, his sniper rifle, an M-40, and extra clips for each, all on top of a Kevlar vest. His body screamed to take a break. Slowing down, he tried to do a regular-paced walk, but even that taxed his lungs. He ground to a stop, bent over with his hands gripping his knees, and gasped for each precious breath that he took in.

As he felt the blood drain from his head, the light-headedness affected his stance. The assassin realized that some things had to be shed. The vest only covers the vital parts of my chest and gut, he rationalized. I could still get shot in the arm, shoulder, hips or legs. Even if it allows me to kill whoever is left, I'd have no way of getting back to Otter Creek for medical help. I'd be a dead man walking and I'm not going to be flayed alive by a pack of crazed wolves. He took off his parka and discarded the cumbersome vest. His gaze next locked on his sniper rifle. "I'll guess I'll pick your sorry ass up on the way back," he growled in disgust as he leaned it up against the nearest tree. He reached into the left pocket of his parka, pulled out its extra clip, and tossed it in the snow at the base of the rifle. Looking at the clips, he sorted out the Beretta clip and took off the holster that included the silenced 9mm. "You ain't looking for quiet, pal," he said to himself. Snapping a low branch about two inches off the tree that held his sniper rifle, he hung the holster above it. He stood back and looked at them with a yeoman's sense of pride. Stringer pulled his parka back on, slung the M-40 over his shoulder, and pulled his NOD's back on. He took off at another military trot. "Not to worry, I've still got three weapons. If that can't cut it, then I need to get out of this business," he said.

Julie's knees screamed in pain. She wanted to get up, grope around the cabin, and try to find a towel to put under them, but she didn't dare. If she were to knock something off a counter or shelf, the noise could cause Devon's whole strategy to be ruined. Instead, she shifted her weight to one side, slid one leg straight out, and sat on her right thigh. With the sound of a low whine, Oscar's head slid out from under the bed and lay on her thigh. Julie looked down and gave Oscar a soft stroking of his head. Her thoughts returned to her father and his sacrifice for her. Wanting to remain in charge of her emotions, she pushed Oscar's head back under the bed. She was determined that she would remain vigilant … death was on its way.

CHAPTER 45

OUT OF BREATH AND HUNCHING LOW, STRINGER MADE HIS way to Polnich's snowmobile. His trek didn't take as long as he thought, which meant that Polnich might have heard the sound of his machine. Was he close? He doubted it, but he couldn't take a chance on it. He pulled his glove off and felt the engine covering for heat. There was none. He wasn't surprised—he felt kind of foolish for even bothering to check—not in this kind of cold.

Stringer looked around to see if the Russian's tracks veered off from the large track left by the Weston's' vehicle. They didn't, so he took off running again down the snowmobile's path.

As McKenzie's cabin came into view, he looked down at his watch. He had been on the move for about an hour since leaving the snowmobile. Strange, he thought. There's no sign of Polnich. Stringer decided to make a large sweep around to the back of the cabin. "No sense in stirring the bees if you're not ready to take the honey," he whispered to himself.

Rounding the opposite side of the cabin from where Devon was, Stringer had a field man's instinct that eyes were trained on him. The question was whose eyes? If someone had seen him, there was nothing he could do to change that. But he widened his sweep of the cabin, nonetheless.

Devon didn't need his trip wire this time around. His eyes were riveted on the stalking assassin. Killing a CIA agent went against his grain, but this man was here for no good. In the pit of his stomach, Devon knew this was kill or be killed. He had his night scope zeroed in on Stringer. The bead was drawn and it was sure—an easy head shot that any hunter worth his salt could pull off. But something, he didn't know what, held him back from squeezing the trigger. The assassin vanished around the corner of the cabin. Devon was tempted to leave his blind, and had tightened the muscles in his legs to get up and begin his tail, but he stopped. He drew deep into his bucket of experience and thought a better plan through.

Yes, there was a window to the rear, but Julie would not be visible. If Stringer were dumb enough to try to gain access through it, Julie would greet him with a hail of bullets. No, the killer would come around full circle and try to gain access through the front door. If he did, Devon had a clean shot, no problem. Stringer could also stake himself outside for the duration of the night and try to pick them off in the daylight as they exited. But for this to work, he would have to find shelter—both for camouflage and for warmth. He would see Devon's blind and make his way toward it. Either way, one of Devon's guns would have the last word. Stringer stopped in his circle about twenty yards around the back of the cabin. The lights were off, but his instincts told him there was someone inside. He decided to move in close and catch a glimpse through the window. The terrain dropped toward the house, so he walked bowlegged, trying to keep himself in a low-crouched profile. He heard a slight rustle in the tree to his left. His Glock, pointed downward in a two-handed grip, raised and pointed in the direction of the sound. As he took his next step forward, his foot caught on a heavy clump. He lost his balance and tumbled forward to the ground.

"Damn it!" He growled, as he lay in the snow trying to regain his stealth. He rolled over and looked backwards to see what he had tripped over. He was startled to see the bloodied face of Gregor Polnich. Years of witnessing death up close kept his body and mind still. I was right, you were a body of iron, but a brain of mush, he thought.

After assaying that no one had heard his failed approach, Stringer decided to move back up the hill to a wider perimeter. He adjusted his shouldered rifle to his backside and put his Glock in his parka pocket. He crawled military style to higher ground.

As he advanced to a point wide of the cabin's front corner, he spotted Devon's blind. He chose to check it out to see what options it afforded him. He arose halfway. With another bowlegged, crouching walk, Glock in two hands, he headed toward the blind.

Stringer reached the edge of the blind and looked back toward the front of the cabin. Sure that Devon was in the blind, he aimed his gun to blast the cover. Without warning, hard pressure from another Glock pressed into the back of his neck. Stringer froze. He knew he had been had. He said, "Before you pull the trigger, you might want to invite me in for coffee."

"Why would I do that? If I pull the trigger, my problems are over."

"Over with me, yes … but they're not over with Grayson and Carey."

"Well, at least you and that scumbag, Polnich, will be a good start."

"Polnich was freelancing on his own—guess that means you must be well loved."

"So who sent you?"

"… Grayson and Carey—who else? And I might add, Hatcher himself."

Devon shoved the gun harder into Stringer's neck. "What are you talking about?"

"Hold on, I'm going to give you my weapon." Stringer raised his open hand with the Glock over his right shoulder. "It's cold out here. Couldn't we talk inside where it's a little warmer?"

Devon took the Glock and put it in his pocket. He hissed, "Take one step forward and take your rifle off your shoulder and throw it on the ground. Empty your pockets and throw any extra guns or clips on the ground. And I assume you have a knife strapped as well. Take it out and get rid of it. Remember, I have no reason not to blow your miserable head off."

When Stringer was done, he stood erect and spread his legs with arms raised. "Go ahead and search. I assume you're from Missouri?"

Devon found no humor in the man and frisked his body. With his left hand, he gave a quick, hard push and shoved Stringer toward the front door. "Move it! But if I were you I wouldn't take a step onto that porch. That is, unless you have wish to eat a mouthful of lead!"

Within a minute, they arrived at the porch. "Hold it," Devon said. "Julie!" He hollered out. "It's me Devon. Light the lamp and open up the front door. We have a guest."

As the lamp lit, the massive damage to the front door became apparent as light streamed through the holes. Julie creaked the door open, just enough to see out. Stringer smiled and said, "Hi, sweetheart. I found this goon behind me and invited him for supper."

Devon cracked the Glock over his head—hard enough to hurt, but that was all.

"Ouch!" Stringer said. "But you'd better be careful, he's a nasty goon." He ducked his head again, waiting for the next hit.

"Shut up and get inside."

As they both stepped inside, Devon kicked a chair from the table over toward Stringer. "Sit down and put your arms behind you." He looked over at Julie and said, "Pick up your gun and keep it on him. If he even twitches, open it up and waste him."

Devon tied Stringer's arms and legs together. Devon leaned in and hissed in his ear, "You say one more word without permission and you'll taste the back side of duct tape for the rest of the night. Got it?" Stringer nodded.

Devon turned to Julie. "I'm going outside to pick up the loose hardware and load the sled. Keep your gun pointed straight at him. Don't be swayed by his comedy routine. It's the oldest trick in the book. I won't be long." As Devon turned to go out the door, he paused, and turned back to Julie. With an apologetic face, he said, "I wrapped your dad in visqueen and buried him in the permafrost. You were asleep and I didn't want to wake you. I think we should leave him buried here till things get sorted out. We can't be taking him to Otter Creek and have to meet with the police—at least not yet."

"I know. Go do what you need to do. I'll keep an eye on the creep."

When Devon had everything on the outside secure, he reentered the cabin. Walking over to Stringer, he grabbed another chair and placed it in front of the agent. "You can talk, but remember, I've also been doing this for years, as has Ms. Weston. So we will be listening ... to every word."

"How about we start over?" He asked. "You get rid of your preconceived notions about me, for the moment, and I'll tell you everything."

"Deal ..."

"You may think I was sent to kill you, and you would be right. That's because Grayson and Carey did sanction me to do it. Difference is I don't work for them. I work for DCI Hatcher. The Agency big brass has been looking into those two clowns for years. The problem has been that they've been laying low. My job was to keep an eye on them. Hell, I've been running surveillance on them for four years, and each year the trail kept getting colder—till now."

Devon noticed that Stringer never made direct eye contact with him. His eyes remained over his shoulder or down at the floor. "Go ahead, I'm still listening."

"So you see," Stringer continued, "that's why The Agency's been looking for you all these years … to get those account numbers you've got. You know, the ones in Zurich that Grayson and Carey were dumping the money into."

Devon's eyes lit up and focused on Stringer's. "Who told you that there were account numbers in Zurich?"

Stringer shifted in his seat. Two beads of sweat showed from beneath his scalp. "Uh, Hatcher did. Yeah, it was Hatcher … he briefed me on it … years ago."

"Really …?" Devon leaned in on the agent. His face was about six inches off that of his captive. "There was one person that I gave those numbers to, and he was killed because of that information." Devon's stare remained focused on Stringer. "Julie, did Tim ever give you any Swiss bank account numbers to check for him?"

"No," she said.

"Did Tim ever tell you that Grayson or Carey had been siphoning off money into any Swiss accounts?"

Julie's focus became keen. "No," she repeated.

"You were running surveillance on Tim Daniels, weren't you?" Devon bellowed out. His rage was consummate. Small pellets of spittle pelted the agent's face.

"No … no … I swear, the DCI briefed me on it. I swear!"

"You killed Tim Daniels, didn't you?"

"No, I had nothing to do with that guy—whoever he was!"

Devon rose from his chair and looked down at Stringer. "He was my friend and he was her fiancé." Walking over to the table, he took his silenced Glock into his hand. With a quick snap of his wrists, he chambered the first round. He walked back over and sat down in his chair. Placing the barrel of the gun next to Stringer's knee cap, Devon leaned in to Stringer's nose. He snarled, "I should have put that bullet in your head when you first arrived. You're going to tell me the truth, or it's going to get painful—one body joint after another. First your right knee, then your left. When you pass out, I'll get a bucket of water. It'll be your right elbow next, followed by your left. If you haven't told me the truth by then, I guess we'll have to work on your ankles. Understand—I won't stop until either the bullets run out or you run out of joints."

Devon knew that second stringers either lacked the necessary talent or they didn't try hard enough. He was sure in Stringer's case, it was the latter—he wasn't willing to become a cripple for the likes of Grayson and Carey. Stringer saw the look of hate in Devon's eyes. He was running out of precious time.

"Okay … I was running surveillance on the guy, but that was my assignment. It was just another job for God's sake."

Devon pushed the steel barrel harder into his knee. "Who ordered you up?"

"Grayson did."

"Who ordered Daniels killed?"

"It was Grayson."

"Who killed him?"

"It wasn't me, I swear. I was in the van monitoring the situation."

"But *you* ran the show, didn't you?"

Stringer's head dropped toward the floor and he muttered, "Yes."

Like a lightning strike, Devon's hand rose and smashed the Glock across Stringer's face. Stringer's body, with the chair still attached, turned over onto the floor. Julie screamed. Devon knew that with the death of her father, she was trying to hold herself together. With a look of shell shock, she sank onto the bed.

When he realized the consequences of his actions, the anger that exploded in Devon diminished. He moved to Julie's side and held her hand in his. It took a couple of minutes comforting her to bring her back in control. "Julie, I can't tell you how sorry I am … it's been four years of hell since Tim's death. I've been living alone like an animal and—anyway, I'm sorry."

"I'm sorry too," she whispered. "I hate this fiend, and I hate the fact that I want to see him dead, like you do."

"I know," Devon said, "it's just that I know he ordered up Tim's murder. I couldn't deal with that. But I can now. I'm ready to leave in the morning if you are."

Lying sideways on the floor, Stringer peeked open his one eye closest to the floor. He strained to hear the whispering over at the bed.

"What about that animal?" She said, pointing to Stringer. He closed his eye.

"If we leave him alive, he'll still come after us," she said. "But I can't kill him and I don't want to see you do it. I don't want to be a monster like him."

"Don't worry. I'll make sure he's tied up tight so at least we can get through the night. Let's sleep on it and decide what to do with the vermin in the morning."

CHAPTER 46

DEVON AWOKE TO FIND STRINGER STILL LYING ON THE floor. He was awake and grimacing over his sheer discomfort. He may have been an agent of many years and had been trained to survive extreme treatment, even torture, but until he had to experience it, nothing could have prepared him for the pain of having his hands bound behind him for a long period of time. Worse, Devon had cinched them tight to the rope that bound his ankles. Devon looked at him grimacing in pain, but didn't care. Moreover, it pleased him. "So, how are you this morning, scum-bag?"

"That the best you got? This is nothing," Stringer lied.

"Good, I'm glad! Because you're going to stay that way till you figure out a way to get free. You can enjoy your walk back to Otter Creek. The vehicles that you and Polnich brought will be disabled—permanently."

"You know damn well nobody could make that trek on foot. You're condemning me to certain death and you know it."

Devon looked at him straight in the eyes and glowered at him. He raised the corners of his mouth into a pleased smile and went out the door.

When the snowmobile was ready, Devon hooked up the sled and gave one last check on all the bindings. He turned and gave a long look at his cabin in resignation. It wasn't much and that was an overstatement. But it had been his home for the last four years—his protection from the outside world. He had to leave it behind and reenter the sick world of violence and corruption. Deep in his heart, he comprehended that he couldn't stay. It would mean that he would never get another night's sleep and moreover, certain death. But its bond was overpowering and he didn't want to leave.

With his mind wandering, he thought, Am I about to start a new life … with this woman? How would that affect my memory of Cathy? Would I even be able to protect Julie? The shadows were professional killers who would stop at nothing short of his death and that of Julie's. He looked heavenward and felt the communion of his spirit with Cathy's. She told him that this was God's plan, a course he must take. She also gave him her blessing. Like it or not, he could do nothing to change the circumstances, only the end result. He lowered his head and went back into the cabin to gather Julie and Oscar.

Opening the cabin door, Devon stopped dead in his tracks. Stringer stood defiant with his arm around Julie's neck. He had a Glock shoved into her ear.

"Come on in, scar-face! Oh, and do shut the door. It's so cold outside. We wouldn't want to freeze our little sweetheart here, would we?"

In a shocked state of resignation, Devon stepped in and shut the door. He didn't know how, but he needed to stall. "I guess the worm has turned," was all he could come up with.

"That's right, stupid. You see, I *am* the professional, and you …? You're some has-been piece of crud hiding out in the sticks of nowhere. Sooner or later, gutless cowards like you are found hiding like a woman. Pull your weapon out with your left hand and drop it on the floor!" Stringer shouted.

Devon eased his Glock out of its holster and let it drop to the floor. "Let the woman go, it's me you want," said Devon.

"Yeah, right. Well, guess what? Grayson and Carey want you both dead—no loose ends—get the picture? And that *will* happen."

"Is killing women in your little book of tricks?" Devon asked, trying to buy time, for what he wasn't yet sure.

"Don't even think of playing those mindless, little, stalling games with me. And, oh by the way, it was me who garroted that wimp buddy of yours. Want to know something else? I enjoyed every second of watching his body twitch while the wire in my hands sucked the life out of him. And here is the good part: Yes, I kill women, after I have my way with them." He paused, and his eyes widened with a perverted joy. A demonic look appeared on his face. "I like it most when they start crying and begging me for their lives. I teach them who's in charge of their pleasure. I guess she'll know 'who her daddy is.'"

He growled in sheer contempt, "Kick that gun over to me before I get pissed off!"

Julie listened to every sick word that came out of his mouth. She felt like her eyes were going to spit blood. With a rage that she had never experienced in her life, she hit her boiling point. She wanted this monster dead. Worse, she wanted a hand in his death. The thought of him shooting her meant nothing. This fiend was going to kill her anyway.

She may have been an analyst, but she still had her training at The Farm to draw upon. She cleared her throat to get Devon's attention. His eyes at once meet hers. She twisted her whole body. She raised and thrust her right heel into Stringer's scrotum. She jerked her head away from the Glock. He pulled the trigger. His gun discharged. The slug lodged itself into the wall. Devon was on the floor with his weapon aimed at Stringer's head. He squeezed off two rounds. The first embedded into Stringer's left cheek. The other missed. The back of Stringer's skull blew out. Pieces of brain and skull splattered against the wall. Stringer's body stood motionless. Devon squeezed off two more shots. They landed in the killer's chest. Stringer crumpled to the floor.

This time she didn't scream. This time there were no tears. She was filled with an angry satisfaction. Her father's image, lying dead on the cabin floor, flashed through her mind. With a sense of pride, she ignored the sharp pain in her abdomen. She picked herself up and stood over the dead assassin's body. Julie straightened her blouse by shifting her shoulders. Her father's death had been avenged. She raised her chin up high, looked down in contempt, and with a burning hatred, spat on the bloodied mass.

A strange sensation came over her. She no longer felt like a bit player. She was Devon's partner. Maybe not his equal, but a full-fledged partner nonetheless. Stretching her arm downward, she offered Devon a hand up.

With her ears still ringing from the sound of gunshots, Julie stood there, not knowing what to say. Her soft green eyes looked at Devon and he at her. She wanted to offer an excuse for Stringer getting the edge on her, but words escaped her. After what became an embarrassing pause, he raised his arms up, wrapped them around her, and whispered in her ear, "I don't want to know what happened. I just thank God that you're alive."

After Devon went through and doused the cabin with gasoline, he told Julie to take the first shift driving the snowmobile, and to move it about seventy-five feet away. With a forlorn look, he stared at his cabin, paused, and lit the Molotov cocktail. Angry, he threw it into the place that had been his refuge. As the vehicle picked up speed and with Oscar riding the rear sled, Julie stopped the vehicle. She turned her head to look at her father's makeshift grave. Devon knew that the sight of it would be like a dagger to her heart. Devon also turned his head backward and took one last look at the raging fire. Another chapter in both of their troubled lives was over. He turned forward and tapped her on the top of her helmet. With tears in her eyes, Julie bit her lower lip, turned her head into the wind, and sped off.

CHAPTER 47

BEING OFF THE GEORGE WASHINGTON PARKWAY AND JUST outside of the city, Fort Marcy Park had been a safe spot for Tom Grayson to get in his weekly outdoor exercise. Because it hosted a small number of visitors, he liked the feeling of its overall seclusion, and was sure that at least his workout regimen wouldn't be disturbed by any of his colleagues. Having labored all these years for the CIA, he was smart enough to know that there was no such a place as a true "safe haven." Any person, anywhere in the world, at any time, could be accessed—either for assassination, kidnapping, or general surveillance. The question was how much money a person or organization was willing to spend and how they wanted an operation carried out. Grayson was aware of this as he was one of the great perpetrators of this axiom.

The intelligence community was one of the largest, yet closest fraternities in the world. Everyone pretty much knew everyone else's business. Information, no matter how secret it was intended to be, could never be held in total secrecy once it left one person's mouth and traveled to another person's ear. Power may corrupt, but it is money that makes power, and it is money that makes the world turn. Grayson was aware of this and knew that no matter how much money he and Carey had put aside over the years, there was always someone that had more. And because of that, keeping their treasonous activities going and yet secret was akin to unraveling a Gordian knot.

When he arrived at the park, the clouds were low in the sky. Diffuse light cast a gloomy pall over the landscape. In the early spring months, with all of its leaves missing from its extensive array of trees, Fort Marcy Park appeared so stark and bleak that it exuded an ominous and foreboding appearance. The slow-moving clouds caused shadows to creep over the sidewalk like spilled ink moving through cloth. As Grayson continued his late afternoon run, he gazed around at the naked woods and the shadows gave him a feeling that a threatening presence was stalking his every move. Every stride made him more and more uncomfortable. Why should I feel this way? I've run this course a hundred times.

He thought back to that day in July 1993 when the body of Vince Foster was found with what the park police determined was a "self-inflicted" wound. Foster was not just a lowly bureaucrat. Some said that he was the keeper of the keys to a closet filled with illegal deals.

If Foster's death could be covered up with such ease, how would that apply to his own situation? Grayson slowed his pace and came to a stop. As he bent over, wheezing for breath, he looked around at all the possible places that someone could be watching him. He heard a rustle in the bushes—his blood ran hot. His head snapped around to check his backside. Had he heard someone? Was someone watching him? Over the last several days, Grayson, the career CIA spook master, had lost his feeling of invincibility and had become tentative and afraid. His nerves were a jumbled mass that were starting to short circuit his ability to stay ahead of the game.

As he started up his run again, he thought of Stringer. Why hadn't that stinking vermin contacted him? He was twenty-four hours late in doing so. Grayson was ready to jump out of his skin. Damn, he thought, why hadn't I pushed Carey to use that Russian killer? We should have used him, and had Stringer eliminate the Ruskie—end of story.

Like a fire alarm going off at midnight, his cell phone announced an incoming call. His whole body jolted and he stumbled coming to another stop. Pulling the phone out of his pocket, his hand shook as he looked at the caller ID on the screen—it was Stringer. He paused, took a deep breath for strength, and hissed into the phone, "You're twenty-four hours late!"

Grayson's knees buckled out from under him when he heard a female's voice.

"I'm sorry, Mr. Grayson, but Agent Stringer seems to be indisposed. As a matter of fact, he and a nice gentleman named Polnich are feeding the wolves. Would you like me to call you on Mr. Polnich's cell phone so you could verify?"

Grayson was so taken aback that he couldn't force a word from his gaping mouth. The voice continued, dripping with sarcasm.

"I didn't think so. After all, I may have found these two phones along some deserted road … but I digress. Mr. Grayson, I think the game they're playing is called 'dancing with wolves.' Yeah, poor Agent Stringer said he'd give his left arm to play that game … or was it his right leg? Hmm … arms, legs, full carcass … oh well. What does it matter when *you* are what's on the menu? But he did have a pleasant conversation with us. That is, before he started playing that silly wolf game. He also had nice words to say about you and Mr. Carey. Well, maybe not the nicest of words, but a lot of words anyway. I had no idea that the CIA was allowed to be involved in domestic assassinations! Oh, and did I use the term 'us?' Yes I did. Ex-agent McKenzie sends his regards and is anxious to tell DCI Hatcher about all the lucrative work the two of you have been doing over the years—all for the sake of your country."

"Listen here you bitch-slut—" was all Grayson could say before the connection went dead.

Grayson's face blanched. He felt light-headed and dizzy; his legs became weak like jelly. There was a park trash canister to his right. He stepped over and grabbed its rim, using it to steady his listing body. His left hand reached up and wiped his brow, lingered, and began rubbing his temples. He tried to swallow, but his tongue and throat were parched bone dry. He tried to think, but nothing sorted through this confusion. "Fuuuuuuuck!" He screamed in rage. His knees buckled and he dropped to the ground and vomited.

**

Sitting in the great room of her father's house, Julie flashed a look of satisfaction at Devon as she rang off and handed him Stringer's cell phone. Devon's mouth was agape—he looked at her in total awe. "Lady, you don't need a gun. Your tongue is the most lethal weapon you have. Please, remind me never to cross you."

Julie smiled again, acknowledging the compliment, but she was all business and her smile turned flat. Pointing to the phone, she said, "We need to smash this and dispose of it on the way to Anchorage. You haven't been gone long enough not to know that they can track us through the phone by GPS. I'm going to book the first flight I can get to Seattle. We'll catch a flight to Atlanta, and from there we'll work our way to Washington. I'm afraid that if we don't catch a plane now, Grayson will have us on a watch list through Homeland Security."

Devon sat across from Julie and had a pensive look on his face that said he hadn't heard a word she had said. She cleared her throat to get his attention and asked, "You *do* know about the Department of Homeland Security … don't you?"

"Oh, I'm sorry. I was trying to extend your plan forward, that's all. And yes, I know about DHS … hello … short-wave radio?"

Julie's face turned red. "No, I'm the one who should be sorry. I'm acting like I'm still in Grayson attack mode. That was sarcastic and I didn't mean it. What I'm trying to say is that time is of the essence, and that's one commodity we have little of. Do you still have a current driver's license?" Julie asked.

"Yes … but not in my name. I kept all my fake passports, birth certificates—all the tools of my trade. I've got stuff that goes out to 2020."

"I may not be that well equipped, but Tim gave me two sets before he was killed. It wasn't that he was a paranoid person, just well prepared."

"Do you think he had a premonition?"

"I don't know, but give me the set you want to use, and I'll book the flights. After that, you and I are going to work on a major disguise. A shave and a dye job will do you well."

"Remember, they know what I look like from the newspaper, but I can't be clean shaven like I was in the old days, either." Devon pointed to his long scar and said, "This is an ugly trademark and pretty obvious."

"It's not as bad as you think … we'll work with your stubble and my makeup."

"I like your auburn hair … it'd be a pity to see that go," he said, while turning his eyes away as if he expected to be ignored.

"Flattery will get you everywhere," she replied with a devilish smile.

CHAPTER 48

ILLANOV CONTINUED SEARCHING HIS EXEC'S QUARTERS. Sandwiched between two books on a shelf next to his bed was a folded advertisement out of an entertainment magazine. He opened the paper up and saw that it was for a Norwegian electronic rock band named Danica. The captain remembered that Kashnikov had made several points of stating his extreme dislike for hard rock music. Putting the folded paper back in its place on the shelf, he made a mental note of the name Danica. He couldn't figure out why, but his instincts told him this had to play into whatever scheme his exec was working with.

Sounds of footsteps coming down the hall caused Illanov to jump back and place his back tight to the wall. The footsteps slowed down and stopped outside the of the EO's quarters. His heart leapt into his throat. Illanov could hear the loud thumping of his heart, and he swore the person outside would hear it and would know he was in there. The door crept opened. Illanov pushed his body off the wall and stood with a commanding presence in the opening. Feodor jumped back, as startled as the captain. Both breathed a heavy sigh of relief.

Illanov was the first to react by placing his hand on the seaman's shoulder and motioning him back into the corridor. "Go down to my quarters—now!"

Feodor Strivnych stood at attention in the captain's room. The last eight hours had been hard on him. Over and over, the image of Alex's strangled body flashed in and out of his mind. The images were followed by his last words: "I know the FSB killed them Feodor, and I think deep in your heart you do too." Alex was his friend, maybe the only true friend he had ever had. And his brother Batu was a good man. Worse, Feodor believed that the FSB had Batu's family killed. God, he hated them and everything they stood for. Alex was gone—murdered because he loved his brother. Because of what was going on around him, Feodor was growing more and more confused. Was there a bigger picture? He couldn't be sure.

Illanov motioned for him to sit down. "I am sorry, Captain, I did not mean to rattle you, and I shouldn't have been sneaking into the EO's room without your permission," said Feodor.

"It is okay, my friend. We're all you and I have. But if we ever get out of this mess, don't pull that on your next captain's boat. He'll have you drawn and quartered."

"Oh, I wouldn't, sir. Besides, I don't want to be on any other boat but yours … that is, as long as you'll have me."

"I would Feodor, but after this cruise I am afraid that a quiet retirement is all I want … a nice dacha in the country to watch my grandkids on weekends."

"You will get that, Captain, I can promise you that."

Illanov smiled and his brow furrowed as he became pensive in thought. When he raised his head, he asked, "Do you listen to hard rock music?"

Feodor was confused by the question. "Well, I don't, Captain, but the rest of the crew sure does. They are into all that weird heavy metal stuff and that American rap garbage. I don't like it because it does not allow my head to even think. Why do you ask?"

"I found a folded up magazine ad for a Norwegian rock band called Danica in Kashnikov's room. He once told me that he hated rock music. If so, why would he squirrel away an ad for an electronic band?"

"Well, Danica means Morning Star in Danish tongues, Captain. Does that help?"

Illanov paused, muddling the name Morning Star through his mind. He muttered, "Morning Star is a common nautical name for ships—used the world over, but in the merchant marine."

"You think maybe there's a Morning Star ship or trawler that's to pick the traitors up after they do their dirty deed, Captain? You know, like their escape route?"

"But how would they get off this boat without us knowing that they're trying to escape? There is no way for that to be possible."

"Pardon me, Captain, but that is an easy one. You see, they are not figuring for the rest of us to be alive. That is what the fuss with the ventilation system is all about. They are going to try to use some sort of poison gas on the rest of us!" When Feodor said this, he was startled by his own words. Could this scenario be possible?

Illanov cursed while pounding his fist on his desk. "But Kashnikov is the executive officer of a Russian nuclear submarine—he swore an oath to protect his country!"

Feodor put his index finger over his pursed lips and frowned at Illanov. "Your voice is getting too loud, Captain. We've got to keep this low." He motioned backward to the door and whispered, "Maybe he's taken a more sinister oath. Maybe he's made a pact with the devil to line his own pockets. You and I both know that half of the weapons from our old Soviet days have been siphoned off and sold on the black market by our own crooked countrymen. They're dirty buggers, Captain, and whores to boot. They will do anything and they've got footlockers full of money to do it with."

"You're right, Feodor, and that kind of money makes the weak of soul do insidious things." Illanov sighed in frustration and said, "I guess we *are* copying the Americans."

"Amen to that, Captain. What kind of gas do you think they got hold of?"

"Probably a supply of VX gas—the supply of it in our military warehouses is endless. Of all the WMDs that we stockpiled, this was the most prolific. It has also been the easiest weapon to smuggle out of our inventory. It's small and can be transported without much attention to handling. The only reason more of it hasn't been taken is that terrorists seem to be obsessed with the greatest amount of people killed in each attack. That is why all the attention has gone to small nuclear devices."

"Or in our case, big ones," said Feodor.

Illanov straightened back up to get to the business at hand. "Alright, let's get back to what we have to deal with. This gas is odorless, colorless, and wears off within an hour of its killing spree. Even on a boat of this size, one canister the size of a small thermos bottle would be enough to kill everyone. Once people are infected, they keel over and fall to the floor in a retching, vomiting stupor—two minutes later, they are all dead."

Feodor grasped the gravity of the situation. "Is there any antidote, Sir?"

"Yes there is ... atropine. The person who is inoculated will still go into a vomiting seizure, but within a short period of time he will recover. I am positive we have a supply in the ship's pharmacy, but I don't know how much we have stored."

"Would it be enough for the whole crew, Captain?"

"I can tell you with great certainty that there isn't—it's not standard protocol to have a large amount on board. So the greater concern becomes, who is to receive it. Are we giving to friend or foe? Are we going to inoculate a crewman who will survive and turn around and kill us?"

The captain took a deep breath. "Alright, Mr. Strivnych, let's review those ventilation drawings and see if we can figure out where and when they are going to strike … and how in the hell we can prevent it."

"Can't we lock them up, Sir?"

"No. We don't know how far this conspiracy has gone into the crew. We can be sure that they will keep it small, but they will have at least two others working with them. It will do us no good to nab half the conspirators and tip off the rest."

"But Captain, Sir … don't we arrive at the gas fields in the early hours of morning?"

"No, Feodor, I instructed Mr. Kashnikov to slow down and let the gale pass over us. We've still got about thirty-six hours before we arrive. In any case, time is running out, and we need to look at the ventilation plans to find the most vulnerable points of entry. After that, we'll make a visit to the ship's doctor … let's pray that he's one of us."

CHAPTER 49

THE ENDLESS GALE WINDS FAILED TO ABATE, AND THE fleet of tugboats struggled to keep pace. Peter Jorgesen felt better about their chances of putting the platform down and it showed in the calmness of his demeanor. He wasn't a Stoic. He was one of those rare individuals who could look for and feel the fourth dimension that enveloped and permeated his being.

Never one to be satisfied with external pleasures, Peter had spent a lifetime developing and honing a spiritual force from which he could draw upon in any of life's crises. He was neither a zealot, nor did he consider himself an overt evangelical type of person. His voluntary faith in God was his own and its strength was ingrained in his psyche. Whenever someone would take umbrage over his quiet devotion or challenge his beliefs, Peter would reply that his core trust in God was what rounded him out as a person. It raised him to a level in life that gave him meaning and purpose and filled his empty cup. If someone else failed to grasp that simple concept … well, that would be their loss, and he wished them well on their own journey.

With his eyes never leaving the images on his computer screen, he said, "Greta, I need numbers."

"…Distance to tugs holding firm at one hundred twenty-five meters. The release rate of their cables is matching our rate of descent. The distance to hardpan is closing in on one hundred fifty meters. Our rate of descent is still high, but staying within upper limits of design safety. I think we need to begin letting out more cable on the tugs."

"Bjorn, what's the readout on that port bow tower stress crack?"

"Nothing has changed, Skipper. No further cracks showing anywhere else. We're going to have a hard landing, but we should hold intact."

"Status on the port infill pumps?"

"No change in the pumps … we still need the pull of the tugs to balance our descent."

Peter's speakers rang out with alarm. "Gimli, this is Alpha tug—Charlie has taken on too much water—the bilges are not able to stabilize. She is listing heavily to port side! We are releasing her cable! Repeat—we are releasing Charlie's cable!"

"Alpha tug, that's a Roger! Notify all tugs to go to Alert Status One! Repeat—Alert Status One!"

Peter felt the release of Charlie's cable through the sudden jolt that vibrated through the deck of the platform. He raised himself from his chair, desperate to get a better visual through the window. "Greta, I want numbers status hollered out every twenty seconds!"

He looked again at his monitor screen, pushed the button to send, and said; "Alpha tug, this is Gimli. Can you save Charlie, Stellan? Repeat, can you save Charlie?" Seconds went by and the lack of response by Alpha tug made it seem an eternity. Peter's mouth was dry. More and more it was becoming difficult to talk. He leaned into the window and cupped his hands around his eyes in an attempt to see Charlie tug, but the horizontal rain made it next to impossible. "Alpha tug, this is Gimli—do you copy?" More precious seconds ticked by, but still no answer. A flash came through Peter's mind. He could visualize the faces of the men from Charlie tug and the horror of their drowning in the turbulent water. Nothing mattered but the men of the listing tug.

Greta shouted out the numbers: "One hundred meters to tugs and dropping fast. One hundred twenty-five meters to impact! The tugs are reversing at too great a speed, Peter, we could lose them all! They need to let out more cable!"

Peter pulled out the crucifix from around his neck and gave it a kiss, asking God to give him courage and bless his decision. "Alpha tug, this is Gimli. Stellan, can you move in Bravo and Delta and secure lines to its aft sides? Repeat! Can you secure Bravo and Delta to the aft sides of Charlie?"

The speakers rang out, "We can try, Gimli. But it may be too late! Repeat! We will attempt to secure Charlie!"

As it become apparent by stacks of papers sliding on the desktop, Bjorn hollered out, "Decreasing infill of water in towers 2, 3, and 4, Skipper, but I don't have anything left to work with—I'm at minimum infill. We can't land on one tower—she won't handle the impact!"

Ten excruciating minutes went by, but Peter held steadfast. He felt crushed by the weight of the world on his shoulders. He had drawn all he thought he could from his faith in God's will, and was at the point of even questioning that. Nothing was working and it was ripping his gut out. Was his well of strength empty? He wasn't sure, but he decided one more quick prayer couldn't hurt.

Beads of sweat had formed on Greta's face. "… The tugs are fifty meters out and seventy-five meters to impact," she blurted out, her eyes afraid to make contact with Peter's.

"Skipper, we need more power from the tugs." Bjorn's voice tailed off as he completed his sentence. He too was aware that Peter was backed into a corner.

Peter knew that time was running out. He looked at the send button, hesitated, and pushed it down. "Alpha tug, this is Gimli. Stellan, I need a report on Charlie tug. Repeat—need report on Charlie!" The speaker remained in numbing silence.

Greta began to call out her numbers again, but was interrupted by a voice breaking on the speaker. "Gimli, this is Alpha—do you copy?"

Peter's body jumped in anticipation. "Go ahead, Alpha."

"Gimli, we have secured Charlie. Repeat, we have secured Charlie! Do you copy?"

Tears welled in Peter's eyes and his voiced stumbled with emotion. With his left hand he pushed the send button while crossing himself with his right. "Praise God, Stellan. Can you give me a twenty-five percent increase in power in Alpha, Bravo, and Delta only?"

"That's a Roger, Peter. Repeat—up power twenty-five percent in Alpha, Bravo, *Charlie* and Delta."

"Alpha, did you say Charlie?"

"Roger that Gimli … Charlie's back in the hunt!"

"Alpha, change that to a twenty percent increase. Repeat—twenty percent ramp up in power and release more cable at a ten percent increase!"

"Twenty percent increase in power and ten percent up on cable release, Gimli. And Peter … thanks for thinking of my men."

"God speed, Stellan." Peter's voice cracked again with emotion. He whispered to no one, "God speed."

Greta wiped the tears from her cheeks and looked Peter straight in his eyes. "Tugs are holding at one hundred meters and fifty meters to hardpan—rate of descent back under safety redline." A small smile broke on her face.

Bjorn started to talk before holding his breath to steady the wavering in his own voice. "Port bow tower is raising to level, Skipper. It looks like we're going to have a four-point landing!" He turned and with the back of his palm, wiped away his own tears of joy.

Peter Jorgesen slumped back down into his chair and lowered his head to his chest. He closed his eyes tight to prevent his tears from flowing. With a quivering chin, he gave thanks. He knew that one more time, he hadn't been abandoned.

CHAPTER 50

AFTER LEAVING FOR THE AIRPORT, JULIE MADE A QUICK stop at a FedEx store and purchased three medium-sized packages for shipment. She paid cash. With Devon driving, she put the Glocks in separate packages, distributing the ammo and silencer between them. Two different hotels at the Atlanta airport were the mailing addresses. Devon had stated his case for keeping the package weight low and that having two destinations would improve the odds that at least one gun would get through.

Before boarding the plane to Seattle, Devon and Julie outfitted themselves with angler's caps, hiking boots, jeans, and Carhartt jackets. The angler's caps with their elongated bills would help to restrict overhead shots from airport security cameras.

Their outdoor gear wore well on the short flight to Seattle, as most people who left Alaska were the adventuresome type. Although to a lesser degree, the same held true as they made their way through Seattle's airport.

On the long flight to Atlanta, Devon's mind processed everything and everyone like a computer. He even scanned the stewardesses before dropping his eyes as they passed. Devon knew, however, that Julie's body needed the rest, and she slept most of the flight.

***

The weather in Atlanta was dreary and overcast, which suited the pair just fine. They hoped that anything that might challenge airport security cameras would be their friend and give them an advantage. Julie thought the seven a.m. business flights would present the greatest test for the screeners from Homeland Security, they chose to land in Atlanta. What she couldn't be sure about was if Grayson had alerted Homeland Security. She believed that Grayson would never risk having them picked up by anybody outside of The Agency who wasn't within their control. Julie was passionate that Grayson would come up with some bogus alert so if they were seen, they would be monitored with tracking reports sent to Grayson. In the end, Devon bowed to Julie's better counsel.

After disembarking the plane, Devon split with Julie to pick up a rental car for the drive to Washington. He used a different alias and credit card than he used for the flight travel disguises. Julie proceeded down to the luggage carousel to pick up the bags that contained the balance of their necessities.

Exiting the airport, Devon and Julie made quick stops at the two hotels they had registered with from Anchorage. They checked in early using two of his credit cards, ruffled the beds, and returned to the front desks to claim their "mail." For breakfast, they chose a Cracker Barrel restaurant because of its continuous overload of hungry travelers, and it would also serve as a way of killing the time needed until most retail stores would be open for business.

Sitting through their third cup of coffee, Devon reminded Julie that heavy crowds would be their ally.

When they paid their bill, Devon got back on the road and proceeded to the nearest Verizon store. Under the guise of buying two phones, one for her daughter and one for her son, Julie purchased a plan with the fewest number of minutes available for both. Neither phone would be kept long. To get clothes fashionable enough to blend in with Washington street life, they drove to the Atlanta suburb of Buckhead, a case study in the trendy suburban aesthetic. They chose small haberdasheries and ladies dress shops as the chance of those establishments having security cameras was low. When they had finished with the last ladies store for Julie, Devon drove around to a local Mexican restaurant that hadn't as yet opened, and dumped the outdoor gear in its rear dumpster.

Devon had nixed the idea of having a navigation system in the rental car. The presence of one meant that their vehicle could be tracked at any time by Homeland Security. After purchasing maps of Georgia, North Carolina, and Virginia at the nearest gas station, he and Julie set their sights on the I85 East out of Atlanta. Without having enough time to prepare a viable plan of attack, the pair understood that further running and hiding out was not any sort of long-term solution. By necessity, their current plan had to have an evolving and fluid strategy. For the moment, that line of attack had them in Washington, D.C.

As he looked over to move his car back into the slower lane, Devon's eyes locked onto Julie. With her knees together, she was hunched over, studying a map of North Carolina. He was taken aback by the sight of her. This naturally, beautiful woman, with her self-reliant attitude, still appeared vulnerable and in need of his protection. But that was the smallest part of his attraction. He could feel her spirit moving within his own. It was soft and loving, yet strong and loyal. It was that moment when he realized he was ready to take another chance on love. Not love as some detached, esoteric feeling, but as the essence of life itself.

Julie never turned her head but she could feel the long presence of his gaze. She too was feeling a merging of their souls, and to her, it also felt right.

Devon mustered the courage to speak the first words other than "take the next exit," since leaving Atlanta. "You know that I lost my first wife … and she was the love of my life, but—"

Julie's face saddened and she turned her head to look out the side window. Not because Devon had mentioned his first wife, but because of the void that was in her own heart over the loss of Tim Daniels and her father. "I know," she responded, cutting his words short. "I also lost Tim, and he was the love of my life." She hesitated and looked over at Devon. "We've both had the good part of life kicked out of us … not once but twice. You lost your best friend and your wife. I lost my fiancée and my father. These three people were murdered as a result of some connection to us. They were either loving us or trying to help us. I will carry this guilt for the rest of my life, as I'm sure you will. I don't know what is left for two people like us." Turning her head to the side, her eyes returned to a faraway look.

Devon saw a blue rest area sign approaching and pulled off the highway into the exit. He stopped the car in an unused area of the truck parking lot, leaned into Julie, and put a comforting arm around her shoulders. "What I was trying to say is that I … I've fallen in love with you. You are all that matters in life to me."

"Devon … I'm not sure, but I think I fell in love with you when my

Dad and I came out to your cabin."

Devon turned away, a puzzled look on his face. He said, "Look, I'm a screwed up and broken piece of work, but if you're willing to try to put ol' Humpty Dumpty's pieces back together, so am I."

Julie placed her head onto his chest, tears streaming down her cheeks.

CHAPTER 51

AFTER HIS BREAKDOWN ON HIS KNEES IN FORT MARCY Park, Tom Grayson pulled himself up and walked to his car. He wanted to call Dennis Carey but his emotional state wasn't up to another sarcastic duel of words with that major prick, his wretched partner in crime. It was all he could muster to get in his car, drive back to his condo, and take the elevator up to his fourth floor unit.

He had chosen the condo for convenience rather than security. Like most mid-level bureaucrats in the CIA, Grayson had no real enemies that would have him on some sort of hit list. Unlike a field agent who had been exposed, these bureaucrats seldom required protection beyond a sophisticated security system and sundry debugging devices. His white collar job was to direct a certain number of people whose primary function was the main work of the spy business—the gathering of intelligence. Grayson believed that the only reason he had ever become involved with the agent named "Trojan Horse" was because his boss, Dennis Carey, liked to keep his soft hands clean. Whenever a project came to the front where an agent had to step out of intel work to carry out a mission, Carey seemed to passed the grunt work down the line to him. Grayson was convinced that this way, all successes would be claimed by Carey and all failures would be blamed on him.

Punching in the code to his security system, Grayson entered and looked over at his wet bar. He made a bee line for the bottle with the racing horse and jockey stopper on top. On a normal night, a double Blanton's over ice was all the Kentucky bourbon he needed. But this was not going to be a typical night. After he finished the first glass that was filled to the brim, he poured another full glass and eased himself into his oversized leather chair. He began to wind down—the single barrel bourbon was doing what it was meant to do. But for Grayson, these drinks were going to be a warm-up.

Leaning his head backward into his cushy chair, he kicked off his running shoes and put his sore feet on an ottoman. Realizing that he hadn't alerted Carey of the cell phone call from that bitch, Weston, he grunted as he reached down and struggled to get his cell phone out of his pants pocket. He swished the drink in his tumbler and was pleased when he listened to the ice cubes clanking against the crystal. "God I need you," he mumbled to the glass and untied the drawstring waist of his jogging pants. After dialing the number, he hesitated before pushing the send button. He would have one more belt before he had to explain this latest fiasco to that prick-nose. That was the last thing he remembered.

Tom Grayson woke to a blistering headache that felt as if his head were going to spin off and explode. He looked around and scrunched his bloodshot eyes, trying to get his bearings. Seeing the empty bourbon bottle lying on the floor next to his chair was all he needed to know that he had screwed up. He laid his head back and tried to think with a clear mind. If there was any possibility to nail the bitch and that bastard turn-coat while they were still in Alaska, calling Carey was imperative. It may be true that Stringer was no longer viable, but they still had other options to kill, delay, or at least track the threatening couple and eliminate them later. How was he going to explain Stringer screwing up, let alone his own bad action of getting drunk by himself, passing out, and taking no action at all? And what is this garbage about that Ruskie Polnich … who the hell brought him into the stinking mess? He reached for his cigarettes, but the package was empty and lay crushed on the table next to him. Grayson wiped his sweaty face with his hand, and in turn, wiped it on the arm of his chair. Pulling himself up, he opted to make a stiff Bloody Mary before calling Carey.

When the Bloody Mary was finished and he had wolfed down the celery stick, Grayson made the call he dreaded most.

Dennis Carey's voice was terse and dripping with sarcasm, as it always sounded when Carey answered his phone calls. "What is it? Did Stringer decide to run off with our 'Amelia Earhart' and live in sin?"

The hair bristled on Grayson's neck, his upper lip turning into a snarl. He held the phone away from his ear, mouthed a four letter expletive, and directed his middle finger at the phone. When he finished, he calmed down and informed Carey of the status of Stringer. "FYI, I got a call from Stringer's cell phone."

"… And let me guess, there was another problem?"

"You're damn right there was a problem! *He* wasn't on the phone, that bitch Weston was."

Carey's voice no longer dripped with derision. "What are you trying to tell me?"

"I'm not *trying* to tell you anything. I am telling you that she was using Stringer's cell phone and she said that he was dead. Get it? He's dead!"

"How can he be dead for God's sake? Are you telling me some do-nothing analyst broad took out an experienced assassin?"

"I don't know who did it or how it was done. Are you forgetting that I'm here in Washington like you? And Stringer's not the only one dead, or 'feeding the wolves' as she put it, but so is Gregor Polnich."

"… Polnich! What do you mean Polnich?" Carey's voice was up several decibels and at the point of rage. "Dammit, Grayson, I never gave you any authority to bring that Ruskie swine in on this."

"I didn't! He just showed up. I don't know whether he was working rogue with Stringer or what. All I know is she said they were both dead and she was using Stringer's cell phone to back it up. She also asked me if I wanted her to call me on Polnich's cell phone."

There was no response from Carey. After a long pause, Grayson said, "Hello?"

"Yes, I'm here—where do you think I am? I was thinking, you idiot! What about McKenzie? Tell me that at least *he* is dead."

"That's the rub … he's not, and it gets worse. She said Stringer told her that he was sent by us to kill her and McKenzie. On top of that, McKenzie has filled her in on the details of our Russian ventures."

Carey bellowed out, "Stinking son of—"

Grayson's hand jerked the phone away from his ear. The sound was so piercing that his eardrums vibrated in pain. But he knew better than to utter any sound at this moment. As he waited for Carey to resume the conversation, his body relaxed. After another long lull, Carey's voice broke the silence. This time it was calm, but direct. "What have you done to recommence the sanction?" He asked.

Knowing that this was coming, Grayson squirmed in his chair. He was aware that his real problem was about to begin. "Well, nothing yet, but I've been working on a plan."

"Working on a plan? Well that's perfect, isn't it? When did you get that call and where are the 'Bobbsey Twins?'"

"I got the call yesterday afternoon after work—I was running in Fort Marcy Park. And no, I don't know where they are."

"You got that call yesterday afternoon and you've squandered thirteen precious hours to inform me?" Carey seemed to reach the end of his rope. Like an orchestra playing a classic concerto moving to a clash of symbols, with each sentence his voice exploded louder and louder. "We could have traced the cell phone within minutes! We could've had two men there within hours! They would already be dead and buried! And all you can tell me is you've been *trying to work out a plan*!" With his voice gone hoarse, Carey began again in a lower tone. "I'm done with you Grayson. You've been a life-sucking millstone around my neck since I took you in. Get new black ops onto this mess and get them now!"

Grayson stood with his mouth open. After a short pause, he tried to respond, but the phone connection was already dead. With shaking hands he dialed his office and took a breath to steady his voice. "Mrs. Franks, clear any appointments that I may have today. I'm a bit under the weather and I'll be working from home today." When he rang off, he made another Bloody Mary and left the bottle out for the next several rounds.

***

Carey had been in his BMW on the way to Langley when Grayson had called in, and he had pulled out of traffic into an open parking space. The phone call had infuriated him and he felt spent. He wondered how a twit like Grayson could have ever been accepted into The Agency in the first place … and to rise up and become a department head? It was beyond his imagination, yet confirmed his belief that The Agency was on a bumpy road to becoming irrelevant. The self-examination of him choosing this idiot to become his accomplice set in. "What in the hell was I thinking?" He muttered. "I guess it doesn't say much about me either."

But he had to refocus. He had to wrestle with the specifics of what to do and in what order. It was obvious that Grayson was losing it—he was cracking under the stress. If I don't get a firm hold on the situation, and damn quick, this whole fiasco is going to blow up in my face, he thought. He'll be getting former black ops on Weston and McKenzie … but I need to get some of my own on him. There's no other way. I'm not going down the stinking toilet because of that spineless maggot. He's a weak-kneed crybaby, but this time he's gone too far. I'll have to get the names of his black ops before I take him out, however. I'll give him about two hours lead time, and I'll do a follow-up call under the guise of getting the dope on the sanction. After he gives me the names, he'll have a "nasty little accident."

Tapping his fingers on the steering wheel, Carey frowned as he worked out the specifics on how to do it. I'll wait till he goes home tonight and has a few drinks, he thought. I'll call him and ream his prissy ass something fierce … that'll push him to have a few more drinks. Then we'll go in and over the balcony he goes. Will it be an accident? … Suicide? Who gives a damn? He'll have been so loaded anything could have happened. I'll get the Hadley brothers. They're local, quick, and won't charge but a hundred thou'—money well spent.

Not a bad deal. I won't have to listen to that pantywaist anymore and my retirement portfolio will double. With a smile that would make a Cheshire cat proud, Carey mused, damn good thing those accounts are in both our names with one signature needed to withdraw.

CHAPTER 52

YURI DOLGORUKI

CAPTAIN ILLANOV LOOKED INTO THE INFIRMARY AND SAW the ship's doctor bent over his compact desk. He slapped his open hand twice on the frame of the opening to announce his presence. The doctor looked up and rose to his feet. It wasn't to attention, but more of a casual sign of respect. "Captain ...?"

"While you are up, Doctor, I would appreciate it if you check your supply of atropine and give me a quick inventory."

"Now, Captain ...? And is there a reason for your interest?"

Illanov chafed at the doctor's response. "Let's say I have a small curiosity ... no reason given and no reason needed. Doctor ...?"

The doctor's face contorted to an odd look. Illanov hoped it was one of piqued interest, not nervousness. "Yes, Captain ... you do know that whatever we have will be in self-injectors?" Illanov acknowledged with a nod of his head. The doctor turned and went into the pharmacy section.

Illanov heard the opening and closing of several cabinet doors. Within minutes, the doctor returned with a quizzical look on his face. "I do not understand, Captain, there must be some sort of mistake. The atropine seems to be misplaced. I took a full inventory on all the medical supplies before we shipped out, and I do have it logged in. But for some reason, the whole supply is not where it is supposed to be. I ... I don't know what to say. It is missing!"

Illanov stood, frozen. The reality of the situation had alarmed him, but he was not surprised. In his heart, he had already suspected what he had just heard from the doctor, but even that had not prepared him for the bald truth. His hopes sank. "Doctor, is there any other place that this supply could have been ... let's say, misplaced?"

"No, Captain. I remember organizing all of the medicine myself and I do it by the book. No one else is allowed to organize my pharmacy."

Andrei Illanov felt a bead of sweat curl down his left temple. He feigned scratching his ear, removing the evidence of his concern. His mind was in overdrive, sorting his remaining options. Was the doctor in on the plot? Or was the atropine stolen without his knowledge? He wasn't sure, but decided that he hadn't had enough time to read the doctor's face. He extended his chin upward and regained his command composure. "Doctor, I want you to initiate an immediate search for the atropine. If you logged it in, and I have no doubt that you did, then it was stolen by someone on this boat, and it will be on board. I want it found! There is only one other crewman that I want involved. I want Feodor Strivnych to conduct the actual search of the men's bunk areas, but I want you present to tell anyone who asks that it is under my direct orders. By 1800 hours, I want the report of your findings delivered to me in person in my quarters. It is imperative that only you, Strivnych, and myself know of this! Do you understand?"

The doctor responded with a sharp salute, saying, "Yes, sir."

The captain made his way to Feodor's work station and slumped into Alex's chair. He clasped his hands between his knees and lowered his head in frustration. He paused before speaking, as if he were confessing his sins to a priest. "The atropine has already been stolen," he whispered.

"Captain, maybe if I were to rough the doctor up a bit … maybe he would talk?"

"No," said Illanov, "something tells me that he didn't know it was gone. I can't be positive, but I feel it. He may be an arrogant man, and anyone can be bought, but I don't think he is one of the conspirators—not him."

"Did you let him in on what we know?"

"No, Feodor. That may be an option, but not yet. I told the doctor that he was to conduct an immediate search of the ship. I also told him that you were to accompany him and would do the physical search. He is to report back to me at 1800 hours."

"But Captain, we could be running out of time and it's a big boat!"

Illanov rose and said, "I know, my friend. Do your best and we will reevaluate when the doctor finishes his report. Go ahead and get started. And Feodor, search the EO's quarters first—I will delay his watch for about thirty minutes."

***

Anton Kashnikov looked down at his watch. The captain was long overdue to stand him down from his watch. Rubbing his sore eyes, the EO was beginning to wilt under the tension of his mission. As the zero hour approached, his sleepless hours grew. He was desperate to take a much needed a break, but knew that was wishful thinking. He could handle the questions of either self-doubt or the validity of the mission, but two other questions returned over and over again: How long could he keep up the charade before Illanov might catch on? Moreover, had he already?

Kashnikov was startled when he felt the heavy hand of the captain on the back of his shoulder. The EO stiffened. Had he been reading my thoughts? "Captain!" He said with a look of deceitful embarrassment. Illanov recognized the flushed look of a traitor. This was the first moment that he was sure his EO was in on the plot and was, in fact, its ringleader. It was one small look, but Illanov read it and his heart sank in disappointment. "Mr. Kashnikov, you may step down after we reexamine our location."

"But Captain, nothing has changed since we last reviewed our position."

Illanov shot him a stare that would kill, and said, "Mr. Kashnikov ..."

The EO read the meaning of the glare and moved over to the large horizontal flat screen that replaced the table where maps and charts used to be displayed.

Captain Illanov was all about delay. He needed as much time as he could garner to give Feodor and the ship's doctor the time they needed.

As their location came up on the monitor, Kashnikov pressed a little further. "As you can see, Captain, we are still in the same location as we have been. It is just as I had—"

With a thunderous clap, Illanov slammed the flat of his palm onto the monitor. "Mr. Kashnikov! When I want to listen to your self-ingratiation, I will ask for it. Do I make myself clear?"

"Yes, Captain."

"The discussion I wanted to have was the route we would take to get to this position." Illanov pointed to a location halfway between the new Gimli Field and the existing Troll Fields. "I do not want to take a direct course to this point. I prefer to take a route that makes our behavior appear erratic. This way we can come up with some bogus reason for our actions. Perhaps we will make, say, three stops along the way holding for about an hour. During these periods we will submerge to random depths and rise up again before proceeding on. Our excuse can range from engine malfunction to testing of equipment … whatever our politicians would like to use. Plot me out a course before you retire. I'll be waiting."

Illanov calculated that a few unaccepted calculations should give Feodor and the doctor sufficient time to search his EO's compartment one last time.

CHAPTER 53

JULIE AND DEVON WAITED ABOUT TWENTY MINUTES UNTIL a car went through the gate of Grayson's condo complex. Before the gate closed, Julie swung the rental car around and zipped it through unscathed. She turned to the south end of the complex while Devon concentrated on any shadows that might be watching. She caught an address and passed to the next building around the corner.

Continuing the conversation that had been interrupted by the opening of the gate, Julie said, "Devon, we've been through this a dozen times. We can run and try to hide for the rest of our lives or we can go to the one person at The Agency I can turn to. I know Mike Connors, and I believe I can trust him with our lives. If I'm wrong and he rats us out, it's over. I can't live the other way. I'm a woman and I want us to have children … and I want them to have a free life. I love you, and we'll get through this together. You've got to learn to trust again, and that means trusting me."

While Julie talked, Devon stared ahead. When she finished, he looked up and over to her. With a twinkle in his eye, he said, "I don't remember asking for your hand in marriage."

"Yes, you did—but I was smart enough to hear the unspoken words." It was her turn to smile back and she said, "By the way, I accept."

Devon feigned a defeated stare and replied, "Was it a tender proposal?"

"Let's say it was as good as I deserve."

Devon grabbed the door handle and opened the passenger door with his right hand. With his left, he squeezed her cheek. "C'mon fiancé, let's get on with your plan."

His body froze as Julie's hand shot up and grabbed his wrist. "Look! Who are those two men entering his building?"

Devon reached into the glove box and pulled out his Glock.

As he exited the car, she whispered, "Wait, I'm going with you."

He knew better than to waste his time arguing with her. He reached back into the glove box and pulled out Stringer's Glock and handed it to Julie. "Hurry up—we may not have enough time." Devon checked the clip and butt-shoved it into the Glock. He screwed his silencer on the gun and pulled the top slide back. As she watched him slide the gun into the outer pocket of his jacket, Julie followed his lead and did the same.

Running low, they made their way to the parking structure below the condo. Devon pulled up, whispering in Julie's ear, "He's on the fourth floor right above us. We've got to take the stairs—stay close behind me. C'mon!"

Reaching the fourth floor, Devon eased the stairwell door open. Grayson's unit was one over from the staircase, just past the elevator. He pulled out his Glock and began his ingrained, gun-in-hand duckwalk to Grayson's door. He nodded to Julie to follow suit. Placing his fingertips on the handle, he turned it to the left. He couldn't believe his luck—the deadbolt was left unlocked. He motioned Julie to put her back to the wall right of the door. With the gun barrel over his lips, he signaled silence, and starting with his index finger, motioned the starting count of three. When his middle finger raised itself up, he grabbed the handle and swung the door open.

He saw two men wrestling Grayson over toward the balcony railing. One man had Grayson's head locked under his armpit with his spare hand over his mouth. The other man had his arms around Grayson's waist and upper thighs. Devon saw that Grayson was horizontal and limp, as if he had been knocked out. When they began to raise his body higher to clear the rail, Devon squeezed off two shots in succession. The first bullet lodged into one man's neck; the second shot exploded into the side of the other man's skull. Grayson's lifeless body dropped to the balcony side of the railing, landing atop his assailants' crumpled bodies.

Julie and Devon pulled Grayson off the assassins' blood-soaked bodies. Devon reached down to the man who had been shot in the neck. He was still alive, but barely. Devon slapped the man's face to get his attention. Placing the silencer next to his temple, Devon growled with a sneer, "Who sent you?"

The dying man opened his mouth and with blood oozing through his teeth, smiled, and whispered, "… Carey." His head sank to the left and he breathed his last.

Devon searched the bodies of the dead men, pulling one phone out of their collective pockets. He slid it into his own pocket and dragged Grayson to the bedroom, where, with the help of Julie, they hoisted him up onto the bed. She went into the bathroom and returned with wet towels. Devon stood rigid over the comatose-like body, gun in hand.

After wiping the attackers' blood from Grayson's face and neck, Julie examined his clothes for evidence of any bullet wounds. There were none. "He's passed out, but there doesn't appear to be any sign of trauma."

Looking around and into the living room, Devon spotted the empty booze bottle. He bent over and lowered his nose to Grayson's mouth. The rank stench of bourbon was enough to make him gag. "It's because he drank himself into a stupor before those two goons came in," Devon said. Looking back down at the disheveled mass on the bed, he continued with a sneer of disgust. "This guy is a real piece of work."

"I'll go make coffee," she said.

Devon handed her the gun and replied, "Hold on a second." He went into the living room and returned with the ice bucket that was half filled with water. He threw the entire amount of water on Grayson's face.

Grayson jolted upwards and rested his upper torso on one elbow. He shook the water off his face and ran his hair backward over his head, removing as much water as he could. Blinking three or four times, Devon came into view. He gasped and growled, "It's you—you turncoat puke."

Julie handed the Glock over to Devon and demurred, "You idiot, you owe your life to this 'turncoat.' Your would-be killers had your drunken body hoisted over the railing when this 'puke' shot the two of them. Care to walk over to the balcony to verify?"

"No," was all he could whimper.

"… Guess you and Carey must be tighter than you thought. Or is there someone else at Langley that loves you more?" She asked.

Grayson's face showed that his house of cards had just collapsed around him. He looked down at the drenched bed and back up at Julie. "What do we do?"

Julie opened her mouth to talk, but Devon beat her to it. "You're going to shut your stinking mouth and listen to every single thing we tell you. And if I feel even one twinge that you're not cooperating, I won't give you a second thought before I put a bullet between your eyes faster than you can blink. Nod if you understand."

Grayson nodded twice, to be sure.

"All right, Julie, make the coffee … and make it so a spoon stands straight up." Devon's Glock rose until it pointed at Grayson's forehead. For emphasis, he wiggled the barrel of the gun and feigned sighting in to between the quivering man's eyes. He looked over to Julie's backside and said, "I don't want 'Mr. Potato Head' here to have to have a third eye because he didn't understand what we're going to tell him to do."

When Grayson finished his second cup of coffee, Julie cleared the cups, and Devon yanked him into the bathroom to relieve himself. At first Grayson complained that he couldn't urinate while someone watched. When Devon reached out and pressed the silencer of his Glock on his ear, a steady stream appeared.

Once back in the dining area, Devon motioned for Grayson to sit at the table. Julie placed his cell phone in front of him and said, "First things first. Call my boss at The Agency, Mike Connors, and get him over here. I don't care what excuse you use, get him over here."

When Grayson rang off and set the phone down on the table, he looked up at Julie and stated, "He said he would drop what he was doing and come over. He can be here in about thirty minutes."

Grayson shifted his weight and with the back of his hand wiped the sweat ball that hung on his nose. "But if Carey ordered this up, he'll be looking for confirmation of the sanction. If he doesn't get his answer right away, he'll send someone over to verify—maybe even come himself."

"Exactly," replied Devon. "There's nothing like having your boss and a few friends over for some wine and cheese." He shot a clever smile over to Julie, thinking that he was keeping pace with her barbed tongue.

Her look back said, don't even think about it.

CHAPTER 54

YURI DOLGORUKI

ANTON KASHNIKOV WALKED AWAY FROM THE CONNING tower with a conscience that was void of all feeling. The thought of what he was about to set in motion gave him no reason to pause, and the fact that his shipmates were about to die en masse caused no feelings of remorse within him. His head told him the amount of money was too vast to turn down. There was graft everywhere you turned in Mother Russia—politicians, labor unions, businessmen, and men in all branches of the military. He kept salving his conscience by reminding himself that even members of his own admiralty were cashing in … but were they committing the kind of crime that he was about to unleash? Of course they were—they were the ones who recruited him. In any case, did it matter? It's just a count, he told himself—a numbers game. People die all the time—hell, he was in a business that taught him to kill. Any one missile that this submarine fired would kill more people than what was being asked here. Besides, he was committed to doing this—there was no going back. But, this captain had gotten under his skin. He was old school—he still loved his country.

Sucking it in, he ventured into the radio compartment and said to the radioman, "This message is to be sent to Admiral Vedeyev on this code. It is to be destroyed. You will mention this to no one. Proceed." The message read: Danica 0900

***

Admiral Popov was ecstatic. He jumped up from his chair, raised both arms in the air, and danced a working man's version of a traditional Russian dance. The millions of dollars that would soon be flowing his way boggled his mind. "We are about to cross the finish line and we will be as rich as Arab potentates," he half sung to a broken melody. "After all this time, Vedeyev, it is going to happen." He clenched one fist and smacked it into the other, looked up at Vedeyev and gave a wide smile of satisfaction. Opening the large drawer of his desk, he pulled out two shot glasses and an open bottle of Stoli. He filled the glasses and said, "We are almost there, my friend ... almost there. Soon we will be living like two Sultans in our own seaside villas in Spain. And believe me, our harem will be stocked with many whores. They will flow in and out like the ocean breezes." He raised his shot glass and toasted, "To Morning Star!"

Vedeyev acknowledged his toast, and snickered in response, "To many whores *and* a stockpile of that American Viagra!"

When the shots were downed, Popov gathered the glasses from his desk, threw them back into the open drawer, and placed the vodka bottle next to them. Closing the drawer, he sat back in his chair, and with a sinister look, he said, "Now, Mikhail, let us make sure we have covered ourselves with Illanov's EO. When the submarine is boarded by the rescue team, we must be certain that he is dead ... beyond any shadow of doubt."

"But we have paid the Chechen dog to kill him after the missiles have been fired. He has already made a film claiming this act in the name of al-Qaeda. It is retribution for all the war crimes committed by Russia in Chechnya and NATO's role in Afghanistan. That tape is already on board. He *wants* to die a martyr, and it will be found on his body by the rescue team. There is nothing more that we can do but assume that everything works as planned."

Popov's stare became more intense as he gnashed his teeth. "That is why I am an admiral and you are a vice-admiral. I leave nothing to chance. We must pay someone, someone that we can trust, to go in first on the rescue team. We will command that no one can enter until our man gives the all clear signal. He will enter with a hazmat suit to make sure there is no poison left. If Kashnikov is still alive, he can kill him on the spot."

"But can we trust *that* man to keep his silence?"

"No. Of course not," Popov said with a twinkle in his eye. "But *you* can kill him when you pay him."

Vedeyev winced in uneasiness. "No. Killing a man outside of combat is not what I am comfortable with."

"What is the matter with you? We are killing everyone on that boat! Tell me what the difference is."

"The difference is that the gun will be in *my* hand!"

Popov cracked a twisted smiled and said, "Good, have him come to me for final payment. The pleasure of killing him will belong to me. But ...!" He slapped his hand on his desk and pointed his index finger at Vedeyev. "It will cost you two whores—two whores and one box of Viagra, my timid little friend."

CHAPTER 55

YURI DOLGORUKI

WITH THE DOCTOR WATCHING THE HALL PASSAGE, FEODOR left no stone unturned in the EO's compartment. His frustration was evident in his voice when he said, "We must go—there is nothing here." Feodor was sick that he had again come up empty-handed. Alex's encounter with the EO again played over in his mind and gave him a burning conviction that Kashnikov was front and center in the plot, whatever it was, and was either responsible for Alex's death, or had murdered him himself. He loathed the man and wanted to strangle him with his bare hands.

As they walked down the hallway, the EO came into view. Passing became awkward. Feodor lowered his head and eyes and gave a scrunched salute, while the doctor did nothing more than acknowledged the exec's presence.

***

Kashnikov stopped and looked back at the receding pair. Why were they so close to his sleeping quarters and what were they up to?

Entering his room, he gave a thorough scan to every detail. His footlocker looked the same way he had left it—his Makarov sidearm was still in his desk drawer—nothing appeared amiss. He looked back over his shoulder to his closed door and strained to hear any sound. Comfortable that no one was near, he raised his foot up onto his bed and pulled his pant leg upward. The covered syringe of atropine was intact and still secured to his ankle. He gave it a pat and pulled the pant leg back down, but his tension was not eased. The same question came back to nag him: Why had he passed the doctor and that seaman so close to his quarters?

***

The ship's doctor suggested they go to the galley for their next search.

Feodor wanted to go to the torpedo section and confront the Chechen, but since the galley was on the way, he acquiesced to the doctor's suggestion. The galley was a hub of perpetual activity. The feeding of one hundred and thirty men with differing shifts meant round-the-clock activity.

As Feodor busied himself with the investigation of every cabinet and every possible hiding place, the doctor took care of the grousing crew that was insulted by the intrusion into their pandemonium. After a complete search, there were no more places to look. Feodor felt helpless. He knew that a two-man search of a submarine the size of the Yuri Dolgoruki would take the better part of a week, and, if word got to the traitors, they could shift the antidote to a spot they had already searched. And what of the VX gas … where was *it* hidden?

Feodor didn't think like an aristocrat, he was raised a man of the wharfs. If I had my way, he thought, I would act on instinct alone and put my knife under that EO's throat, and watch the little coward squirm for his life. It would be so easy—me and the captain alone in the EO's room. Oh, he'd talk alright … sing like a canary, he would. It's alright, Captain, I'll continue your little charade. But I'm telling you, time is running short, and when we have no time left. You will have no choice but to listen to ol' Feodor. Then, I'll get you the answers you need, and real quick. You don't seem to understand, Captain, when it comes time to kill a snake—you start by cutting off the head.

CHAPTER 56

FAIRFAX, VIRGINIA

RIDING THE ELEVATOR TO THE CONDO'S FOURTH FLOOR, Mike Connors was still grousing over the call that brought him over on short notice. Unlike many of the other department heads, Mike had tried to maintain some semblance of a decent family life. He had avoided the promotions that would have dragged him into the "darker" side of the CIA. Even he had a general disdain for "the spooks" in The Agency … they disgusted and frightened him. Having a strong set of moral values, this was his way of contributing to his country yet not having to cross any ethical lines, and falling into a morass that blurred one's vision. He liked the analytical side of the business, and was content to ride out a normal bureaucratic career, retire with a nice pension, and never have to "get his hands dirty," so to speak. The black-ops people wore black hats. The people in his division wore white. In his mind it was all clear.

But, here he was, riding an elevator to meet one of the "black hat" people, Tom Grayson. Worse, the meeting was at the man's residence … after hours! The arrogant prig got under his skin, and he avoided contact with him whenever possible, even though Grayson was his boss. The call to his wife, Molly, hadn't gone well. She was angry and reminded him that his twin boys, Tracy and Danny, were in a game at their high school in Fairfax. The game started at seven and—

The ding of the elevator announcing the fourth floor broke his grousing. As he prepared to knock, he reminded himself that Grayson had ordered him to come. When the door opened, Connors was taken aback. A man with a long scar on the side of his face stood before him. He paused and studied the man's face, but couldn't connect the dots. "I … I've seen you somewhere before," Mike said.

From somewhere inside in the condo, Julie Weston's voice rang out. "Mr. Connors, thank you for coming. Please, come in and don't be shocked, everything's okay."

The man with the scar retreated, but not enough to make it easy for Connors to enter without sidestepping him. When he did, he was startled again. He saw Julie with a gun in her hand, pointed at Tom Grayson. Taking one step backward, he blurted out, "Julie? What the hell …?"

"Mr. Connors, please don't be alarmed. Everything is under control … please, you must believe me." Her gun never left the direction of Grayson. With a broad sweep of her left arm she motioned toward the man with the scar. "Mr. Connors, this is Devon McKenzie. You may remember him as an operative named 'Trojan Horse,' but I can assure you, he is on our side—unlike this dirt-bag sitting over here." The direction of her hand and arm returned to point to Grayson.

Connors' eyes looked back at the scarred man. He was still standing near the door, but there was something different. He had a silenced Glock pistol in his hand. It may have been pointed down at the floor, but it was still in his hand. Connors didn't like the menacing picture and his anxiety rose. He nodded acknowledgement to McKenzie and turned his attention back to Grayson without a word spoken. This man, his boss, appeared to be a pathetic worm, sitting with an expression of guilt written all over his face. Even a novice could tell that he had run afoul of something—and it had to be serious enough that a mild-mannered analyst like Julie Weston would be holding him at gunpoint.

Julie nodded at Devon to switch places with her. She lowered her gun, walked over to Mike Connors, and gave him a small hug. "You know me, Mr. Connors. I have never lied to you nor done anything that was not in the best interest of The Agency. This man is a traitor to his country. He and his partner, Dennis Carey, have been selling Russian arms to mid-east terrorists, and siphoning off the money to their own bank accounts in Switzerland. To keep their dirty little secret, they had Tim Daniels killed—"

Connors cut her off. "Did you say Tim Daniels? I thought he died in some sort of drug deal that went bad."

"No! Devon had given Tim proof of what they were doing, so Grayson and Carey had him killed, and made it look like a drug killing. They had a Russian contract killer named Polnich try to kill Devon and his wife. Devon survived, but his wife didn't. He's been hiding in Alaska ever since."

"But—"

"Please, wait." This time, Julie cut him off. "He was in hiding until I crashed my plane near his cabin and he saved my life. When I called Grayson to tell him that I had found the agent code named 'Trojan Horse,' he sent out a black-ops agent named Stringer to kill us both. But before he was killed by Devon, he confessed that Grayson had ordered the killing of Tim, and had sanctioned a contract on the two of us."

"But why didn't you call *me* with that information—for God's sake, Julie, I'm your immediate supervisor?"

"I wish to God that I had … I made a mistake. You see, Tim was my fiancé, and he was the one who first asked me to try and pull up information on Trojan Horse. He worked for Grayson and I knew our department was under his. I assumed Grayson would be the one to get the information to. When Tim was killed, you accepted the police report, and that killed me. Maybe it was because I was in the hospital in Anchorage … the drugs, I don't know. I wasn't thinking straight—I am so sorry."

"But what will Carey do? What if he finds out that you have his alleged partner being held at gunpoint?" Asked Connors.

"In the first place, there is no 'alleged' nonsense here. We've tried to think it through, and haven't got all that worked out. But you need to come over here. There's a mess that I haven't told you about, and you need to see it for yourself."

Julie grabbed Connors by the arm and led him to the balcony doors. She drew the curtains back and opened the patio door, exposing the two dead bodies.

"…My God, Julie! What in the hell has gone on here? Who are they?"

"*They* are a present from Carey to Grayson. Devon shot them both when they had Grayson's drunken body hoisted in their arms and halfway over the rail. Two more seconds and he would have taken a four-story swan dive into those bushes."

"I … I don't know what to say," said Connors. "I don't know what to do. At this moment, I'm at a total loss." He loosened his tie and unbuttoned his collar. As he tried to collect his thoughts, his stare remained fixed on the dead bodies. His look of bewilderment changed to a look of fear as he whispered, "This could be bigger than all of us combined … this is deep, spook-world stuff. I guess I should consider myself lucky.

Maybe if you had called me first, I would have called Grayson and he might have had a contract put out on me … And what about my wife? … My kids? I don't need to tell you how dangerous this could get."

"Let's go back and talk to 'Good Neighbor Sam' in the other room. I'd like you to hear it for yourself."

"…About your friend in there. Could you tell him I'm on your side?"

"Yes, I will, Mr. Connors."

"We're not on the clock, Julie … just plain Mike will do."

A long hour passed, and Grayson confirmed everything Julie had told Connors. With the attempt on his life by Carey, Grayson admitted that he had come to the realization that at last it was over and there was no place to hide. All during the spilling of his guts, Devon noticed that his eyes never left the floor below his feet. With his head hung like a beaten dog, he looked up at Connors and pleaded, "Please, can I call my lawyer? I want to try and cut a deal with the Justice Department—they'll want Carey over me."

Connors looked over at Julie and said, "I would prefer to take this right to the top of the CIA. Are you willing to have me call Director Hatcher? I would prefer to keep this within The Agency for the moment and let *him* contact DOJ. You never know, there may be sensitive information they need to get first. I'm not sure—I'm looking for advice."

Devon looked at Julie. "I don't know, I've been hunted for so long, I think like a stalked animal wanting to run and find safe ground. But I don't like the idea—what if there are others above Carey in on it? What if Hatcher himself is involved?"

Julie stood up, went to the bar, and opened a bottle of water. She took a swig and rolled the cold plastic bottle across her forehead. "We can arrange to have the evidence mailed to DOJ if something should happen to any one of us, so I'm not worried that this *won't* blow up in Grayson's face. I'm not sure that we can protect ourselves from getting killed. Devon, I trust Mike will do the right thing. If he wants to take this to Hatcher, I guess I'm alright with it."

Devon looked down and used his gun to point at Grayson. "I'm still worried about Carey. What happens when the snake comes to eat the rat?"

The phone from one of the killers began vibrating in Devon's pocket. He pulled it out and checked the caller ID. He looked over and the gaze of all three was fixed on him. He grimaced and said, "By the way, that may not be too long." He turned the phone to face the three. "… It's Carey!"

Mike Connors spoke. "Muffle your voice by holding the phone away from you. Answer it with hello. When he asks if Grayson is terminated, say yes, and click off—it'll buy us some time."

When Devon hung up, he looked at Julie and said, "I can't say for sure, but I think he bought it." Looking over at Connors, he said, "I hope Julie and you are right. Now it's your turn. Get hold of Hatcher—ball's in your court."

CHAPTER 57

SVEN GUNDERSEN WAS RELIEVED TO BE BACK BEHIND THE controls of his P-3C Orion surveillance aircraft. The hunter was again doing what he needed to do—stalk his prey. Because of the gale in the North Sea, he had two days of downtime and that had him crawling the walls. Fearing that he would lose the Russian sub, Yuri Dolgoruki, Sven pressed hard with command to be the first plane up.

After about an hour, his concentration was running at full tilt. He hadn't located his prey and his tension was mounting with each minute that passed. When one of his three sensor operators whistled through his mike, Sven jumped out of his skin.

"Gotcha, you Ruskie puke!" The radar man shouted.

Sven was startled and he wanted to holler back at the tech, but he was so relieved to make contact again that he let the boisterous intrusion pass. Besides, he wanted his crew hungry. In a calm, yet stern voice, he said, "What's the routing pattern, Max?" Hoping his delivery would sink into the tech's youthful head.

"There's some kind of weird stuff going on down there, sir … and it's nothing that we've evidenced before. It's some kind of a strange zigzag pattern with stops and starts thrown in. Also their depth level changes with each stop. If I had to guess, it appears that they're conducting some sort of test. But I'm grasping at straws."

"Usually I'm comfortable with your hunches, Max, but we'll let MIU make that kind of call. We have to assume their intentions are sinister at best. Let's not forget that they're Russians we're dealing with. They're not the kind of people we want to invite over for a nice evening of wine and cheese. Let's keep the chatter down and stay focused and on course."

"Roger to that, sir."

***

Leaning back in a stiff chair in the debriefing room, the officer from MIU had just finished his last question with Sven. Squaring his chair to four legs, he again opened his notebook and reviewed the streaming data from the day's flight. Sven was anxious for him to finish his review so he could hear the man's opinion and venture his own.

"This is odd," was all the man from MIU muttered. He sat with a pensive stare at the data and drum rolled his fingers on the desk beside his notebook.

Sven had reached the extent of his patience and with a hint of sarcasm queried, "And your conclusion is …?"

"My conclusion is that I'm glad I'm not this Russian captain. I don't think I'd want to be trapped in his head. None of this makes any sense at all. I mean, you go out of your way to provoke both the military and political bodies of Norway—and hence, NATO. It sets off a global juggernaut of ugly consequences." He stopped and looked up at Sven. "And they are doing all of this for what … theatrics … a power display … a silly war game played by one? It defies all logic."

"I'm not with you on this one," Sven ventured. "The risks of major political fallout are too big. I think all this zigzagging and starting and stopping is nothing more than a cover. They think it gives them a variety of excuses for whatever it is that they are planning." Sven frowned while gathering his thoughts. He raised his hand and shook it by the side of his head for emphasis. "But … there is something unsettling about this one. It doesn't feel right. If they wanted to demonstrate a show of power, they could have done that with a quick sail-by. You know, sort of a 'thumb your nose,' or the universal middle finger in the air. But! And here's the key: The sail-by would nonetheless be quick. They would blow right by us and leave us in their wake. Norway bitches to the UN and the rest of the world pretends they give a damn."

The MIU officer scratched the back of his head and said, "Let's say you're right and they *are* up to something. The question still is: What would it be?"

"I'm not sure, but you can believe it has something to do with both of our gas fields," said Sven. "Why park a nuclear sub right between the two? They could take them out from anywhere. No, this is an 'in your face' statement that is meant for worldwide exposure. Could it be someone on that boat is about to go rogue?"

"Okay, this one's going upstairs on priority alert, then on to NATO." The MIU officer looked back at Sven as he went through the door. "About to go *rogue* …?"

Sven grimaced, tilted his head to the left, and raised both palms up in mock disbelief. "Got anything better?"

CHAPTER 58

DENNIS CAREY DIDN'T WANT TO MAKE HIS NEXT CALL from his house. He decided instead to go back to his office. As the CIA was a round-the-clock complex that worked 24/7, there would be nothing out of place for him to be there at ten o'clock at night.

He had already reviewed his plan for the umpteenth time and was certain there were no holes in it. In his mind, any chance that the Hadley brothers had left a trail at Grayson's condo was slim to none. He'd used them many times before and they had never screwed up. They were required to do this for their outrageous fee and they knew the drill. The "accidental death" had to show as that—nothing more. He may have had a slight twinge of insecurity, but he dismissed it. He reminded himself that they did say it was done and besides, no one survives a four-story fall. In the morning, he would call Grayson's secretary, Mrs. Franks, pretending to be looking for her boss. Feigning an urgent meeting, he would call every ten minutes. When she failed to reach him, he would instruct her to call Fairfax County Police and have them go over to his condo to check it out. It would be an open and shut case—another booze-head trips on his balcony and bites the dust. He dialed Hadley's secure cell phone one more time, he wanted the sordid details.

***

Ernest Hatcher was making notes for the next morning's staff meeting at the CIA when Mike Connors' call came in on his secure line. He grimaced when he looked up at the Regulator Clock on his den wall. Hoping to get to bed early for a change, his first reaction was annoyance at being disturbed. That feeling faded as Connors laid bare the details of his urgent call. Hatcher was stunned. He felt like he had been hit over his head with a baseball bat. "Dang it," he whispered away from the phone mike to himself. The last thing he needed at an agency he had worked long, hard hours to clean up was two of his supposed "trusted" department heads committing traitorous acts. The acid in his stomach started to burn. He knew heads were going to roll and this could become a black eye that would take him down and ruin his career. He slid his desk drawer open and pulled out the anti-acid pills.

"All right, Connors, I want to thank you for coming to me first. My first reaction is to keep everyone alive and safe. Can you handle your family's safety, or do you need my help with a safe house for them?"

"For the moment, I don't think so. Grayson, the two agents, and you are the people that know I'm involved. I believe my family will be safe, but I would appreciate continuous surveillance of them."

"You've got it. Next, McKenzie and Weston need to go to a safe house … the one near Manassas. That safe house also has a holding room in the basement. We'll use that for Grayson. I'll have a special agent named Koehler contact you and make immediate arrangements. But I want you to stay at the condo until he arrives and keep everything secure. As top priority, I want this to be handled by the book. First person I'm going to call is the president's Chief of Staff, Richards—I'll let him brief the president. Then, Attorney General Baylor—I'll have him call FBI Director Kearns. Bottom line is their people should all arrive at about the same time. Listen, I'm going to invoke national security to keep the circle as small as I can, so I want you to say as little as possible. If Carey is in on this, I need to know if their cancer has gone further. If anybody has questions, tell them they're to call me. Koehler will get the four of you out of there without on-site harassment from the Feds. I'll arrange surveillance on Carey within minutes. Is there anything I've missed?"

"No sir. We'll await Special Agent Koehler's arrival."

***

Presidential Chief of Staff Neil Richards was still in his office at the White House when Hatcher's call came in. He had just finished a call with NSA Director LaSpesa and was about to call Hatcher. Unlike the CIA director, Richards didn't mind a call coming in at any time of night. A self-professed workaholic, Richards' ego was well stroked being the gateway to POTUS. He also understood that the downside meant his being available 24/7. Having been married three times and divorced the same number, he had no illusions about ever having a stable home life.

Hell, the truth was, he didn't want a home life that might interfere with his own limelight.

"I'm glad you called, Ernie," Richards said, sitting up straight in his chair and taking control of the conversation. He cleared his throat to deepen his voice and said, "I was about to call you regarding a meeting at 11:00 tomorrow morning in the Situation Room. NATO's got its shorts in a wad over a Russian sub sitting in Norway's gas fields off their North Sea coast. Bring whatever you've got on a sub called … uh, wait a second … yeah, that's it—the Yuri Dolgoruki. And of course, any other intel you've got on all this Russian activity that's been going on in the North Sea."

Hatcher paused, an obvious three seconds went by, and he stammered in. "Neil … yes, I'll be at that meeting, and with all the intel, but I've got a major problem … one of my directors has been killed. His death may have been ordered up by his superior—here at The Agency." He waited for Richards' response. Silence was all he heard.

Neil Richards *was* silent, but it wasn't out of incredulity or irritation. This news was big and he also knew that within a short period of time, it would be known by everyone, including the president. It wasn't the fact that there was loss of life or that reputations would be ruined, to him that was how it was in the piranha-filled waters of Washington. He was calculating how this chain of events might increase his stature within the president's inner sanctum when he would be the first to hand him the information. A warm feeling of occasion crept over him. Every crisis, large or small, was an opportunity to skewer every trusted aide but himself, always with a bent for brokering the primacy of his counsel. He collected his thoughts and said, "Okay, Ernie, get yourself prepared for the eleven o'clock and I'll call you back as soon as I make contact with the president. But for the moment, let's keep this tight between us and don't call Baylor or Kearns until I've gotten back with you. Oh, and by the way, have all your intel to the Situation Room by ten—the usual number of copies."

"Understood," said Hatcher as he rang off.

CHAPTER 59

YURI DOLGORUKI

WASTING MORE TIME THAN FEODOR WAS WILLING TO allow, the incessant nit-picking of the ship's doctor had Feodor about ready to reach his breaking point. "We don't have enough time for you to close every door of every cabinet we search. I don't care that everything we disturb is put back in its proper place! We don't know when or where these crazies are going to release their horror on us, so if you want to spend your time walking around like a cleaning lady, you'll have to do it alone." With that, Feodor turned on his heels and headed for the torpedo man's quarters. He knew the crewman would be coming off duty in ten minutes.

The doctor straightened up the small boxes that were toward the front of the storage locker and shut the door. He appeared irritated as he watched as Feodor speed down the narrow passageway. He began chasing after the computer man.

When the doctor arrived at the torpedo man's quarters, Feodor threw a cassette case at him. The doctor's reflexes were quick and he caught it with one hand. Feodor whispered that it looked like it was going to be some sort of demand or threat tape. As the doctor turned it over to view its contents, he read the handwritten sticker on its side: Send out 0900 hours.

Feodor next found the air duct system blueprint. He unfolded the large drawing and saw two spots that were marked with an "X." He knew it showed the two locations for the nerve gas to be placed. In one swift motion, he grabbed the drawing, crumpling its center as he turned to the doctor and said, "Let's go! We've got to alert the captain."

Ducking to go through the passage door, Feodor stopped. He turned and faced the startled doctor. "Doctor, this atropine that we haven't found ... what does it do?"

The doctor responded in a surprised tone, "Well, it can be administered by injection in the thigh or arm, but that is, say an hour or so before exposure. It can still be injected within seconds of a person coming into contact with VX gas, but the person who takes it will need to inject the atropine into his heart. In any case, he will still suffer much of the effects of the gas and pass out into a semi-comatose state. The difference is he will not die. Depending on how much gas is ingested, a short time later, he will again gain consciousness. He will be nauseous and will vomit, but he will be alive."

Feodor stood and frowned, as if contemplating a decision. He turned and began running down the passageway. He made sure that the doctor never saw the atropine self-injection syringe that he had slipped into his pocket before the doctor had caught up to him in the torpedo man's compartment.

CHAPTER 60

DIRECTOR OF NATIONAL INTELLIGENCE JIM LASPESA opened the eight o'clock meeting by walking in the door and taking his seat at the center of the conference table. This was a working meeting called to discuss the Russian submarine, Yuri Dolgoruki. NATO's reaction was quick to move the latest intelligence information forward to all member nations. NSA was well aware that the Defense Department was conducting its own meeting as were CIA and the Departments of Homeland Security and State.

In spite of the former president's mandate to smooth the flow of intel under the banner of Homeland Security, bureaucratic "turf wars" were still a fact of life in Washington and the subsequent paralysis that ran through the body politic was hard to exorcise. Sharing occurred, but after each department had first deciphered, then given its own take on any given situation. Security may have tightened up to a degree, but all agency heads had learned to accommodate the others while keeping their own intact. The major difference between pre-9/11 and post-9/11 intelligence was another, more massive layer of paper trails and people, all vying for supremacy in a barely functional, bloated bureaucracy.

Attempting to interpret the streaming data from Norway's P-3C submarine hunter aircraft was challenging at best. The readings of zigzagging patterns were hard to formulate into a definitive plan that confirmed sinister intentions by a submarine captain, let alone the navy he represented. But no one in the NSA meeting had any question of the gravity of the activity of the Yuri Dolgoruki. Like its Norwegian partner, MIH, those in the NSA were piecing together the reasons behind the Russian submarine's action. Once all the evasive "peripheral noise," the shifting actions meant to deceive the observer, were stripped away, the Dolgoruki's intentions were easier to comprehend. Believing that Russia would take the risk of such a high stakes poker game was hard to swallow by the NSA. What was not lost, however, was Sven Gundersen's hypothesis that the submarine meant to attack the gas platforms. This was the sticking point ... the five-hundred-pound gorilla in the room, and it couldn't be ignored.

But it was easier to gain consensus on the target than it was to find a reason why. When the CIA's intel on its Trojan Horse operation was brought up, the waters became even murkier and the meeting debased into a free-for-all of opinion and snide accusations.

CHAPTER 61

YURI DOLGORUKI

STANDING IN THE FORWARD TORPEDO AREA, RUSLAN Petrova raised his wrist and looked at his watch. The time was 0650. When he started his shift, the boat's executive officer had given him the signal that the time for action had arrived. Their watches were synchronized and the agreed upon time to release the two canisters of VX gas was to be at 0700 hours. Ruslan's tasks had been reduced to two: At 0650, he was to take the cap off his injection syringe, press it to his thigh, depress the top button, and count off ten seconds to allow the atropine to enter his system. The timing devices he had set to explode the VX canisters would take care of the rest. His second task would occur after he woke up. With the entire crew dead, save the executive officer, he was to rise, make his way to the radio room, and send out the video that he had prepared. The EO was to handle the firing of the missiles. Soon, the infidels of the West would know the fury of the sword of Allah.

Time crept the last hour of his shift and he spent the greater part of that time reminiscing ... his mother Issa weaving in and out of his memory like threads in a fine piece of lace. In spite of their abysmal poverty in Chechnya, she had been the one bright spot in his otherwise miserable existence. But within that bright spot was buried the perpetual nightmare that had shaped his twisted life. He could never remember that joy without the accompanying pain, and that pain was what lingered last. Ruslan recounted the scene of the Russian soldiers taking their turns savagely beating and raping his mother to death. Over and over, she screamed for him not to watch and not to come near her. He was just a child, but the shame of his inaction haunted him his whole life and defined his existence. If only he had been able to fight the drunken animals ... her face, bruised and bloodied, her eyes swollen shut. Tears streamed down his cheeks and he wiped them in case a crew member came near.

Ruslan knew that his Russian father had loved his mother, but that man was a colonel in the Russian Army and was stationed in St. Petersburg when the savagery occurred. His father came to get them, which was true, but he came too late! *He* should have saved her! Sure, his father took him to Russia and gave him a Russian name, but that was after her tortured death. Did the man not understand that he was born a Chechen and would never fit into a Russian life?

The retreats from the endless wars in Afghanistan and Chechnya were hard on the spirit of the Russian people. Like the quagmire the United States faced in Viet Nam, the conflict was never declared a war, nor was it ever explained to the populace as being vital to their interests. Worse, the losses of young men increased every year and seemed destined to go on forever.

As in all foreign wars, soldiers brought home children. But these children reminded others of their own losses. They were never accepted, and were hated and blamed for something of which they had no control. Ruslan's father Sergei had him placed in school after school, but his son's swarthy complexion betrayed his roots. The discrimination against him was relentless and he grew to loathe the term "darkie."

"I will never stop hating my father—even in Paradise I will curse him!" He whispered.

His rage peaked and began to ebb as he remembered the mosque that his father reluctantly allowed him to attend. Sergei had made a promise to Issa that although he could never renounce his Christian faith, he would allow her and their child to practice their Muslim faith so that their family could live as one when he brought them back to Russia. But he had lied. He broke his sacred promise and tried to raise Ruslan in his Orthodox Christian faith. For six years, Ruslan fought him in his faith, until Sergei relented and let his son attend the largest mosque in St. Petersburg.

***

From all external appearances, the Imam in St. Petersburg was a man of peace. But within the followers, there was a group, led by this same Imam, which contained the "true believers." They understood the real meaning of the tenets of the Holy Koran. Not the creed that the fools of the West quoted to substantiate their convoluted beliefs that Islam was a "religion of peace." No, these were the righteous tenets that took Islam to a higher calling ... a political system that would destroy the West and all other nonbelievers until the entire world was under the sword of Sharia Law.

In spite of the fact that hatred smoldered within the young man, the true believers were in no hurry to cultivate Ruslan's spirit and open his mind to these truths. He was still young and they would bring him along at a slower pace. When they knew that the time was right and his immersion was complete, they decided that a trip back to Chechnya was in order. There, another Imam and another band of cohorts would further purify him, making him ready for a virtuous cause—a cause that would give him an eternal place in Paradise. All they needed was Sergei's permission, and out of ignorance and perhaps a weariness of the constant tension between him and his rebellious son, he caved in and agreed to Ruslan's long visit to Chechnya.

***

In the quiet of the torpedo room, Ruslan's mind continued to drift and he no longer was gritting his teeth. His tears had dried and a slight smile broke on his face. He was in Chechnya, the land of his birth. He remembered the creed that was ingrained in every Chechen from birth: "Free and equal like wolves." He was the wolf that would never be tamed, of this he was certain.

The mosque in his village was small as compared to the mega structure in St. Petersburg, but it was Chechen, and in his mind that alone made it special and even more holy. His mind was filled with the glories of a Chechen jihad. He was told the story of how three hundred and thirty-four infidels were killed at an elementary school in Beslan, North Ossetia on September 1, 2004. The fact that one hundred and eighty-six of the slaughtered were children was never included in the narrative. No, the butchers were portrayed as martyrs that died in a holy war and were in Paradise with Allah. Their names and the glorious deeds of these wolves would be told for generations to come and would never be forgotten.

When his next level of indoctrination was nearing its completion, the Imam introduced him to Mohmad Kazbek. In and around his village, Kazbek was well respected by the Chechens as a man of deep Islamic faith. Surrounding Kazbek was a small army of men whose loyalty to him was unquestioned. He had a unique ability to get things done and this made him a man of great power and influence. For the villagers and the Imam, he was also a man of great benevolence, and for this, whispers of his corruption or of his being a warlord were ignored or at least never mentioned. The Russian mafia knew Kazbek well, but they called him "Kazbekov."

Ruslan was pleased that a wolf such as Mohmad Kazbek would embrace him. For the first time in his life, Ruslan felt as if he belonged. That the country of his birth needed him, and this gave him self-importance and a sense of mission.

Mohmad Kazbek made the connection as to what Ruslan's bond with St. Petersburg could do for him. When it was brought up that Ruslan's father was a colonel in the Russian Army, Kazbekov envisioned a golden river of rubles flowing his way. He convinced the Imam that Ruslan's true worth was that of a sleeper cell in St. Petersburg. Ruslan would go back, continue his life, and begin a career in the Russian military. Ruslan's chance to share in their glorious jihad had to wait until his full potential could be realized. Through Kazbekov, the Russian mafia would be patient, for they had other plans for Ruslan.

***

A clanking noise from down the hall jolted Ruslan from his long daydream. Raising his wrist again, he saw that the second hand was ticking down to two minutes to detonation. With his anger still intact, he straightened up, reached into the pocket of his dungarees, and pulled out the syringe of atropine. As so often occurred, his mother Issa's loving smile reentered his consciousness. Her presence warmed him and he longed to be with her. He felt her tender arms enfold around him and draw him tight to her breast. He weakened, slid down to the floor, and began crying once more. He looked at his watch again, and as the second and minute hands reached 0700 hours; his grip released the unopened syringe and let it fall to the floor at his side.

CHAPTER 62

YURI DOLGORUKI

AS HE BOUNDED FORWARD, FEODOR USED THE OPEN PALMS of his hands banging off the left and right walls of the passageway to steady him. Where's the nearest wall phone? He screamed in his mind. I've got to let the captain know—there it is! He tripped from his sudden stop, as his hand fumbled to pull the phone off of its wall cradle and dial the bridge.

"...Captain? Captain, its Feodor—I've got the locations of the VX gas. I'm on my way to the first location—it's in the missile compartment, down the hall from my station. You've got to get to the second. It's—"

The captain's voice was hoarse and interrupted by coughing. "It's too late, my friend. Try and save your own life—the gas has already been released."

Feodor glanced at his watch. It was two minutes after 0700 hours. His eyes rose from the wristwatch and looked down the hallway. He saw seamen staggering out of their compartments. They were doubled over and hacking for breath. One by one they fell, like a trail of dominoes coming at him. He ripped his shirt off his back. With buttons flying, he wadded it up and placed it over his mouth and nose. With his other hand, he pulled the injector syringe out of his pocket and ran the colored bottom cover up to his mouth under the wadded shirt. He pulled the bottom protector off with his teeth. In one swift motion, his hand rammed the injector onto his heart. His thumb pressed the top release downward. He heard the first click and waited until he heard the second. Feodor's eyes rose to the carnage in the hall and he too went into convulsions. Blackness overtook him.

CHAPTER 63

JULIE WAS ABLE TO UNWIND AND FIND SOME CALM AND comfort in the CIA safe house. Devon, on the other hand, was not. They were told that they had the "run of the house," but that was not the case. Certain rules and restrictions were laid out. Unless they were approached regarding meal selections, they were asked to avoid personal contact with the staff. The lower level where Grayson was being detained was off limits. Either alone or as a couple, they could go outside and stroll the grounds. But they were required to notify Agent Koehler and he would provide for an armed escort. Koehler said it was for their protection, but Devon wasn't buying the spin. No charges had been leveled against them at this point, but they were material witnesses in a major scandal involving the CIA. And it was still unclear as to what involvement Devon had in the arms smuggling charges that would be made against Grayson and Carey.

It wasn't like Devon was back in his twenty-by-sixteen, one-room cabin in the woods. But the comfortable quarters that restrained him couldn't satisfy his agitated spirit. At least in his hideout in Alaska, he had unfettered access to the wilderness he had come to love. But his adrenaline rush from the past weeks was still on the fast track and the present accommodations chafed him.

Walking around like a caged animal, he grimaced, pounding one tight fist into the other open hand—over and over. He needed to know what was going on, what his next move would be. Would the honest people at the CIA be able to remove the cancer from its own body, or would The Agency close ranks and sweep the dirty mess under the rug? Would he and the woman he loved be hunted like he was before? There were too many questions … he had seen too much corruption flow under his bridge. He was involved from start to present and he knew too much. Worse, he trusted no one except Julie. And even with her, he worried about her naiveté and her own willingness to trust Mike Connors.

Devon McKenzie had both his palms raised and placed flat against one of the large windows in the main living room. He may have been standing there, forehead resting on the glass, but his attention was miles away. He was staring at the bleak, rolling Virginia countryside when the cell phone in his pocket vibrated. Devon jumped and unbuttoned the flap of his cargo pants to retrieve the irritating device. He looked at the number on the screen. It was the same number that called him the night before, and that number belonged to Dennis Carey. Devon paused—he knew the call would be gone before he reached Agent Koehler at the far end of the house. He cleared his throat and answered the phone in a low whisper. "Hello."

Carey recognized that the gravelly voice was not that of Robert Hadley. "Who is this? You know that Robert is the one I talk with ..."

Devon said, "Who do you think ... it's Sam—Sam Hadley."

"I said I only talk with Robert."

"Well, call him back when he's done with that broad in the other room."

"No. Go in there and tell him it's me and I want to talk to him. Do you hear me?"

"Piss off, if you want to talk to him that bad, you get your ass over here and you break in on him."

Carey was desperate to know the details of Grayson's death and decided to proceed. "Alright. Was it clean ... I mean, did you confirm his death?"

"Of course. How many times have we done this before?"

"The apartment ... it's wiped clean? And did you leave a broken glass on the porch?"

"We never miss a detail. It was handled as you ordered."

Carey ended the conversation. As he set the phone down on his desktop, questions began haunting his troubled mind. Did he tell them to leave a broken drinking glass on the porch, or had he told them to throw it onto the ground, as if it had been in his hand? Why hadn't Robert answered the phone? Was it even Robert that he talked to last night? He couldn't be sure. Sweat broke out on his forehead. He noticed his hand was shaking as he tried to pour a drink. Mrs. Franks ... yes, I need to start calling Mrs. Franks, he thought. He picked up the phone and began dialing. That voice—was it even Hadley's?

***

When the phone rang, Mrs. Franks looked up at Mike Connors, who was huddling over her desk. He held up his index finger to give her pause. "Go ahead," he said. "You know what to say."

Mrs. Franks was an old pro, but she still calmed herself before speaking. "I'm sorry, Mr. Carey, but he's still not in. I've tried to reach him at his condo several times and I've also called his cell phone, but he is not picking up. If you happen to make contact, would you please tell him that Director Hatcher has already called four times this morning? Perhaps I should transfer the director's call to your office next time—?"

There was no need to finish her sentence—the connection was already broken. The fox had been flushed from his den.

CHAPTER 64

FOR THE MOMENT, THE TENSION IN THE SITUATION ROOM was moderate, as the magnitude of the threat level was still undetermined. The bickering that Jim LaSpesa had encountered in his NSA meeting subsided when consensus formed that the strange behavior of the Russian sub was secondary to its suspected target. LaSpesa, like the other members present, brought a consensus of his own group with him.

When the president entered the room, he signaled for the people at the long table to remain seated and he himself sat down and opened the top folder in front of him that contained the report from State. After thirty seconds of silence, President Coleridge closed the cover of the folder back over. With eyes never leaving the stack of intel in front of him, he said, "I understand the Ruskies say that this submarine run was within their rights under international law and that it encountered some 'difficulties' for which they need a little time to iron out. Some issues, due to its maiden voyage." Raising his trademark bushy eyebrows and exhaling for emphasis, he scanned those present at the table and continued, "But does anybody in this room *buy* into this nonsense? I mean Norway's got its shorts in a wad, NATO is concerned but perplexed, and the French are flapping their wings in the air. Anyone care to comment?"

Jim LaSpesa was the first to respond. "Mr. President, NSA believes that the Norwegian gas fields are a decoy. We neither accept their right to be there, nor do we buy the Russians' lame excuse about 'difficulties.' But it is inconceivable that the Russians would dare provoke a world war by attacking these gas fields. The Russians have been ramping up their submarine activity in this area ever since NATO announced that it will deploy our Patriot missile batteries in Poland. It is NSA's conclusion that this maneuver is a strong-armed tactic to remind NATO that *any* missiles, even if they're defensive, in any ex-Warsaw Pact member will never be tolerated. This, we believe, is their way of further ratcheting up the heat in the hope that NATO backs off."

"Dammit, those missiles are defensive—*defensive*! They are our primary battlefield missile-defense system—targeted against the Iranian missiles and they know it!" Thundered Coleridge. "How the hell can we calm down our Eastern Bloc allies without those missiles? Hell, since we let them into NATO, they have helped us more in the war on terror than any country outside of England. None of the other original allies have stepped up to the plate. And the Brits' support is on the wane." Turning his head, the president looked at Admiral Booth and with a quick nod of his head, signaled to him that he wanted the opinion of the Joint Chiefs of Staff.

"The problem, Mr. President, is after we were the only ones to scrap the installation of the long-range missiles, the Russians mistook that as a major victory. We're going in with defensive missiles, but manned by American troops ... first time for American troops deployed on Polish soil. Having our troops that close armed with missiles is driving them over the edge—simple as that. Back to the matter at hand, we concur with the opinion of NSA, but the gravity of the theatrics is something that still requires an equivalent response. However, at this moment, a military response is not the central issue ... it is the problem of *backing up* whatever response we choose. We believe that a military response is neither warranted nor in the interest of NATO. This situation may be best handled by a formal complaint to the United Nations and handled by the Department of State. In short, the JCOS believe our strategic forces are stretched too thin."

Before Admiral Booth had finished his last sentence, he no longer held the president's focus of attention. The president's eyes turned downward and he opened the report from the CIA in front of him.

Earlier, he had read the report regarding the agent called "Trojan Horse" and his clandestine mission that corrupted the computer systems of the Borei class submarines. The room again fell quiet as he scanned the first page. "... And what are the ramifications of this Trojan Horse encryption? Does this not have some sort of bearing on our decisions?" Coleridge turned his head to Ernest Hatcher and gave him his cue.

The CIA director paused. His mind was still preoccupied with the drama of the Grayson-Carey situation. "Excuse me, Mr. President," he said as he fumbled to open his own report. "As I'm sure you are aware, we had an agent, code name 'Trojan Horse,' that did, in fact, corrupt the missile system of the Yuri Dolgoruki. But, our problem gets complicated by two factors: In the first place, the first thirteen of their sixteen missiles can be fired in a normal sequence. Thereafter, the virus aborts the system and shuts it down. If, however, they choose to fire them all in one salvo, and they can, the system goes into an overload and no missiles will fire. Our second problem is thus: In all subsequent Borei class submarines, after the first missile is fired, no subsequent missiles will fire whatsoever. Their systems are all tied together for security, and this virus will travel, undetected, to the rest of their Borei fleet. And if any newer classes should happen to share this system, they too will receive this virus."

Coleridge scanned the table and returned a quizzical look to Hatcher, saying, "So what does this mean to our immediate situation in the North Sea? If the Yuri Dolgoruki can still fire thirteen missiles, I think you can appreciate the amount of destruction that could be wreaked on not just the two gas platforms … but London or Paris … and how about we throw in New York or Washington, D.C.?"

"I do, Mr. President, but—"

President Coleridge interrupted Hatcher's response by looking over to his JCOS admiral. "Admiral Booth, is it true that each of these Borei missiles can carry multiple warheads? And can't each of these multiple warheads be targeted?"

"Yes, Mr. President, that is true, but it gets even worse. Our intel says the Bulavas possess advanced defensive capabilities which make it resistant to NATO's missile-defense systems."

Coleridge's eyes narrowed on the admiral as his brows turned to a frown. "How so?" He asked.

"We show that each individual missile has evasive maneuvering, mid-course countermeasures and decoys. And if that isn't bad enough, the warheads are shielded against both physical and electromagnetic pulse damage. In short, Mr. President, this is the one missile we have prayed that they would never be able to produce. And, here it is, sitting on Norway's doorstep."

Coleridge dropped his pen on the conference table to gain attention. When all eyes returned to him, he said, "Well isn't that just a bucket of spit!" He picked his pen back up and scratched out the multiplication by hand. "We could be looking at up to seventy-eight missiles going God knows where …"

Hatcher was reluctant to put himself on the hot seat, but replied anyway. "With all due respect to everyone in this room, the central point is being missed. Having that encryption unbeknownst to the Russians could be a major trump card that we should protect at all costs. With the mothballing of their Akula class fleet, we cannot chance that they may fire these missiles at anything that isn't a part of the United States. In the future, if a major exchange between our two nations should ever occur, we could nullify more than one-third of their total offensive capabilities. I don't believe that the Russians would ever risk hitting our cities on a first-strike basis. Maybe those gas platforms, but …" He let his words hang and shrugged his shoulders in a gesture of uncertainty.

The room fell silent again as its ramifications settled in. Then an explosion of sound occurred as all members tried to advance their thoughts. The president raised his hand for silence. "Does this encrypted 'virus,' if you will, require us to take this submarine out before any action can be advanced on their part? We … I mean … NATO countries still have the right of first response to these provocations."

Admiral Booth raised his hand and was nodded permission to speak. "The waters where the sub is maneuvering have a maximum depth of three hundred meters. We believe this is shallow enough to where the sub could be eliminated by a NATO-sanctioned attack using a Norwegian Ula class sub, but we will need the support of a British Vanguard class sub. The Russians, however, are claiming both the right to be there and that its erratic movement is due to possible malfunctions in its navigation system. Due to the fact that it *is* a maiden voyage, they are positioning themselves to have their cake and eat it. With France and Germany in the mix, I'm not sure that NATO would do anything but squawk. We would not be able to gain consensus on blowing it out of the water and time is of the essence."

Showing frustration, the president bellowed out, "Well, short of puckering up and kissing Putin's ass, what the hell *are* our options?"

Without any viable options to proffer, all at the table looked around to someone else. Ernest Hatcher again raised a tentative hand. "There could be one more complicating factor, Mr. President. This encryption was written four years ago, so we can't be one hundred percent sure that it hasn't already been discovered by the Russians and that they haven't removed it. Even if it is still in place, we have no way of knowing what happens to the rest of their submarine fleet, should this first-in-line sub be destroyed. What we do know is that this encryption was meant to start a domino effect. *But*, and this is critical, only when it is used. What we *don't* know is this: What if that first standing domino tile is never pushed over … because we have eliminated its existence?"

CHAPTER 65

PETER JORGESEN WAS IN A MUCH BETTER FRAME OF MIND since the gale had passed and the platform was resting secure on the floor of the sea. It wasn't as if his job was finished. All the inspections of its great, conical legs were still ongoing, and the multitude of startup connections to get the platform up and running had begun. The crews to perform these tasks were flown in by helicopter and were in place. On the surface, everything appeared to be running as it should and Peter was enjoying an uncommon respite that included his trademark cup of steaming hot cocoa with one floating marshmallow.

Kicking his feet up onto his desk, he reached over and grabbed the communiqué from Vats that reminded him that the Norwegian Navy was chomping at the bit waiting for him to do another demonstration of the SRDRS mini rescue sub for NATO. Holding the paper in one hand, he took a sip of the cocoa with the other. God, how I want to do that demonstration, he thought. I could use the break. Working the schedule out in his head, he reckoned that two more days work on the platform and he should be able leave. I'll even be able to take Bjorn and let Greta run the show.

That welcomed lull was ruined when his assistant Bjorn came in and placed the latest wire from Norske Shell on the desktop in front of him. As if it were toxic, Peter sensed that something wasn't right. He picked up the wire and read its contents. His breathing became shallow; he couldn't believe what he was reading.

He felt powerless as he read the transmission. The Norske Shell wire was terse and brief:

Russian nuclear submarine parked twenty-five miles east of Gimli platform—intent unknown, situation unclear. NAF on high alert, NATO apprised, awaiting direction. Situation dire— suggest you place platform on code level red.

Peter Jorgesen leaned back, crumpled the paper, and sagged in his chair. He sensed that a red alert meant nothing to him and his crew. Death was knocking at their doorstep. They were in danger. This time—there was nothing he could do. "God help us," he whispered.

CHAPTER 66

YURI DOLGORUKI

THE SHIP'S EO, KASHNIKOV, WAS THE FIRST TO AWAKE. AS the first bits of light entered his eyes, his insides wretched and he doubled over and vomited. His eyelids opened again, and once more he coughed and more vomit spewed from his mouth. The pain in his stomach was horrific and he remained doubled over. His body felt as if he'd been hit by a car. Anton Kashnikov had been forewarned about the aftereffects of the atropine and inhaling the VX gas. But nothing could have prepared him for how he felt. He was, nevertheless, alive, and for that he was grateful.

As he lay on the floor of the bridge, his body was in a fetal position and his two arms were wrapped around his stomach. When the pain ebbed, he felt well enough to get on two knees and begin surveying the damage. Without a full inspection of the boat, he had no way of knowing for certain, but he was sure that the only two people alive would be himself and Ruslan Petrova. He fingers gripped the top of the table next to him and he strained to raise his body to a wobbly, standing position.

Turning his head in a left, center, and right sweep, his mind began to work again. He had expected that everyone on the bridge would be dead, but seeing it firsthand was like Dante's Inferno. The captain, still in his chair, slumped over backwards, his face distorted, vomit covering his uniform, and bloody spittle cascading down his cheek. The sonar man, as well as the others, was on the floor, each in their own unique, wretched position. For a brief moment, he wondered what he had done, what form of evil he had made a pact with. But his lack of conscience returned, his cold, reptilian eyes again stared straight ahead, and he remembered the timetable that had to be adhered to. In forty-eight hours, he would have all the riches he needed to sustain a lifetime of excesses.

Anton Kashnikov turned and navigated his way over the strewn bodies. He had three things left to do: Make sure the video had been sent out, fire the missiles on time, and kill Ruslan Petrova to corroborate his story of saving London and Paris. He guessed that Ruslan was awake and on his way to the radio station.

When Kashnikov reached the radioman's compartment, he saw that the operator must have stood while he convulsed for air. His body was laying facedown across his chair which still supported the man's dead body. The EO was nervous about touching the radioman for fear of possible recontamination. He was certain that it would be okay to move him out of the way, but the mere thought of having to go through what he had just experienced made him grab papers to cover his hands.

The transmitter stood in front of him, but there was no tape in its slot. Had that worthless Petrova already sent out the video? He might have, but Kashnikov worried that he hadn't. His first thought was to go find Petrova, but he changed his mind and decided to wait and find him later. Timing was critical, so he pulled a copy of the cassette out of his pocket and slipped it into the slot for transmission to the outside world. A small monitor to his left displayed what was being broadcast. The streaming images were striking and they chilled him to the bone.

***

Feodor Strivnych had never felt such horrid pain in his whole life. Sitting on the floor, his legs were curled out in front of him with his back leaning against his bed. He had neither the strength nor the inclination left to pull himself up. He had crawled and scraped his way back to his quarters. His body was drained, and he was still in a state of mental shock. Twenty years of being at sea had not prepared him for the carnage he dragged himself through. Bodies were strewn everywhere in the most bizarre array of contorted positions. Men's ashen faces, dripping with a putrescent concoction of spittle, blood, and vomit bore witness to the ghastly deaths they had succumbed to.

He had, however, the presence of mind to pull the video tape out of the cold, clenched fist of the ship's doctor as he struggled to crawl over him. Feodor looked down—it was in his own fist. As he rolled his wrist over and turned his palm upward, he felt a sharp spasm of pain in his heart that reminded him of the atropine injection that had saved his life. For what purpose he had been spared, he couldn't know, but he was certain that the secret lie in the tape in his hand. He needed to get to his station and put the tape into his computer. His mind said to move, and he tried to grab the side of his bed, but his body wouldn't respond. At that moment, he heard the awkward dragging of feet coming down the passageway.

As the ominous sound grew with each step, he again tried to move. Closer and closer, the dragging feet came. Still his body would not respond except to roll his wrist and turn the tape downward and out of sight. As the sound stopped at his doorway, Feodor closed his eyes. He prayed he could hold his breath long enough for the danger to pass.

CHAPTER 67

WASHINGTON, D.C.

AS PRESIDENT COLERIDGE WAS WINDING DOWN FROM another lengthy diatribe on not trusting the Russians, his Chief of Staff reentered the Situation Room and whispered in his ear. The president pulled his head back in irritation and barked, "Confound it, Neil, you don't have to whisper in my ear. Hell, everybody in this room knows what we're talking about. Go ahead … spit it out for everyone to hear."

Neil Richards puffed up like the banty rooster that he was. "Gentlemen, please address the screen, this has just come in from NATO." With that, he clicked the remote and the demand tape began to play.

Ruslan Petrova was clothed in the dress of an al-Qaida combatant. He wore a black and white Keffiyeh and had an AK-47 strapped across from shoulder to thigh. He delivered his threat first in broken English, then in his native Chechen tongue:

> *"Because NATO has supported the scurrilous dogs of America in Afghanistan, two demands are being made. First, all prisoners of war being held in the Guantanamo detention facility will be released in twelve hours starting from this broadcast. If they are not released in their entirety, the two Norwegian gas platforms will be destroyed.*
>
> *Second, the Satan that is the President of the United States will apologize to the world community at the United Nations and declare that the illegal occupation of Afghanistan is over, and all troops will be withdrawn immediately. If these demands are not met, all sixteen missiles will be launched and targeted to explode over the cities of London and Paris. An electromagnetic pulse will occur that will bring the economies of the West to its knees. It will take months, maybe even years to recover from this disaster. By the use of nerve gas, all crewmembers of this submarine have been killed, save one. This officer has been tortured into releasing both keys and codes needed to*

establish all targets and the firing sequence. Those targets have been established and await my command. Unless all demands have been met within twelve hours, I will release all missiles to rain destruction upon you. I will cut the head off this serpent for the entire world to see. If any attack upon this submarine occurs, I will release all missiles.

Allahu Akbar!"

The next clip on the video showed a bound and gagged executive officer in a kneeling position with his head held up by his hair.

There was dead silence in the room when the tape finished. The president was the first to speak. "Well, I guess we have our reason." He looked over to his defense secretary and asked, "What about that first domino, Henry? Do we try to take it out or not?"

Henry Dilworth was still biting the base of his index finger. The sound of his name startled him. "Uh, I'm sorry, Mr. President." His face scrunched into a pensive frown as he gathered his thoughts and said, "I'm feeling that there's some sort of a disconnect here and I can't seem to put my finger on it. Why *start* with the gas platforms? Why set off an EMP over London and Paris' financial centers? Why not let the missiles hit and incinerate the cities? Hell, al-Qaida doesn't give a rat's ass about human life ... the more casualties, the better. None of this seems to add up ... unless money is involved."

Howard Irving, from State, was anxious to insert a calming word. "I think the reason that they would do an EMP is because of the heavy Muslim populations in those cities. They don't want to kill their own."

Henry Dilworth looked at President Coleridge and gave an incredulous look. "Really?" He drawled out with dripping sarcasm. "According to the Koran, a Muslim warrior is allowed to kill any Muslim that is not committed to a jihad, or if they are living in harmony with any infidel population. I mean, that could include any Muslim population in America or Europe."

The president raised his voice and said, "The point I am trying to make is that he said, 'if attacked, he would fire all the missiles.' He didn't say *some*—he said *all*! Director Hatcher, does that not shut the whole system down?"

Ernie Hatcher could only offer, "Maybe ..."

CHAPTER 68

YURI DOLGORUKI

FEODOR THOUGHT THE MAN IN THE PASSAGEWAY WOULD never move on. *Maybe he suspects that I'm still alive—I can't tell.* The pain in his chest and the urge to vomit was again overwhelming. But he held his position and, after what seemed an eternity, he heard the scuffle of the first step as the man moved away. Feodor cracked one eye open. In spite of blurriness from his eyelashes, he was able to recognize the intruder. It was him, the ship's executive officer. Fighting off rolling spasms of pain, Feodor lay frozen in his feigned death position until the dragging footsteps had faded.

Even though it was safe to move, his body refused to respond. He didn't know how long he had been lying this way, but his left leg twitched and curled out from under his other leg. He felt a rush surge through his cramped body. He reached his arm up to the top of the bed and pulled himself up, and fell backward onto the mattress. Lying there, staring at the ceiling, Feodor rolled his wrist one more time, exposing the tape that was still clutched in his hand. *The tape! He thought. I need to get to my station and play the tape.*

Pulling his body upward, he thought of the Chechen torpedo man. *Is he still alive … are we the only three left on the boat?* He couldn't be sure, but his wits were collected enough to know that the exec had headed in the opposite direction of where he suspected the Chechen terrorist might be.

Opening the lid of his footlocker, he slipped his hand underneath. He dug down until his hand found its target—his sheathed knife. He pulled it out and strapped it to his lower leg. With a look left and right to stabilize his wobbly body, he gathered his bearings and proceeded in the direction of the forward torpedo room.

His progress was slow, but it was no longer his addled mind or his pummeled body that was the cause. It was climbing over the strewn bodies of sailors, sometimes stacked one over the other, that proved difficult to his sense of balance. Feodor used extreme caution, ducking into each open compartment so as not to stay exposed in the passageway for any time longer than necessary. The main torpedo room came into focus. He felt as if he had been on a long journey.

Once past the racks of torpedoes, Feodor stopped as he entered the wider space that allowed for the loading of the deadly missiles into the horizontal tubes … nothing. As he turned to exit, he saw the body of Ruslan Petrova, slumped over with an unopened atropine syringe lying next to his opened palm. Picking up the syringe, Feodor paused. He couldn't comprehend why the Chechen had not used the atropine. He had chosen death over life. A sense of pity overcame Feodor as he concluded that the kid had a last minute change of heart. His blood ran hot as his thoughts moved to the EO. What kind of man would make a pact with the devil himself, when at the last second, even this fanatical boy passed on entering the gates of hell?

Feodor put the auto-injector into his pocket and was at his missile station. His computer was still on and he slipped the tape into its slot. The outrageous demands of the terrorist came into view. The ramifications of the tape shook Feodor. He glanced at his watch but didn't panic. He wasn't sure, but he guessed there were at least eleven hours left. Reaching down the leg of his pants, he reassured himself that his weapon was still there. I've got plenty of time to slit the EO's throat, he thought. He pondered if there were other ways that he could torture that monster in a slow, agonizing death. The images that entered his mind sickened him. What kind of a fiend am I becoming? He asked himself.

So much had happened in so little time. The death that was everywhere had fogged his thinking and Feodor still felt the lingering in-and-out pain in his heart where he had stabbed himself. He dropped his head and made the sign of the cross with his left hand. He had never given God any quarter since he had entered the Navy still in his teenage years. With his eyes closed, he begged forgiveness and prayed to be given direction. Sitting with his head hanging low, the vision of his longtime friend, Alex Sigua, came out of the fog. The first picture started with him and Alex sharing laughs in their shared compartment. That image was ruined when it rolled into the killing fields wrought by Stalin on the land of his birth. He saw the slaughterhouse that his ship had become, and himself holding a knife under Alex's throat as he begged for mercy while telling him of the American agent named Trojan Horse.

Like a blinding beacon of light, Feodor snapped his head upward as everything crystallized and his mission became clear. "The radio room," he whispered. "I've got to get to the radio room. I've got to send out a message before it's too late!"

CHAPTER 69

WASHINGTON, D.C.

THE MEETING IN THE SITUATION ROOM WAS DRAGGING ON without any forward direction. Opinions drifted further apart, rather than toward a consensus. At that moment, the door burst open with Neil Richards again interrupting the meeting. "I have another broadcast from the sub ... but this time it's strange ... a different sounding voice and no video to go with it." He pointed his arm at the screen and clicked the remote once again.

"... Cough, pause, another cough ... this is Feodor Strivnych, of the Yuri Dolgoruki, missile compart—garble, pause ... Trojan Horse ... cough ... Trojan Horse—garble."

With the last garbling noise, the transmission ended.

"What the hell was that all about?" Asked Coleridge.

The room remained silent while they all acted befuddled by the strange and incoherent message. Ernest Hatcher broke the moment. "Sir, this is a message from the Dolgoruki missile compartment ... he's the head computer man. I think he knows about Trojan Horse. Remember, Batu Sigua was the scientist that worked with Devon McKenzie—aka Trojan Horse. His brother was Alex Sigua—he worked in the missile department with Feodor Strivnych. Alex *must* have told him about the encryption. It's even possible that this Strivnych was in on it with him."

"How can you speculate that?" Asked Coleridge.

"There *has* to be a reason that he sent that specific message. He was either sending it to us or to the Russians. But I'm still not sure the Russians know about the virus, otherwise they would have eliminated it. Hence ... why would he send it to the Russians? The more I think about it, I am convinced that message was meant for us."

The room again exploded with a cacophony of sound as all tried to speak at once. The president called for order. "Wait a darn minute. Ernie, what *if* it was meant for us?"

"Well, sir, maybe he's trying to get Devon McKenzie on board the sub … maybe before it's too late. He might even think this Trojan Horse fellow could get on board and disable the system, not allowing it to fire. Let's not forget that you saw the EO bound and gagged, and that makes it a big boat for one man to monitor and keep secure." "I have one simple question: If we wanted to get him on board, *how* would we do that?" Coleridge asked.

"To answer your question," Hatcher replied, "NATO has an SRDRS that was scheduled for another test demonstration in Vats, Norway as we speak. One of the holdups has been waiting for the Norwegian operator, Peter Jorgesen. He's the man that conducted the previous test, Bold Monarch—which was successful, I might add."

"Refresh my memory, an SR … whatever is what?" Asked the president.

Hatcher pointed over to Admiral Booth to handle the question. "The acronym stands for Submarine Rescue Diving Recompression System. It's the newest toy to replace the old Mystic and Avalon rescue mini subs … you know, Hunt for Red October and Gray Lady Down? Well, all that crap was fiction. The difference, Mr. President, is that this new one works, is sitting in the fjord of Vats, and happens to be available."

Coleridge looked again at his CIA chief. "Ernie, you aren't suggesting some sort of Hollywood stunt—another USS Dallas scenario? … Or are you?"

"Oh, I am, Mr. President. Devon McKenzie is in a safe house in Manassas and Peter Jorgesen is on the Gimli platform as we speak. Give us two Navy Seals to fly over with McKenzie and we can have them all there with maybe a little time to spare."

Coleridge looked around the table, more or less begging for differing opinions. "Can anyone tell me again why we don't eliminate the domino and take the Dolgoruki out? I mean, look, if you say that you don't think the Russians know about the encryption, let's take the safe way and take the sub out. The Russians will bitch, maybe even threaten, but the world will know of this terrorist broadcast and NATO has jurisdiction in its own waters … end of story."

Admiral Booth chimed in, "Let's not forget that any attack on the Dolgoruki will be known by them long before any first strike hits. It will give them ample time to get the missiles launched. We're talking seconds."

Henry Dilworth from Defense was the next to speak. "Sir, with all due respect, I have to agree with Director Hatcher. I am sure the Russians are in conference like we are, and they may already be sending their own rescue sub to the Dolgoruki. If this Feodor Striv-whatever gets into Russian hands, it will be certain that our encryption will be exposed. If we take out the Dolgoruki and the domino effect doesn't take place, we're back to square one and all of our covert work will have been for nothing. Don't forget, we lose our potential ace in the hole in any kind of nuclear exchange. I think the best plan would be to at least *try* with the SRDRS and use a NATO submarine to take the sub out as a backup plan. Either way, we risk this terrorist nut-job setting off the firing sequence. It is critical that this Trojan Horse character get in before the Russians do and verify that the encryption is still viable. And as Ernie said, perhaps he could make the encryption darker, less able to be detected. After all, it's been four years since we put it in, and there has been one hell of a lot of technology that has advanced in that time—on both sides. I think it is worth whatever risk we have to take."

"Do we have one of our subs in the region?"

"No sir," said Admiral Booth. "Not one that *we* could get there in time."

"The Brits, the French … the Norwegians?"

"I can have an answer in minutes, but I'm sure there will be at least one that can get there in time."

"But this McKenzie … he's been in hiding the last four years. He won't be in tune with any of the latest technology," Said Coleridge.

"Mr. President, if he's half as good as we think he is, a team of our people could bring him up to speed within several hours."

"We don't have several hours!" Said an exasperated Coleridge.

"They can brief him on the plane ride over."

"No pun intended, but this is like playing Russian roulette," said Secretary of State Irving. "I recommend we talk to the Russians first and see what we can work out together … you know, in our mutual interest."

Ernie Hatcher raised his pen in the air to get the president's attention. When Coleridge gave his approving nod, the CIA director cleared his throat for emphasis. "There is one more complicating factor … When VX liquid is aerosolized, it is in its deadliest form. Its adhesion qualities rend it impossible to remove it from any surface that it comes in contact with. Every square inch of that submarine has been contaminated and will kill any person that comes in contact with it. By the way, the 'V' of VX signifies its long life. Not trying to be dramatic, but I dare say that the Yuri Dolgoruki is more than a death ship, it's a ghost ship. Salvaging it would assume a massive cost, if it can be salvaged at all."

"I rest my case! Let's blow it out of the water and end this nonsense. I know damn well that NATO—hell, even the United Nations would support that!" Coleridge said.

"But wait!" Interrupted Hatcher. "We still don't want to lose our strategic advantage with the computer program. Why not see if we can make sure that the encryption has transferred, as it exists to the next boats in line. The Yuri Dolgoruki was the first of three that are being built. The second, the Dmitri Donskoi, headed out to the White Sea thirty days ago to conduct a missile test. For whatever reason, the launch was cancelled and the submarine was ordered back to port. Our intel says it is sitting there with no activity being reported. I must remind everyone that they plan on having five Borei class subs by 2015. Why not get Trojan Horse on board, make sure the encryption is moved, intact, to the Donskoi. Then it's our option to destroy the sub, and if we do, the world will thank us. It's worth the risk."

Coleridge leaned back in his chair, pushed his glasses upward, and rubbed the corners of his sore eyes. When he sat back up, he looked at Henry Dilworth and Admiral Booth and said, "Gentlemen, go with the rescue sub plan. Howard, do what we have to do to pacify the terrorist. Get with Charles at DHS and set up a charade at Guantanamo. Tell the United Nations I will be addressing them in eleven hours. Henry, notify NATO to keep the PC-3 moving and check with NATO to see who has a sub available for option two. Ernie, get that McKenzie fellow on the fastest jet to Norway with the right number of Seals to do the job. Also, get that minisub operator off that platform and ready to go. Oh, Jim, best brief Treasury on what's at stake. If we're not able to stop this, the global economy is headed for a deep freeze. And gentlemen, may I remind you, there can't be any screw-ups."

CHAPTER 70

DEVON MCKENZIE WAS SITTING BY JULIE'S SIDE IN THE living room when Special Agent Koehler approached with Ernest Hatcher at his side. After the introductions were made, Koehler left and the CIA director sat down with his two troubled agents.

Hatcher made an attempt to wave Julie out, leaving them alone, but Devon would hear nothing of it. The slighting of Julie became awkward, with Hatcher's eyes staring in on whom he considered to be his subordinate. But she held her ground, and the director was forced to turn his focus on the man he knew as Trojan Horse. Devon's return glare grew ugly as the moment turned into a test of wills. Short on time, Hatcher decided to let their perceived acts of defiance pass. Opening the manila file that he brought with him, he handed it to Devon.

"I understand you know a thing or two about computers," he said, hoping to break the tension.

"Don't start playing the fool, Hatcher," Devon replied in a raspy voice. "It doesn't become you or your agency."

Hatcher grimaced and shrugged his shoulders, acknowledging that the ex-agent was no longer impressed by the CIA or his title. "Fair enough," he said, nodding toward the folder. "McKenzie, the file in your hands contains all the intel we have on the Yuri Dolgoruki … I know you remember that submarine and the encryption you placed in its computer over four years ago. You worked a dissident scientist named Batu Sigua, who in turn arranged for you to meet with his brother, Alex, aboard the Dolgoruki. Okay so far?"

Devon perused the folder and gave a passive look, telegraphing an uninterested acknowledgement. Nonetheless, he continued sifting through the papers until he pulled up the specs of the SRDRS. "What the hell is this and what does it have to do with me?" Devon asked, holding the SRDRS photo up for Hatcher to see and passing it on to Julie. He knew passing it to Julie would further anger Hatcher. But Devon felt it important to establish his independence of the CIA.

Julie scanned the photo and turned her head back toward Devon. "I've seen this—it replaces the old Avalon submarine rescue vehicle. This one's as good as they say."

"Quite so," said Hatcher. "Study it well 'Agent' McKenzie, we hope to have you aboard this sub within a matter of hours."

"I'm not your *agent*, Hatcher. Nor am I anyone else's," Devon growled. "If you recall, my life was destroyed by The Agency and I want no part of it ever again."

"Well, you *are* a part of it—by order of your Commander-in-Chief, I might add. That is, unless you refuse your president's order in your country's hour of need. Here are the facts: The Dolgoruki is sitting smack dab between two Norwegian gas platforms, its entire crew has been killed by a terrorist using VX gas and he is threatening to use its torpedoes to destroy the two platforms and rain its missiles over Paris and London in an EMP attack. Other than that, no, your country doesn't need you." Hatcher slid his hand into his suit coat inner pocket and pulled out a copy of the terrorist tape. As he slid it across the coffee table, he looked at Devon and asked, "Interested?"

CHAPTER 71

PETER JORGESEN STOOD AS THE DOWNWARD DRAFT OF THE helicopter blades hurled the cold air with such ferocity that he found himself at about a sixty degree list, with his hand straining to keep his sailing cap snug to his head. As the chopper rocked back and forth, its wheels touched the deck and Peter heard its screaming jet engine begin to wind down. Within seconds, Sven Gundersen exited the chopper and helped the other passenger out of the helicopter that continued to bounce from the heavy sea winds.

Sven ran to Peter and they gave each other their customary bear hug. "Damn! It's been too long, Sven."

"Yes it has, my old friend, far too long." As they separated, Sven looked over to his traveling companion and said, "Peter ... this is Anders Neilssen from MIU. Anders, this old polar bear is the famed Peter Jorgesen."

After they shook hands, Peter stepped between them and put his large arms around both and shuffled them toward the warmth of the platform offices. Waiting on the reception room table were three steaming mugs of hot cocoa with one marshmallow in each. Sven took notice and said, "It's nice to know that in a world filled with change, some things remain the same, Peter."

Peter shifted emotional gears as he sipped his hot chocolate. "Sven, we're old and great friends, but I suspect you came out here to grease the way for something ... something that I might not want to do. Care to comment?"

"You're right ... as always." Sven's head turned to the man from MIU and motioned for him to open his briefcase. "Peter, we need you to pilot the SRDRS."

"I know that, but can't it wait? We all know that there's a Russian bogie sitting out there and it's armed and dangerous. I can't leave here to do another demo."

Sven's eyes diverted to the floor and Anders Nielssen's never left his briefcase. Peter looked at one, then the other. "Oh ... sounds like someone's got another thankless job for the old, expendable Viking. Damn! I knew it! This has got something to do with that Russian sub sitting out there, doesn't it?"

This time the man from MIU took control of the conversation. "Mr. Jorgesen—I mean Peter—that Russian sub has been turned into a toxic ghost ship. What I am saying is that the crew members are all dead—that is, all but a terrorist, the missile compartment's computer man, and the ship's EO. But we ... uh, can't be sure if the EO is still alive or not. You see, the terrorist set off canisters of VX gas, and ... well, he's threatening to take these two gas platforms out with torpedoes and launch its payload of missiles after that. The intended targets are Paris and London and the method is an EMP blast."

Peter was speechless. He looked over at Sven with a look that only a true friend would understand. Sven looked back in painful sincerity. "Peter ... NATO needs to send in a team of Americans. They're going to try and disable the sub's ability to fire these weapons before the terrorist's deadline. Whatever else they are going to accomplish is classified. They need someone to pilot the SRDRS. Plain and simple—you're the best man for this job."

"What's the downside, other than getting fired on by a torpedo and getting blown to kingdom come?" He tried to laugh, but it sounded hollow.

"When we say that the interior of the sub is a toxic time bomb, Peter, we mean it. When VX gas is vaporized, it clings to every single surface it comes in contact with. It was exploded in the main air ducts. There's a strong chance that some of that VX contamination could come back into the SRDRS. If it does, that could be a severe risk to you. We don't know what might happen if there's chaos. We'll have you in a hazmat suit, but there is no guarantee that you might not become contaminated if the suit is torn in any way. You will be given an atropine injector, so that suit won't be your only protection. But it will make operation of the rescue sub precarious at best. That's why you're being asked to be the pilot."

Peter stood up and with a quick sucking sound from his mouth, the marshmallow in his cocoa disappeared from his cup. He looked down at the two men and said through a mouthful of melting marshmallow, "Remember the American 9/11 saying? Well ... let's go rock!"

Sven looked over at Anders and back to his old friend. He shook his head with a look of feigned pity and said, "Peter, I believe the words were: 'Let's roll!'"

CHAPTER 72

DEVON WAS IN A STRANGE MOOD. ON THE ONE HAND, HE was exhilarated. Hatcher was smart, he thought, asking me if I was interested. Hell, it's why I joined the CIA in the first place. This was a mission any good field agent would die for. A chance to save the world from a meltdown of catastrophic proportions, an opportunity to deal terrorism a major blow, maybe save two cities from annihilation should several of the missiles not detonate until they reached the ground. On top of all that, he could stick it to the Russians one more time and that sat well. The sum total of all of this made him feel needed, and he hadn't felt this way for over four years. Interested? My ass!

On the other hand, Julie had entered his life and she had made all the difference. He had never been successful balancing his life as a field agent with his first wife, Cathy … why did he think he could make it work now? But the thought of screwing up with Julie was unacceptable. Hell, she's my last chance.

And The Agency itself, they were the bastards responsible for Cathy's death and all of my misery. But they were coming to him, hat in hand … begging for his help. Even more, he was being asked by the President of the United States, no less. The feeling of vindication was powerful and fought hard for dominance.

A set of car lights rounded the circular drive and its beams broke Devon's trance. A black Suburban had pulled up in front of the Manassas safe house, and its driver was out and had the rear tailgate opened before Devon had a chance to switch his thoughts. He knew he had to go, he could never let his country down, but he wanted to tell Hatcher to take his mission and shove it.

"Damn it!" He whispered. He bent over and grabbed his duffel bag. As he reached the rear passenger door, Devon turned and saw Julie standing in a window on the second floor. Tears flowing, she watched him walk to the awaiting vehicle and waved. He felt his heart ripping out of his chest, but he turned without a return wave and got into the Suburban.

As he started to get in, he noticed the other half of the seat was occupied by a rather geeky looking guy in his late twenties. Devon was startled and stopped his forward movement. Director Hatcher's head appeared from around the front passenger headrest.

"Good evening Agent McKenzie, this is Special Agent Aaron Cohen. Like you, he has a doctorate, but it's from CalSci. I'll let the two of you fight it out over which is the better school. Unlike you, though, he's never been in the field … research—just research. We're sending him with you on the plane ride to Bergen. We thought maybe you two girls might talk this encryption problem through."

Hatcher broke out into a laugh and continued with his words streaming through more laughter. "Cohen here says you two can work on a few algorithms—heh, heh. Lord, help me! What has this world come to?" As Hatcher continued his horselaugh, Devon looked at Cohen and Cohen at Devon. They shared a look that said it all: What a dick! Hatcher wiped his eyes with his handkerchief, and when he finished, he noticed no one else was enjoying the inside humor. "Well anyway, if he can be of help, all the better … if not, tell him to shut up and sleep the rest of the way. My point is, he's here to help … it's your call. Oh, by the way … we picked up that traitor Carey and he and Grayson are singing like two little songbirds in a love nest. It looks like the cancer stopped there. By the way, this may sound hollow, but I *am* sorry about your wife—and what we've put you through. I'll do my best to make it up—I promise."

***

The CIA had a Dassault Falcon 7X fueled and waiting. Their seven-hour flight would take them nonstop to Bergen Lufthavn Flesland Airport in Norway. Walking up the jet's flight stairs, Devon turned to see another Suburban drive up and let two steel-cut Navy Seals out. Okay, the mission just got serious, he thought.

CHAPTER 73

YURI DOLGORUKI

IT WAS A MACABRE SIGHT. LIKE THE GRIM REAPER SITTING atop his stacked pile of bodies declaring that he was king of the slaughterhouse. Anton Kashnikov was sitting in the captain's chair of a ship of war that no longer performed the mission that it was built for. Instead of being a major chess piece in a game of global politics, it had been reduced to a pawn, meant to satisfy a few Russian Mafiosos whose value of life had long sunk in the wake of their own insatiable greed and corruption.

He sat staring, but saw nothing. The initial shock of seeing the dead seamen everywhere around him had been glazed over in his twisted mind and had morphed into nothing more than the landscape around him. Kashnikov sat, pondering the untold riches that were soon to be his. Even as the alarm on his wristwatch went off, there was no jolt. In robotic fashion, it reminded him of the message that needed to be sent to his superiors: The code that told them all was in place and to arrange his pickup on schedule.

Sliding into the chair of the radio room, his hand reached for the frequency dial, but stopped in mid air. He saw the tell-tale signs that a message had been sent—as little as two hours ago.

No! That can't be, he thought. Petrova is dead—I saw him lying there—I felt his neck, there was no pulse. But the evidence before him was incontrovertible. He slammed his fist onto the table as a twisting combination of utter rage and fear rose in his gut. He knew what he had to do, but first he had to send his four-worded code: "Danica ready for sea."

The EO bolted his way out. He jumped over strewn bodies to his quarters. Pulling open the drawer to his desk, he found his 9mm Makarov PM. He reached in again and pulled out two additional clips. He pushed the side button and let the clip in the pistol drop down. Reassured that it was full, he slammed it back in and gave a quick backward pull of the upper slide. With the safety off, he was ready to hunt his prey. He gave a check of his watch—six hours to go. He paused at the door to his quarters—searching for a possible lone survivor was not what he needed to do. It was imperative for him to be in the conning tower watching for possible incoming attacks. But sitting with his face to a radar screen made him an easy target for whoever was still alive on the boat. His decision was made. He would make several forays throughout the ship, and return every fifteen minutes to the Con.

CHAPTER 74

AS THE DASSAULT FALCON 7X BEGAN ITS DESCENT OVER THE airspace, Devon and Agent Cohen finished their common scribbling on a 36" x 24" pad that Hatcher had waiting for them on the jet. In spite of the CIA director's inside joke, McKenzie and Cohen did spend the entire flight working on an improved algorithm to encrypt into the Donskoi's shared system. A lot of water had passed under Devon's bridge, but within a matter of hours, he was up to date and as comfortable as he had ever been.

When the jet's side door opened and the flight steps dropped down, the Seals were on their feet, gear in hand, and stepping by Devon. "Too bad you guys never learned English," said the first. The last Seal patted Devon on the back and said, "Let's go '007,' you're the important package us delivery boys have to make—executive jet to a helicopter to a mini rescue sub ... man, life don't get any sweeter than that."

Devon waited till the Seals got off before hoisting his own equipment bag onto his shoulder. Looking back at Special Agent Cohen, Devon smiled and said, "Wish I had gone to CalSci, Aaron, you've humbled me."

"...That's because you've been away from it for over twelve years, Devon. I do think that between the two of us, we've worked out something good. Bury it deep, brother."

Devon gave thumbs up, turned, and hurried to catch up with the Seals.

One hundred yards away, a Norwegian military chopper sat with its two overhead rotors whirring—ready to lift off. Devon waited his turn and heaved his oversized duffle bag into the waiting arms of the Norwegian corporal standing in the open side door.

"Welcome aboard, sir. It's going to be a bit cold—you might want to zip that parka up a bit tighter. We'll have the three of you out to the gas rig in about an hour."

Devon sat down next to the two Seals, gave a pursed smile, and nodded his head in acknowledgment of "so far so good." The Seal next to him reached into his pocket, pulled out a 9mm Beretta, and handed it to Devon. "We hope you won't have to use this, '007,' and if you do, maybe Chet and I haven't done our job right. Here's hoping not."

Devon took the Beretta and nodded a thank you. All the while he thought, if you knew how much I've been through, that "007" baloney wouldn't be said—even in jest.

The side door slid shut and the chopper lifted off into the biting cold of the fjord. The pilot's voice scratched its way through the headsets: "Next stop, the Gimli platform in the North Sea—keep your straps tight, boys, it's gonna be a bumpy ride! You 'Cowboy' Seals *do* know how to swim, don't you? …Yeeha!"

CHAPTER 75

THE PRESIDENT LED THE OTHERS INTO THE SITUATION Room. The same crowd that was there eight hours earlier was again present, except that the Ambassador to Russia, Allen George, was now included.

President Coleridge looked up at the clock and addressed Irving. "Time is spare, George, what say our Russian friends?"

"Mr. President, I was with Ambassador Gorenkov twenty minutes ago. Nothing significant has happened, other than their pressing us to allow them to use our SRDRS that's in Bergen. The Russian Navy feel they can get there quicker and would love to see the latest technology of our rescue sub. They themselves have an old Avalon, but the soonest it can arrive is about one hour past your twelve-hour deadline."

Admiral Booth broke in saying, "That's in four hours … how can they get it there that soon? It's got to come from Severodvinsk in the White Sea."

Ernest Hatcher broke in. "Well, we've intercepted messages that tell us that Admiral Popov put an Avalon on one of their still-active Akula class subs and had it tail the Dolgoruki because of its maiden voyage. The Norwegians have confirmed an Akula near its territorial waters one hundred and twenty miles away."

"I assume we're staying with the 'operational problem' line?" Asked Coleridge.

"Yes, Mr. President, but the American government will do anything it can—blah, blah, blah."

"Have the gas platforms been evacuated?"

"All but those needed to assist the chopper—Peter Jorgesen left with SRDRS. The chopper will take Trojan Horse and the Seals to it at sea, and drop them into it."

"That leaves two hours forty-five left. Do they have to board the rescue sub at sea?"

"Yes sir," said Admiral Booth. "The mini sub travels at four knots. Because of the time crunch, we put the SRDRS on its tender and sent it ahead. Not to worry, though, weather is projected favorable for calm seas."

"What about the time—are we still going to make it?"

Admiral Booth scanned the table and looked at the president. "God willing … it's the best team we could have assembled, and other than a British takeout, it's the only plan we have."

"Is the sub hunter airborne?"

"Yes, Mr. President—ready and locked in. The Norwegians are the best at this and the data is streaming into NATO control as we speak."

"Tell me again about the submarines to take out the Dolgoruki."

"Sir," Admiral Booth said, "we got lucky on this one. The Brits keep at least one sub in continuous rotation around its isles. When the demand message went out, the H.M.S. Vengeance happened to be about 0200, that's directionally two o'clock in its routine. It's been moved into position to take out the Dolgoruki. In addition, the Norwegians have an Ula class sub that has sneaked in from the south and is also in position to take it out. Both are ready and await your instructions for elimination."

"The French …?"

"Their closest boat, Le Terrible, is in harbor at Brest. It's a Le Triomphant class sub that is neither terrible nor triumphant. They can't seem to work out the bugs … too many labor union problems."

"Could this be an issue?"

"Well … only if you are French, sir."

Coleridge scanned the table. All had a slight grin—some more than others, but all held a concerned face. The president snickered and cleared his throat saying, "Yes, well … Gitmo report?"

Trace Williams from Department of Intelligence was next. "We have completed all the necessary video to pass any test needed. We've even included a before and after shot that shows the place vacant—right down to the cells. We've got close-ups of them boarding a bus and a military transport. I think it was a fine piece of work, considering the time crunch that we had. Hell, we even faked some Mideast-type U.N. diplomats confirming the transfer."

"Howard, what are the Brits and French doing to protect themselves against an EMP attack?"

"This one's been hashed over by every scientist on both sides of the pond. Considering the size of the nuclear missiles, as long as they are set to explode at the right altitude, there is no protection whatsoever. We have protection for our military installations, but no country has set up their civilian infrastructure to withstand a nuclear EMP. If the EO has set it up right, this will be a disaster for some time to come. There is no way around it other than to stop the missiles from launching."

"Have we heard anything further from this Strivnych character?"

"No, Mr. President, our best hope is that he is still alive. However, we did pick up a radio broadcast that was strange. Our people are working on it, but we haven't been able to tie it in as yet. We're not sure, but it could have come from any small fishing village in Norway." Hatcher turned one palm sideways for emphasis, "… just a four-word broadcast: 'Danica ready for sea.'"

"Alright," said Coleridge, "Let's adjourn for awhile. I have to tape my broadcast for the U.N. to play by the demanded time, if necessary. We'll reconvene in one and a half hours."

CHAPTER 76

YURI DOLGORUKI

FEODOR SENSED THE SHADOW OF HIS OWN DEATH AND that feeling of certainty motivated him to come to peace with his God. Crouched in a corner of the pharmaceutical storage room, he reflected on his life and came to the conclusion that although he had sins to atone for, none were egregious enough to deny him eternal peace. Pondering his thirty-five years, he realized that the bulk of his sins were sins of omission and for that he asked forgiveness. But when it came time to promise to do better, Feodor halted, for he knew what he had to do and what he wanted to do. He *had* to stop the destruction his EO was going to wreak on the world. That aside, he *wanted* to kill this fiend. He knew this meant that he was going to deny God His role ... Feodor Strivnych was going to be final judge and executioner. This would be his ultimate sin that would deny him salvation. Reeling from the strain of all the emotions of the past two days, his body slid to a seated position on the floor. His forehead dropped to his knees and he prayed as he never had.

Feodor heard the scuffling of feet long before they came close enough to be a threat. His hand raised his pant leg and unbuttoned the strap that held his knife. As he slipped it out, the sensation of it in his hand gave him pleasure. He knew that Kashnikov was stalking him and would be carrying his Makarov sidearm. Direct confrontation was not going to work. He remembered the deception he had used on Alex. That is what I'll have to do, he thought. He glanced at his watch. He still had time to sneak up on the man, slit his throat, and cancel the firing sequences.

The steps were coming too close for comfort. Because he had had the presence of mind to dismantle the light switch, his instincts for survival told him there was no better place to hide. With great stealth, he slid himself up into a crouched attack position. He waited. The steps came closer and closer. The sound telegraphed that his stalker had entered the doctor's main office. They continued ever closer and were at the door to the compartment he was in. He heard the stalker's fingers fumble with the light switch that refused to work. Two more steps inched the killer into the room. Feodor readied his body for a quick lunge. He knew what he would do. He would plunge the knife deep into the EO's chest with one swift thrust. But the steps stopped again. Feodor could hear his own heart pounding and he was certain the assailant heard it as well. One more step and he would be up and thrusting. One more step and this long nightmare would be over. One more step and he would send this Satan back to the fires of hell. More pounding of the heart … the sound of the beating exploded in his head.

The next step never came. He heard the pivoting of the EO's shoe, followed by his steps that left the room. Feodor breathed a long sigh of relief. He didn't know how long he had held his breath. It was true that he could have lunged at Kashnikov and stabbed him in his back. But something held him back at the last second. Was it God that held his body? Feodor didn't know, but he was sure that it wasn't the right time to attack. The EO wouldn't be able to see him in the low light that emanated from the other room, but he felt vulnerable to the gun that had a full clip of bullets. No, I will bide my time, but I will not let my captain down, he thought. Never! He heard the footsteps fading away in the direction of the conning tower. His instincts told him to go toward the rear, where access to the boat from a rescue sub would have to come. Were they coming? All he knew was that he had to be ready to open the hatch. But had anyone heard his message? Would they come even if the message was picked up? Would Kashnikov resume hunting for him? There were too many questions and not enough answers.

CHAPTER 77

THE SWELLS HAD PICKED UP MORE THAN PETER HAD LIKED, but he was still comfortable that he could steady the mini-sub long enough to receive the three men that would enter suspended from a cable above. As the helicopter approached, that comfort level began to erode. When the chopper centered above him, the downdraft from its massive rotor blades had doubled the swells. It was all Peter could do to maintain any sort of control. He began hollering for Bjorn to open the hatch and pull the men in by their boots.

With the top hatch open, wind and water whirled around Bjorn with the ferocity of a gale. Straining every muscle his body had, he hung onto the rim of the opening and snagged the first Seal's pant leg. Three times the swells pulled him upward with only the spread of his thighs keeping him from being pulled out of the opening. Each dip of the swells crushed his upper thighs and caused the pain in his legs to grow until he wasn't sure that he could hold on.

After pulling the first Seal in, Bjorn signaled the Seal to pull in the next-in-line. Bjorn joined Peter at the controls to help. His thighs were on fire, but he wouldn't let Peter know. Devon was pulled in last. The ordeal was over and the hatch was closed. Peter looked back, smiled at his three guests, and said, "Gentlemen, welcome to the North Sea." For the Seals, it was just another day at the beach. Devon was exhausted.

"Hey 007, where's the chicks?"

"Cute!" Was all Devon could muster in return.

Peter again looked back and said, "Gentlemen, if the banter is over, I suggest you get your gear in order and climb into your hazmat suits … ETA is fifteen minutes, provided counter-measures are not released on us. Bjorn, take control while I get into my suit."

Bjorn frowned as he looked at Peter and said, "You didn't tell me about counter-measures."

"Would it have mattered?"

"No. I go where you go, boss—end of the line or not."

"If you two want to apply to become Seals, let me know," said the closest Seal. "You can cover my backside anytime." He crossed his heart with a closed fist and said, "You've got what it takes." Peter looked at Bjorn and gave him an approving smile.

CHAPTER 78

YURI DOLGORUKI

ANTON KASHNIKOV HAD RETURNED FROM HIS SECOND foray in search of his nemesis that was still an enigma. This search had been as unsuccessful as his first. He was disappointed, yet satisfied by the fact that he had searched half of the boat. As he neared the conning tower, he glanced at his watch. Ninety minutes to go, he thought. One more foray and I should reach the aft end of the boat. That will give me—

Entering the Con, his thoughts were interrupted as he glanced at the radar screen. The screen revealed an incoming vessel above him. Anton panicked, trying to clear his thinking. He picked up the headset and put it on. The blips indicated a small vessel, not a surface ship or another large sub. That's good, he rationalized. His blood pressure began to come down ... but what to do? He looked again at the screen, the bogey was dead square above him, and was close—in fact, too close! He couldn't fire a torpedo—the risk of the vessel's explosion damaging the Dolgoruki by blowback was too great. But what *is* it? He shook his head in a nervous twitch as if he was clearing his mind.

It must be a rescue sub—and Russian, he thought. Kashnikov knew his boat was being shadowed by an Akula sub with an Avalon bolted to its surface. "It's ours—damn!" He whispered. He looked again at his watch—still eighty-five minutes to go! The EO again started to panic. Should I fire the missiles? Damn! They could hit the Avalon and then what? His mind continued to race. I could release the targeted cruise missiles and take out the platforms. Hell, that's all my benefactors wanted anyway. The money's the same—I need to take the shot! He moved over to the firing buttons and put his hand on the buttons. No! I need more time ... they could get into the sub before I set up the scene of killing the terrorist in a final struggle. Yes! That's my only way out ... the access hatch! I've got to block them from opening the access hatch! I'll set up the scene and fire on the platforms. I'll rough myself up and send out a

— 244 —

signal that the sub is contaminated. That will make them go back to the Akula to get full hazmat equipment. Maybe I could set the timing device, get on the Morning Star trawler, and blow this stinking mess to hell.

Kashnikov felt confident that his final plan would work. He turned and headed aft down the passageway. When he came to the last spot he had inspected, he stopped in his tracks. "What the hell?" He whispered. The enigma! Is he real or was I wrong about the radio transmission?

He knew what he had to do. He would continue aft to the emergency access hatch. He knew he didn't have the time for a thorough search along the way, but making noise as he went might flush out his enemy. If it did, he would kill him.

Feodor heard the EO open and close doors behind him. The telltale signs grew closer, but not at a pace that would suggest serious inspection. He figured what Kashnikov was up to. He had spent many summer days hunting with his father. Deer were stalked in silence; quail were flushed with noise. This clanging of doors was meant to spook the prey. Feodor would have none of it.

As the sounds grew closer and closer, Feodor gripped his knife tighter and tighter. He would wait until the sounds passed before making his move. This time there would be no waiting for a better opportunity. The light in his room was off and Feodor stood at the ready behind the door. He was betting his life that the EO would open the door, not turn on the light, and close it again.

The footsteps came and stopped outside his room. Feodor froze— his breathing stopped. The door opened, but the light did not go on. Kashnikov stopped, but didn't move on. For some reason, he decided to check this room. His fingers scratched the wall till they found the switch and turned the light on. Thinking he could make him invisible, Feodor pulled his chest in and pressed the back of his head hard against the wall. Between the hinges, he saw Kashnikov's two-fisted grip of his Makarov cross the threshold of the door. The outstretched arms came into view. Feodor waited and waited until he saw the full body of his assailant cross. He waited three more seconds.

He summoned all his strength and let out as violent a push as he could muster. The door slammed hard into Kashnikov, knocking him off his feet and sending him headfirst into the open shelves to his left. Large heavy cans of detergent and laundry supplies came crashing over him, sending his weapon hurling to the floor. Feodor sprang and leaped onto the EO, his knife thrusting downward, but missing its mark and penetrating Kashnikov's shoulder. The EO raised his knee upward into Feodor's groin. The pain shot upward, causing Feodor to list to one side. Kashnikov heaved upward, throwing Feodor off onto the floor. He looked for his gun—it was out of reach to his side. In spite of the pain in his shoulder, the EO propped his upper torso on one elbow, and with a combination of kicks and digging his elbow in for leverage, he managed to drag his body forward and reach his weapon. Gripping it, he rolled over to fire, but the room was empty— Feodor had disappeared.

Kashnikov grabbed a towel and tore off a long strip, wadding it into a smaller towel and pressing it over his wound. He tied it over his shoulder and wrapped it under his armpit. He again grabbed his 9mm Makarov; this time he crept toward the open door. He popped his head out and snapped it back. Left or right, he couldn't tell which way Feodor had run. There was no choice—he had to gamble that the seaman had moved aft.

Kashnikov moved into the passageway, his one-handed grip pointing the gun toward the floor, and walked forward. There were no compartments for at least thirty feet. He turned and looked behind him—no one. Sweat drained into his eyes, burning them. He wiped it with his sleeve. He approached the first of the open compartments. This time he would be more careful as he passed each room.

When he passed the last of the three rooms, he was both disappointed and relieved. He looked at his watch. Sixty-five minutes remained.

The low-toned, grinding sound of metal against metal caused Kashnikov to spin and throw his back against the wall. He discerned the sound—the mini-sub was docking. There would only be minutes for him to bar the hatch from opening. Running on instinct, he bolted for the compartment where the hatch was located.

Feodor heard the running steps as their sound grew closer. He knew his timing had to be perfect. Instead of being behind the open door, he moved and stood tight against the wall. He prayed he wouldn't be seen. As the EO passed the opening, Feodor leapt out and threw his arm over Kashnikov's wounded shoulder, pulling him in tight and stopping his forward momentum. With his free hand, he reached over the EO's body and stabbed him below his heart. Feodor hung on in piggyback fashion. Kashnikov made no sound—the shock of the knife entering him caused him to stop and take two more steps. His left hand reached and felt Feodor's iron grip on the knife. He wobbled, rolled to his left, and fell over, carrying his assailant with him.

Feodor needed no time to think. He was on his feet racing up the short ladder to the hatch. He reached for his knife, but it was still inside Kashnikov's ribs. He made a fist and pounded three times on the hatch. He waited, his hearing acute—but there was no return rapping. He pounded three more times—again, nothing but silence. Feodor's body sagged under the letdown of emotion. He was dispirited and began to lower himself downward. As if an angel had appeared, the return raps came. Clank! Clank! Clank!

He pounded three more times to make sure the others were ready for him to open his hatch. He placed the flat of his palm on the hatch above him. The return was affirmative—he could feel that it was right on the other side of his hatch. He reached with two hands and wrenched the ring that sealed the hatch. When the pressure let loose, Feodor pushed upward on the hatch and a spray of water soaked his head and shirt. His smile changed as he saw an M1911A1 staring him square in the face. Feodor raised his hands and backed down the ladder.

Through the hazmat suit, the Seal barked his orders in Russian. Feodor moved over to a corner, keeping his hands raised. The Seal slid down and barked for Feodor to lay flat on the floor, arms and hands straight out in front. Feodor obliged. After the Seal did a body search on Feodor, he scanned the passageway and saw Kashnikov lying on his side. He appeared dead, but the Seal took no chances and kicked the gun out of his hand, sending it sailing away.

As the Seal attempted to roll the slain man over, Kashnikov pulled the knife from his ribs and rose up on one knee. He stabbed the Seal in his side, below his ribs, penetrating his hazmat suit. As the Seal fell to the floor, he spit off three rounds into Kashnikov's head. He rolled onto his back and yelled for the second Seal.

Feodor knew the danger the Seal was in from the VX contaminated knife and blood from Kashnikov. He reached into his pocket and pulled out the atropine injector. In one fluid motion, he raised the injector to his mouth, bit off the cap, and lunged to the Seal. This time, his aim was perfect as the injector plunged into the Seal's heart. Feodor held tight till he heard the second click, confirming the injection had been made. The second Seal had just dropped to the bottom of the ladder as Feodor had completed his stabbing leap onto the wounded Seal. He saw his partner's body begin to convulse in what appeared to be choking spasms. All his instincts were to protect his comrade in arms. He drew a bead and let loose two shots. One hit Feodor in his rear right shoulder, causing his body to jerk upward. The other hit below his left shoulder blade, causing Feodor to roll to his right and land sideways against the wall and onto the floor. With blood dripping from a small smile on his face, he looked across, reached out to the fallen Seal, and said, "You will live my friend. Tell my Captain I—" With that, Feodor's last journey began.

CHAPTER 79

WHEN THE FIRST SEAL'S CONVULSING STOPPED, THE SECOND Seal knelt down to help his comrade. He saw the bent injector of atropine lying on the torn hazmat suit. He looked over and down at Feodor. His eyes told the story. The Seal knew that the man had sacrificed his own life to save that of his friend. Reaching down, he closed Feodor's eyes.

He again focused on his fallen comrade. He saw that the Seal's suit had already been breached by the knife wound, so he cut and peeled the suit back to begin dressing the wound. Out of the corner of his eye, he saw Devon come up behind him and stop. He yelled for one of the operators to come down and finish dressing the wound.

Bjorn came down and took over for the second Seal. The soldier jumped to his feet, looked at Devon, and began using hand signals for Devon to get out his 9mm Beretta and follow close behind him. The chilling sight of the wretched bodies strewn everywhere made Devon's stomach want to heave, but there was no time as the Seal continued a steady pace to the conning tower. Standing in front of the firing controls, Devon once more looked at his watch. Fifty minutes remained. Agent Cohen had given him the file that contained the firing patterns used on the Borei class submarine fleet. Even more important was the fact that they had had time to review them on the flight over.

With the aid of the patterns in hand, the firing sequences were cancelled within seconds. Devon pulled a secure transmitting device out of his satchel and sent his prearranged message: "Rising Star aborted."

He repeated the coded message, closed the transmitter, and returned it to his satchel.

Devon's mind was as focused as it had ever been. He looked one more time at his watch. With the missile and torpedo systems shut down, he was racing against the arrival of the Russians in their Avalon rescue vehicle and the ticking seconds were critical. He turned and tapped the shoulder of the Seal who was covering the conning tower entrance.

He spread out the schematic of the Dolgoruki and pointed his finger to Feodor's missile compartment. The Seal nodded acknowledgment and again indicated for Devon to follow him.

Movement in the hazmat suits was difficult at best and their travel time was again hampered by the bodies they had to encounter. In addition, they had to use extra caution so as to not tear their hazmat suits. Devon followed, knowing the Russians were getting close and time was running out.

CHAPTER 80

THE TENSION IN THE SITUATION ROOM COULD HAVE BEEN cut with a knife. Attempts were made at discussing other problem areas of the world, but no one was of a mind-set and so all conversations died, leaving the members sitting and staring at each other while they waited for any news.

When the monitor opened up with an NSA emergency update, all eyes prayed that it was good news. "Mr. President, the crisis is over … the missiles have been shut down and our men are in control."

Everyone jumped from their chairs and either high-fived or embraced one another. Coleridge was the first to back away from the joy of the moment. "Gentlemen, please," He said.

"Neil, what's the condition of our men?"

"No other news, sir. We have to assume that all are okay and that Trojan Horse is doing his encryption work as we speak."

"The Russians …?"

"We're bringing up the latest real-time streaming from the Norwegian PC-3—there it is!"

The side-wall monitor showed the Russian sub to be fifteen nautical miles away.

"They know we are already there," said Coleridge.

"Not necessarily so, Mr. President," said Admiral Booth. "As long as the rescue sub is tethered to the Dolgoruki, their radar won't be able to discern the mini-sub from the larger sub. As long as McKenzie can accomplish the work that he needs to do in say, the next fifteen minutes, it will be up to that SRDSR pilot to get them out of there on an exact course away from the sub so that the mass of the Dolgoruki will block its detection. Our computers can plot that course, but we'll have to rely on his skill to pull it off."

"Will the Akula will still pick them up as it nears the Dolgoruki?"

"That is affirmative, sir, but we can tell the Russians that we fixed our problems with the SRDRS and that it is on the way to help. They will tell us to go away and in the spirit of cooperation, we will be most agreeable to oblige."

"Alright, get a coded message off to NATO that the crisis has been averted, and we'll play our hand out as if we know nothing. Henry, tell the UN that we will not be blackmailed by terrorists and therefore no apology will be delivered. In addition, all detainees are still in holding at Gitmo. Howard, hold a State Department press conference telling the same story. When the deadline passes, it will be up to the Russians to explain their little mess."

"But Mr. President," said Howard Irving from State, "the world is in a panic over this deadline. Is it fair that they have to wait another forty minutes to find out the crisis is over?"

"Howard, they have already waited eleven hours and twenty minutes. I'm sure the world can wait another forty. And there better not be any leaks!"

CHAPTER 81

YURI DOLGORUKI

AS HE GATHERED THE PAPERS THAT HE AND AARON COHEN had worked on in the Dassault, Devon McKenzie checked his watch one more time. The Russians should be here in another twenty-five minutes, he guessed. After he stuffed the papers back into his satchel, he again tapped his Seal and motioned to get moving.

When they reached the fallen seal, they saw that he was unconscious, but still breathing. The second Seal barked the order for Bjorn and Devon to begin hoisting his comrade up into the mini-sub.

"Stop!" Said Devon. "He has been exposed to the VX through both the EO's knife and the EO's blood. We've got to get him into another hazmat suit to keep him from contaminating the mini-sub and ourselves."

"We don't have another suit!" Said Bjorn.

"Well, this is a nuclear sub, so there has to be a certain number stored somewhere."

"No good," replied Bjorn, "those suits will have already been contaminated."

Peter had been listening to the conversation and was growing frustrated. He shouted through the hatch: "Time is up! Bjorn—you climb up here and help me when we pull him up. Devon—you and the Seal stay down and do the hoisting upward."

"We can't bring him into the mini-sub without a secure suit. He's got to be contained!"

With that, Peter unzipped his suit, took it off, and passed it down to Bjorn.

"You can't do that! You will be committing suicide!" Screamed Bjorn.

"Shut up and get him into it. Then get up here and you'll be the one on the top to pull him through."

"But—"

"No buts, someone has to do it! Get moving!"

Devon and the Seal struggled to get their comrade into Peter's hazmat suit. With the final zipping up, they hoisted the Seal up and above their shoulders. They continued pushing, but at some point the rest was up to Bjorn. True to form, he rose to the occasion, pulling the disabled body up and through the hatch of the mini-sub. When the Seal had been laid out on the floor, Bjorn motioned for Devon and the other Seal to pass up their satchels. He was careful as he transported the bags to the rear of the mini-sub. For Peter's part, he stayed as far forward in his seat as was possible.

Peter was nervous. Three men were sitting within touching distance of him and a contaminated fourth was lying between them on the floor—their suits had rubbed up against VX contamination all over the boat. Worse, the comatose Seal would soon be waking, and in doing so, he would be vomiting and coughing inside his hazmat suit. The risk that he could tear his suit with his coughing, causing the contagion to become airborne, was huge. Peter didn't need to be reminded that "no soldier would be left behind." From early in his life, that was also ingrained into his own code of honor.

While the disabled soldier was being pulled up into the sub, Peter had received the coordinates for his return to the tender boat that waited to pick them up. The message warned of the need for strict adherence to that exact path. Peter knew why.

As the SRDRS released itself from the Dolgoruki, Bjorn pointed to the blips on the radar screen. "We're out just in time," he said. "The Russians look to be maybe four miles out and closing fast ... we were damn lucky."

"No Bjorn, we are Vikings—right down to our core," Peter replied, as he turned his head to Bjorn and gave a single wink of his eye.

"Let's not forget the Seals," was shouted out from the rear.

"And the spooks at CIA," added Devon. The vision of the Russian computer man that saved the life of their comrade flashed through his mind. Like a ton of bricks, it hit him hard and his eyes watered over. Through tear-filled words, he was able to utter, "And one courageous Russian seaman—Feodor Strivnych."

***

Forgotten was the long buildup of broken lives that converged to bring about this crisis. They included: Sergei Petrova, his wife Issa, and son Ruslan; Captain Sergei Illanov and the brothers Sigua; his friend Tim Daniels and Julie Weston's father—and yes, his deceased wife, Cathy. Forgotten maybe in the mere snapshot of the moment, but they would haunt and motivate Devon McKenzie's soul for the rest of his life.

EPILOGUE

THE SKIES IN THE FAIRBANKS AREA OF ALASKA WERE AN off-grey color—heavy with a dark cloud cover. A low fog was winding its way through a forest of deep green spruces. It had rained on and off for the last ten hours, but for some reason, the rain held as if it knew the burial ceremony was about to begin. In the background, Mount McKinley stood as an eternal guard.

Jack Weston was a real Alaskan. He lived the life this state had to offer by choice. He could have lived a lot easier and perhaps a lot longer had he chosen to stay in the lower forty-eight. Jack was a man's man and the pastor's words spoke hollow of a man that he didn't know. But it didn't matter. Julie knew him and that is what counted. She stood tall remembering him, and beside her was the man she was about to marry.

Devon and Julie may not have been each other's first true loves, but they would be their last. The CIA had restored Devon's credentials and in so modifying them, he could begin receiving his full pension ... with four years back pay negotiated by Devon, of course.

When the crowd left, all but four lingered. Ernest Hatcher made sure that he was the last to leave. "Are you sure I can't talk the two of you into coming back?"

"Maybe you could talk Julie into it, but that would be over my dead body."

"Well, if you get bored you could call Agent Cohen to come up for a visit. That way, you three girls could work out a few of those algorithm things. Lord, help me! What is this world coming to?"

Devon smiled and gave Julie a strong hug from the arm wrapped around her shoulder. The two watched as Director Hatcher walked away.

Looking at his obedient dog, Devon said, "Let's go, Oscar—we've got a life to live."

Out of nowhere, a chill ran up Devon's spine, causing the hair on his neck to raise. An ominous feeling engulfed him.

Deep, in those green spruces, eyes were watching.